Bloody April

An Airman's Diary

By Gordon Anthony

copyright © 2021 Gordon Anthony

ISBN: 9798729212569

Sunday 1st April, 1917

It's been a long, tiring day, but I made a promise to myself that I would keep a diary of my experiences in the war, and I purchased this lovely, leather-bound journal from a stationer's on Oxford Street before we left London, so I must record what happened on my first day.

Greening, Vanders and I travelled together. We'd been in the same batch of pupils learning to fly at Brooklands, and we'd all graduated at the same time, so we were delighted to join up again for the journey out to France. I won't bore you with all the details, since it involved many tedious hours on train, boat and then train again, until we were finally deposited at Air Supply Depot No.2 at Candas.

It had been a dreary journey, our view of the French countryside hampered by frequent rain and sleet which refused to give way to any sign of spring weather. It had been a long, cold winter, and that dire season seemed unwilling to depart.

Nevertheless, we did catch sight of busy roads as our train trundled slowly southwards. Troops were marching with shouldered rifles, packs on their backs and steel helmets on their heads. Three-ton lorries carried supplies, motorcycle couriers weaved in and out of the traffic, and we even caught sight of a couple of tanks, the great, rhomboid-shaped steel behemoths crawling along at little better than walking pace. Long columns of pack horses and mules had also been employed to help move the vast quantity of supplies being amassed, while others hauled artillery guns to join the bombardment of the German Lines. We also saw a great many troops of cavalry, some with carbines on their saddles, others with steel-tipped lances held proudly.

Amidst all this military traffic, we saw one or two French peasants sitting stolidly on their wagons, their faces expressionless as they did their best to ignore the organised chaos around them.

"I've never seen so much Army traffic," I remarked as I wiped condensation from the train's window and peered out at a road which ran close to the railway track. "And I've certainly never seen so many cavalry."

Greening asserted, "They're getting ready for the breakthrough."

Vanders and I nodded our eager agreement. We all knew the Big Push was coming, and this one was expected to give us the victory which had eluded us so far. Even over the noise of the creaking, rattling train, we could hear the distant rumble of guns as our artillery bombarded the German defences with high explosive and shrapnel.

"I hope we aren't too late to join the fun," I said.

But the guns were still firing when, late in the afternoon, we arrived at Candas. Some other pilots we had met on the way over were going to A.S.D. No.1 at St. Omer, and they were rather jealous since everyone knows the Big Push is about to happen near Arras on the southern sector of the British Lines, and Candas will be supplying men and machines for the squadrons involved in that great adventure.

When we reported to the office of the Depot's Recording Officer, Greening mentioned that he hoped we would receive postings to front line squadrons before the Push began.

The Recording Officer, a middle-aged Captain who looked rather harassed, replied with a grim smile.

"Don't worry. The offensive hasn't begun yet."

"But the guns?" Greening queried, jerking his head to indicate the still audible sound of artillery fire.

"That's nothing special," The R.O. informed us. "When the Push begins in earnest, you'll hear a lot more than that."

It's often difficult to know when a chap is pulling your leg, but the R.O. seemed sincere, so we did our best to take him at his word.

"Postings come through every day," he told us. "You'll be advised when you are needed."

So, for the moment, all we can do is wait.

The camp at Candas is a huge, sprawling place. It has dozens of hangars where aircraft are unpacked from crates and put together. Then they have engines fitted before being tested and sent to front line squadrons. There are huge hangars, many of them built of wood and steel, with aircraft of all types being fitted out. Other sections deal in repairs and salvage, building a new machine from the wreckage of several others, and the place has a constant drone of aero engines as the mechanics test the machines and pilots take them up to ensure they are airworthy. I've only been here a few hours, and I think I've already seen more aeroplanes than at any time in my life.

There are also dozens upon dozens of huts, one of which I am sitting in as I write this. It is dark now, and the only light comes from candles, but I am still aware of what is going on outside. Engines are still being tested, and the artillery still pounds away, a constant reminder that we are at war.

Naturally, the three of us speculated about what type of machine we would fly. After we had completed our training, our instructors put forward recommendations as to which type of flying duty each pupil was best suited to. In the early days of the Flying Corps, pilots took pot luck, flying whichever type of machine happened to be available, but things are much more organised nowadays. Greening and I were both recommended for two-seater planes, while Vanders, a truly exceptional pilot, is destined to join a scout squadron where he will no doubt shoot down loads of Huns.

He said, "I don't mind what I fly as long as it's a single-seater with a machine gun."

I must admit I felt rather jealous even though I have known for a long time that I am not in the same league as Vanders when it comes to flying ability. He even spent a couple of weeks at Joyce Green where he received advanced training in combat flying from experts who have flown at the Front themselves.

Greening, like me, was resigned to the less glamorous task of flying reconnaissance machines.

"The two-seaters do the real work," he said good-naturedly. "You can swan around with your machine gun all you like, but it's we who will help win the war."

"Of course you will," Vanders grinned. "And I'll be there to protect you whenever some beastly Hun tries to shoot you down."

We had spent some time braving the cold to watch aircraft landing and taking off from the aerodrome, and it was clear that there were many different types of machines in use at the Front.

Pushers with the engine at the rear, nimble little scouts with machine guns on the top wing or firing through the propeller and, of course, the ubiquitous B.E.2c, the R.F.C's workhorse.

"I'll be happy to fly anything as long as it's not a Quirk," Greening stated as we watched another B.E.2c claw its way into the sullen sky.

We grinned at that. The Royal Aircraft Factory's B.E.2 series of aeroplanes are known throughout the Flying Corps as "Quirks". That's because, in practice, the B.E.2 has hardly any quirks. The B.E.2c variant is so stable it will fly straight and level even if you take your hands and feet off the controls. But it's a slow, heavy machine, and very few people enjoy flying it.

Personally, I'm not bothered what I end up flying. We all agreed that it will probably be down to pot luck. If your name is next on the list when a squadron requests a replacement pilot, off you go.

"I don't care," I told my friends. "The main thing is that we are here to win the war, and to do our bit for King and Country."

That received unanimous acclaim, so we retired to the Mess to drink a toast to our future.

"We must keep in touch," Vanders declared. "Once we know where we are going, let's exchange details."

That proposal was greeted by another promise and another drink.

And now it is just a matter of waiting.

Monday 2nd April, 1917

We received our orders this morning. Greening, Vanders and I, along with a couple of other newly arrived pilots, were summoned to the R.O.'s office where, one by one, we went in to receive our instructions.

Vanders was delighted with his posting.

"I'll be flying Nieuports," he announced proudly, waving the papers which were sending him off to a squadron based only a short way north of Candas.

"Say what you like about the French," he grinned, "but they build some lovely aeroplanes, and the Nieuport is one of the best around. Albert Ball flies Nieuports, and he's bagged dozens of Huns."

I could understand Vanders's delight, and I was pleased for him. Albert Ball was the most famous aviator in the R.F.C., and it would be a privilege to fly the same type of kite as he did.

Greening was next, but he was less pleased with his orders.

He frowned when he informed us, "It looks as if I'm going to a unit which flies the F.E.2b."

"The Fee is a damned fine machine," Vanders assured him.

Greening wasn't so sure, and I could understand his concern. The huge F.E.2 was a pusher plane, with the engine at the back. The pilot sits high in a pulpit-like cockpit with his gunner in front and below him. The gunner has a clear field of fire because there is no engine or propeller to block his view, but the F.E.2 is another old machine which has been in service for quite a while, and it's not the most agile of kites. Having the engine at the back also poses risks in a crash, because the huge engine is likely to crush the crew to death when they hit the ground. All in all, I'd prefer not to fly one of those bulky kites.

But when my turn came, I felt even less happy than Greening.

"Quirks," I sighed when they asked me what I would be flying. "I'm going up to a place near Arras, so I'll be in the thick of things when the Push kicks off."

"You lucky sod," Vanders said with a grin. "You'll see plenty of action up there."

Our next task was to hurriedly pack our kit and assemble for the final legs of our respective journeys. To the accompaniment of aero engines being tested and planes flying overhead, we bundled into a Crossley tender which whisked us off to our units. Vanders had only a short journey before the driver announced we had arrived at his squadron's airfield. Vanders barely had time to grab his bag and leap out the back of the tender before the driver screeched away again. Greening and I waved farewell, but we had no chance to say anything other than a quick, "Good luck!"

The two other pilots were deposited at their respective airfields, one to fly Sopwith Pups, the other on B.E.2S like me, then Greening was dropped off, leaving me alone in the back of the tender, sitting on the wooden bench with my kit bag lying on the floor beside me.

The roads were still busy, and the weather remained pretty dreadful. I was shivering despite my greatcoat, and I could see puddles of water everywhere. Showers of rain, sleet and even snow gave the French countryside a drab, mournful aspect, and my mood was not improved by the knowledge I'd be flying B.E.2s. I'd put a brave face on it for my friends, but the reality of the situation was now coming home to roost. There's a mock psalm which every pilot learns early on, sung to the tune of "The Lord is My Shepherd", and it pretty much sums up a pilot's view of the Quirk.

The BE2c is my bus, therefore I shall want.

He maketh me to come down in green pastures;

He leadeth me where I will not go;

He maketh me to be sick,

he leadeth me astray on all cross-country flights.

Yea, though I fly over No Man's Land where mine enemies would encompass me about, I fear much evil;
For thou art with me.
Thy joystick and thy prop discomfort me;
Thou preparest a crash for me in the presence of mine enemies;
Thine RAF anointeth me with oil;
Thine tank leaketh badly.
Surely to goodness thou shalt not follow me all the days of my life,
Or I shall dwell in the house of Colney Hatch forever.

When I first heard the psalm intoned, it made me laugh, for I could empathise with it even though I'd only flown a B.E.2 once. It perhaps wasn't as bad as the song made out, but the words certainly went with the plane's reputation. I hadn't been sure what the reference to Colney Hatch meant, but Vanders had told me it referred to the lunatic asylum in the London Borough of that name. Apparently, flying a Quirk for too long could drive you insane.

By the time the driver deposited me at the airfield near the village of Fosseux, I was resigned to my fate. I was a soldier, and I had no choice but to obey orders. I was here to help win the war, and if that meant flying Quirks, then so be it. At least it was a relatively safe machine to fly. Despite the Pilot's Psalm, it was not difficult to fly a B.E.2, and the Royal Aircraft Factory engine was more reliable than many aero engines. Usually.

The airfield was based on farmland. I could see the farmhouse, a low, stone-walled cottage with a roof of old, cracked tiles and shutters on the windows. Nearby was a barn which had obviously been commandeered, for it now bore a sign proclaiming it to be the Officers' Mess. A couple of dozen wooden huts had been erected behind the barn, with the first of these being the Squadron office.

An effel, the sock of light cotton which fluttered atop a tall pole, showed that the blustery wind was coming from the west as usual, and I could see three enormous canvas hangars on the far side of the field. Outside one of them, a B.E.2 stood with mechanics swarming around it.

The squadron's vehicle park was behind the hangars, as were the tents where stores were kept. Beyond them, a row of weather-beaten poplars lined the edge of the field. Fortunately from a pilot's perspective, the other sides of the grass meadow were lined by low hedges rather than trees.

I saw yet more tents beyond the farmhouse, but there seemed to be hardly any people about at all. Other than the activity around the hangars, the field seemed deserted, but I could understand that given the brisk wind which tugged at my greatcoat and chilled my face.

The other thing I noticed was that the thud and thunder of the artillery guns was louder here. I knew Fosseux was ten or twelve miles west of Arras, a town which was almost on the Front Lines. We were safe from German artillery fire here, but the airfield was close enough to the Front for the sound of the guns to be very noticeable.

I took all this in within a few seconds, and then I was hailed by a Sergeant who emerged from the Squadron office and came over to greet me.

Flinging me a casual salute, he said, "Good afternoon, Sir. Mister Kerr, is it?"

"That's right."

"We've been expecting you, Sir. I'm Sergeant Smith. Captain Potter is in the office. If you report to him, I'll see your bag is taken to your hut. You're in Number Three."

He waved a hand, indicating the neat rows of wooden huts behind the barn. Each one had a number painted on its door in bright, white numerals.

I left my kit in the sergeant's care, then strode over to the office, my booted feet squelching on the wet grass.

Beside the Squadron office was the Commanding Officer's hut, with the other huts arrayed in neat lines behind it. I was pleased to see that Number Three was only a short walk from the Officers' Mess.

I went into the office, giving Captain Potter a smart salute. The R.F.C. doesn't go in for a great deal of formality, but saluting a senior officer on first meeting is always a good idea.

Potter was probably in his late thirties. He had a kindly face, his hair cut short, and he wore a toothbrush moustache which gave him a certain air of authority. He was tall and thin, and he spoke with a genial, welcoming smile.

"Mister Kerr?" he enquired.

"Yes, Sir."

I handed over my papers which he glanced at before dropping them into a tray on his cluttered desk.

"Glad to have you with us," he told me.

Looking around, I saw that his office held a couple of wooden desks, with an old typewriter set on one. Maps covered most walls, although one was given over to photographs, black and white images of churned earth and dark lines.

"That's some of our latest handiwork," Potter smiled when he saw my attention being drawn to the photographs. "Rather good, aren't they?"

I nodded, "Yes, Sir. Very impressive."

In truth, I could not tell one picture from another. They all looked very similar, and few showed any feature which stood out from the carnage of craters and puddles. I'd heard a lot about the stagnant nature of the war, but the images shown in these photographs were, I must admit, rather shocking. I'd never seen anything like them in the newspapers.

I had no time to dwell on the images, because Potter launched into an outline of the squadron's role.

"We do photography of the Lines and we direct artillery shoots," he explained. "Sometimes we are required to carry out bombing raids, and no doubt there will be close contact patrols when the Push begins. All the usual stuff. Our main role is to cooperate with the ground troops. Each Army Corps has a close contact squadron assigned to work with it. We work with VII Corps, which is part of General Allenby's Third Army."

With a wave of his hand, he added, "By good fortune, Corps H.Q. is in a chateau just the other side of Fosseux village, so the Corps Commander, Lieutenant-General Snow, and his staff officers are fairly close at hand."

He went on, "You'll be in A Flight under Captain Sibbald. He's very experienced, and you'll be in good hands with him. Come on, let's go over to the Mess and I'll introduce you."

As we walked, Potter continued talking.

"The farmhouse is off limits," he told me. "Old Madame Duprey still lives there. She's a nice old lady. She's a widow, and she's lost both her sons in the war. She can't manage the farm on her own, so she let the R.F.C. use the land as an airfield."

He went on, "The tents are where the enlisted men sleep. Most of them are the Ack Emmas who look after the aircraft, of course, but we do have orderlies, cooks and drivers, as well as our own Photographic Unit."

He gave an ostentatious wave as we reached the old barn.

"And this is the Mess. Don't be put off. It's actually very nice inside. As you can see, we've had proper doors and windows put in."

We entered the front door now. It had been cut into the huge barn doors which were, Potter assured me, kept shut.

Inside, floorboards had been laid to give the semblance of normality. There was a comfortable sitting area with an assortment of armchairs and wooden seats. A piano stood to one side of the room, and the wooden walls were decorated with a variety of posters. Some were official R.F.C. training posters, some were advertisements for West End shows, but I also noticed several pictures of naked women, some of the infamous prints by Kirchner which were big favourites in the Army.

I noticed a phonograph sitting on a low table, with stacks of records beneath it, but the player was idle when we went in, giving the room a somnolent, restful atmosphere.

Potter told me, "Through that door is the dining room. The C.O. insists on everyone wearing proper uniform for dinner. No slacks or shoes. Dinner is usually served just after nightfall."

"Yes, Sir," I nodded, feeling like a new boy on his first day at school.

Then, taking in the rest of the antechamber, he said cheerfully, "Ah, I see most of A Flight is here."

Several airmen, both pilots and observers, sat up and looked at us keenly. They rose to shake my hand as Potter did the introductions.

"Gentlemen, this is Mister Kerr. He's your new recruit."

He then went on to introduce me to Watt, Garrick, Sullivan and Normansby, this last being referred to as "Beano".

I soon realised why.

"Glad to meet you, Old Bean," he grinned as he shook my hand warmly.

The observers, distinguished by their flying badges having only one wing, were Ashton, Long, Howden and Montague. All of them welcomed me to A Flight.

"And, of course, Captain Sibbald. Bertie, I'll leave Mister Kerr in your capable hands."

Sibbald was a stocky, wide-shouldered fellow with a broad, flat face and eyes which suggested he had seen more than he wanted to of the war. I guessed he must be in his mid-twenties, which made him quite old compared to the rest of the Flight. I also noticed the ribbon of the Military Cross on the chest of his tunic, and that showed he was a man who had proved himself in combat, so he gained my instant respect.

He shook my hand firmly enough, although his welcome wasn't as warm as I'd hoped. With a nod, he directed me to the further end of the room where we could sit without being overheard provided we kept our voices low. The other officers made a show of returning their interest to their books and newspapers, but I guessed they were all doing their best to listen in.

Once we were seated, Sibbald did not beat about the bush.

Leaning forwards in a rather intimidating manner, he asked, "How many hours have you got?"

"Twenty-six, Sir."

A pained look flashed across his face.

"And how many of those on B.E.2s?"

I'd checked my log book before setting out, so I was able to answer this promptly.

"Twelve and a half, Sir. They had plenty of Quirks at the training station."

"I'm sure they did," he scowled. "And there's no need to call me Sir. Captain, Skipper or even Sibbald will do. If you are still alive at the end of the month, I'll let you call me Bertie."

"Right you are, Sir," I said, then blushed at my foolishness.

Sibbald affected not to notice my verbal blunder. He frowned as if trying to make up his mind about something, then reached a decision.

"We have a job this afternoon at three o'clock. But I need you to get more hours in before you go on operations. Meet us down at the hangars at fourteen thirty hours. When we go up, you can go too. I want you to get in at least three hours of flying. Go around the local area and familiarise yourself with the landmarks. You can fly as far east as Arras, but don't go beyond there. Understood?"

"Yes, Sir. I mean, Captain."

"Good. Tomorrow, I'll pair you up with an observer and you can get in another five or six hours' practice."

My heart sank. I could tell that Sibbald wasn't the sort of chap you could argue with, but I wanted to get stuck into the job, and he seemed determined to delay me as much as possible.

He must have sensed my disappointment, for he said, "Look, Kerr. It's like this. We have an important job to do, but the Huns do their best to stop us. Some of their pilots have hundreds of hours of flying time. If it were up to me, none of our pilots would cross the Lines unless they have at least fifty hours of flying time, and even then I'd want them to have a couple of weeks' practice out here before they go on operations. But we need every pilot we can get, and time is short, so all I can spare you is today and tomorrow."

"I understand," I told him.

"Righto. Now, get one of the Mess waiters to bring you a cup of tea and some sandwiches. Then go and get ready for a trip. We're off to hold our pre-flight briefing."

So saying, he summoned the rest of the Flight who filed out after him. Beano gave me a wink of reassurance as he passed, and that made me feel a little better.

While I was eating my lunch, I heard the sound of several aero engines outside. Strolling to the window, I looked out to see half a dozen Quirks being guided out to the airfield. One after another, they took off, clawing for height and heading east.

The door opened, and Potter, the Recording Officer, came in, rubbing his hands together for warmth.

"That's B Flight going up," he told me cheerfully. C Flight will be back shortly. Then it will be A Flight's turn."

"There's always one flight in the air?" I asked.

"Weather permitting," he confirmed. "Now, I need some nosh. Waiter!"

A couple of other officers came in, exchanging greetings and saying hello to me in a disinterested sort of way. I finished my lunch, then told Potter I needed to get ready for my own flight.

"Come to the office once you've got your kit on," he told me. "I'll issue your map."

"Will do, Sir."

As I was walking towards Hut Three, I heard the buzz of another aero engine and saw a B.E.2 coming in to land. It touched down in a neat three-pointer, the two wheels and the tail skid coming to earth simultaneously, then it slowed and turned towards the hangars where it was met by a group of Air Mechanics.

Another B.E.2 followed a moment later, and I could see a third approaching from a distance. C Flight was coming home.

Hut Three was small, tidy, and very cold. Just inside the door was a tiny communal area with a wash stand and a Primus stove, with a kettle and some tin mugs. A couple of crudely made wooden stools provided the only furniture, with a small, faded and very worn rug on the floor being the only attempt at making the place homely. A kerosene lamp hung from one of the roof rafters, telling me that the electricity supply which fed the Mess and Squadron Office did not extend to the Officers' quarters.

Through a doorway with no actual door, the hut was divided by thin partition walls into four sleeping cubicles, each with a narrow cot, a bedside cabinet and a chest for personal belongings.

I heard movement, then saw a short, chubby, red-faced Private stepping out from the second cubicle on the left.

"Mister Kerr, Sir?" he asked, flinging me a salute.

"Yes."

"Pleased to meet you, Sir. I'm Etherington, your batman. I've put your stuff away, and hung your flying kit on the pegs. I can brew you a cup of tea if you like."

"No thanks," I told him. "I've just had one."

I'd long ago learned the dangers of drinking too much liquid before flying. Getting caught short was a constant problem, especially if flying a rotary engined machine because of the castor oil used for lubrication. Quirks had in-line engines so were not quite as bad, but the habit of abstaining before a flight saved any potential embarrassment.

"Right you are, Sir. Is there anything else you need?"

"I don't think so. But can you tell me who else stays here?"

"In Hut Three, Sir? Well, there's Mister Ashton. He's in A Flight along with you, Sir."

I nodded. Ashton was a studious-looking fellow who was one of the observers I'd met in the Mess.

"Then there are Misters Vaughn and Tattersall," Etherington went on. "They are both in B Flight. They've just gone out, Sir."

Etherington fussed around for a few minutes, showing me my cubicle and explaining where he'd put my few belongings. That did not take long. Then, after I had assured him yet again that I needed nothing more, he bustled off, assuring me of his best attentions at all times.

I spent some time getting ready. I pulled on an extra pair of thick socks, then tugged on my thigh-length fug boots which are lined with wool. My leather, fleece-lined flying jacket was next, then I wrapped my silk scarf around my neck. One of the first lessons a pilot learns is to purchase a silk scarf. When in the air, you need to constantly turn your head, and the scarf prevents chafing against the rough collars of your shirt and tunic.

I debated whether to take my service revolver. Eventually, I followed the advice of an old instructor and shoved the heavy weapon into one of the deep pockets of my flying jacket.

"It's about as much use as a pea-shooter in the air," he had told me, "but you might need it if you are forced down behind the Lines."

At the time, I'd accepted this as good advice, but Vanders had later told me that, according to comments made by some of his tutors who had fought at the Front, pilots carried a revolver in case their machines caught fire in the air.

"Blowing your brains out is a quicker, cleaner death than burning while the kite falls ten thousand feet," Vanders had told me.

I didn't anticipate dying either by fire or bullet, but I didn't want to look like a complete novice, so I shoved the revolver in my pocket as a way of demonstrating my experience.

Completing my outfit did not take long. I had a pair of silk gloves which went beneath my thick, leather outer pair, and, finally, my leather helmet and goggles. I tried them on, checking they were properly adjusted, then removed them and clumped my clumsy way back to the office. Fug boots are fine for keeping you warm, but they aren't designed for easy walking.

Potter was waiting for me with a map of our sector of the Front.

"We cover a five mile section of the Lines," he explained as he pointed to various sections of the map which was divided into grids.

"The River Scarpe, which flows through Arras, marks the northern part of our sector, so you can't really get lost."

Tapping at some coloured lines which ran across the map in zig-zag patterns, he said, "Our trenches are marked in blue, the Germans in red. Purple shows barbed wire. The Hun gun batteries are also shown by red lines, and strongpoints and machine gun nests are represented by these red dots. The yellow lines show tracks and roads."

He then folded the map and turned it over.

"This section shows our airfield and surroundings. There's Fosseux, with the chateau just north of the village. And that other town just a mile to the south-west is Barly. Even in dud weather, you should be able to get home using those landmarks. The road to

Arras runs fairly straight, so if you find the town, just follow the road home."

I thanked him, shoving the map into a pocket on my thigh, then headed to the hangars.

The rest of A Flight were there, looking over their machines which had been wheeled out of the hangars and lined up in a row, their huge, four-bladed propellers standing still.

Sibbald, decked in his own flying gear, greeted me, directing me to the kite at the end of the row.

"This one is yours," he told me without preamble. It's an old machine, but reliable enough. Once we are away, take her up and stay up for at least three hours. Practise as many stunts as you like, but get used to the machine as quickly as you can."

I nodded my understanding.

"Dunlop and Green will look after the machine for you," he said, indicating a couple of the Ack Emmas who stood nearby, shoulders hunched against the chill wind. "And Sergeant Stirling is in charge of A Flight's mechanics. Any problems, you talk to him."

The Sergeant, a dour-faced Yorkshireman, said, "I've looked over the machine myself, Sir. It's in fine condition. We warmed the engine a little while ago."

Dunlop, the Sergeant informed me, is the fitter. He looks after the aeroplane's engine, while Green is the rigger, responsible for the bodywork, including all the struts and bracing wires which hold the wings together.

"I'll see you later," Sibbald told me before heading off to give the rest of the Flight a final pep talk.

I took a leisurely walk around my plane.

My plane. That thought gave me a thrill. My very own machine. It has the serial number B5268 painted on its rudder, and the Squadron Letter X just behind the blue, white and red roundel of the R.F.C. on each side of the fuselage. At the start of the war, British planes used to have Union Flags painted on the body and wings, but British troops on the ground thought they looked like crosses, so used to shoot at pilots flying overhead in the mistaken belief they were German kites. The R.F.C. soon adopted the

French roundel, reversing the French colours, which means we have red in the centre and Blue on the outer rim.

I did notice a few patches of canvas stitched to the wings, but I made no comment. This showed the machine had been damaged by bullets in the past, but I didn't like to ask which pilot had flown it when that happened.

By the time I'd finished my visual inspection, the engines of the other planes were being started, so I clambered up into the rear cockpit and settled into the wicker seat, fastening my safety belt around my waist.

The B.E.2c has two cockpits, and the pilot sits in the rear one. This is because, without a passenger, sitting in the front would upset the plane's centre of gravity and make it less stable.

"All right, Sir?" asked Green, my rigger.

"Fine, thanks."

I made a show of looking over the controls, checking that the Very pistol and its coloured flares were snug in their holders, and waggling the controls, watching the ailerons move in response. Twisting, I checked that the rudder and elevators did the same.

"Shall we start her up, Sir?" Dunlop called. "Best to let the engine warm up again."

I nodded, running through the procedure of turning off the switches, then activating the petrol feed in response to Dunlop's calls. When he had turned the propeller to suck fuel into the engine, I turned on the ignition and he swung the huge propeller. The engine coughed, emitting a spout of dark smoke from the exhaust pipes, but did not catch. We repeated the exercise, and this time the engine roared into life.

I cut back the throttle, letting the engine slowly reach its operating temperature while the plane bumped against the wheel chocks which prevented it rolling away. Dunlop and Green each took hold of a rope which was attached to one of the heavy wooden blocks which sat in front of the wheels, while a third mechanic draped himself across the rear of the fuselage just in front of the tail unit to prevent the wind generated by the whirling propeller from lifting the tail off the ground.

Fortunately, it did not take long to reach optimum temperature as the Ack Emmas had previously run the engine up for me. I watched as the rest of A Flight waved away their chocks, letting their mechanics guide them out onto the field. One by one, they turned to face the wind, then gathered speed until they lifted into the air.

Now it was my turn. I gave the signal to Dunlop and Green. They yanked the chocks away by hauling on the ropes, freeing the Quirk for movement. I felt the third mechanic release his hold on the tail, and saw Dunlop and Green drop the chocks and run behind the wings to grab the rear struts which joined the upper and lower wings together. They guided me clear of the hangars, then let go as the plane gathered speed. Kicking the rudder bar, I steered the kite to the end of the field, then swung around to face into the wind.

I could see the Ack Emmas watching me, but I did my best to ignore them. They were probably waiting to see if I could get the Quirk airborne without crashing.

"Take it slow and easy," I told myself as I opened the throttle.

I sent the Quirk down the field, gently pushing the stick forwards once I'd gained enough momentum. The tail skid, which acts as a drag to slow the plane when landing, now lifted, freeing the B.E.2 to increase speed. The airflow beneath the wings now provided the lift, and the rumble of the wheels stopped as the plane rose from the grass. I was up, gently easing the stick back to climb higher into the air.

I won't bore you with all the details. The B.E.2c takes over half an hour to reach its maximum altitude of ten thousand feet, and that can be quite tedious. Today, I couldn't go very high because of the clouds, but I did manage to get her up to six thousand, and I spent some time dodging between dark clouds, dipping and rising as I played around with my kite. I also kept an eye on the ground, checking landmarks to be certain I could find the airfield again. Eventually, I turned to follow the road all the way to Arras.

From my height, I could make out the Lines. The sight, I admit, left me feeling in awe. I'd heard about the trenches, but what I could see only a few miles beyond the town of Arras was a wide swathe of ruined earth. In a band several miles wide, the world had been turned to mud and water. Craters were everywhere, often overlapping, most with puddles of water which reflected the dull sunlight. Scars in the ground may have been trenches, but my initial impression was that nothing could live in such a desert of churned earth.

I also now saw the effect of the artillery guns I had been hearing for the past couple of days. All along the Front, great explosions appeared as shells landed, flinging up huge gouts of earth and creating yet more holes. Fascinated, I circled for what must have been ages, turning my head constantly to try to take in the horror of what lay just a few miles to the east.

I noticed an imposing bump of high ground just to the north of Arras. Like the back of a whale breaching the surface of the ocean, this huge lump was, according to my map, Vimy Ridge. It was held by the Germans and, like the rest of the Front, was devoid of vegetation, being little more than an enormous pile of muddy, cratered earth. More shells exploded on or around it as the British artillery continued its bombardment.

Below me, Arras itself was largely in ruins. I could see a few buildings still standing, but most were nothing more than the low remains of walls, and nothing seemed to move in the town at all. That, I supposed, was because the Germans up on the heights of Vimy Ridge – if there were any Germans still alive up there – could look down on the town and direct their own artillery to destroy anything that dared creep out in daylight.

Other than this, the only things of interest were the kite balloons. Moored to the ground by thick cables, these sausage-shaped bags of gas float on either side of the Lines, each with a wicker basket hung beneath it. From these vantage points, observers look down on the Lines, reporting by telephone to the artillery on the ground. I did not envy those observers. Hanging immobile, they were easy targets for any prowling aircraft. Still, I knew the observers were equipped with parachutes which would allow them to jump to safety if attacked. Those of us who fly aeroplanes don't have that luxury.

The sight of the Front fascinated me, but I knew I could not hang around over Arras all day. Eventually, I turned westwards again, doing my best to follow Sibbald's instructions. He had said to perform as many stunts as I liked, but the B.E.2c is hardly a machine for stunting. The whole point of the aircraft is to provide a stable platform for aerial reconnaissance, and it's a heavy kite to fling around the sky. I did a few tight turns, dived and zoomed as best I could, but that was about it. I did contemplate trying to loop the plane as I'd never performed that manoeuvre before, but I decided against it. I'd seen one trainee pilot slip out of the top of a loop and fall into a spin from which he did not recover. Helping lift what was left of him out of the wreckage had rather put me off looping.

Nor did I try to fly into a cloud. That's supposed to be a frightening experience, and the clouds above the Arras sector were dark and threatening. I might have dared fly into a fluffy, white cumulus, but not these towering monsters.

I did test the Quirk's rigging by setting the revs to sixteen hundred and taking my hands and feet off the controls. As the manual described, the plane kept flying straight and level, which showed Green had done a good job of adjusting all the bracing wires. Only the buffeting wind forced me to grab the controls again.

The engine sounded good as well, with very little oil being flung out, and the dials showing it giving good revs.

The B.E.2c can stay aloft for over three and a half hours, and Sibbald had said to stay out for at least three, so I flew back and forth between our airfield and Arras a few times, circling wide to north and south so as to check on local landmarks. I saw the Scarpe river, of course, for it flows through the town, but I also noticed traffic on the roads to the rear of the Lines, including a couple of tanks, and there were several Army encampments where troops were resting or training far beyond the range of German artillery.

As the sun began to edge towards the western horizon, I returned to the airfield, dropping my speed to forty miles per hour and slowly creeping down. I crossed the perimeter hedge, touched down and cursed as I bounced back into the air. Another, smaller bounce, and then the plane stayed on the ground, the tail skid dragging my speed down.

I swung the nose around, heading towards the hangars where Dunlop and Green raced out to meet me. Neither of them said anything about the bounces. There's an old saying that any landing you can walk away from is a good landing, but I still felt embarrassed at my clumsy attempt to put the kite down.

"How was she, sir?" Green asked once the noise of the engine had died away.

"Great. Everything in tip-top trim, although I suppose you'd better check I haven't bent the undercart."

"No problem, Sir. I've seen worse landings."

Other A Flight machines were returning by the time I'd got back to my hut. I filled in my log book, then sat to write this account. I'm sure there will be more to tell as I still haven't met my hut mates, nor have I met the C.O. yet, but I'm not sure when I'll have a chance to write my journal in peace, so I'll leave my account of those meetings until tomorrow.

Tuesday 3rd April, 1917

The Squadron C.O. is Major Jones. He's a short, bull-necked, terrier of a man who speaks with a very pronounced Welsh accent. I spoke to him before dinner, and he welcomed me to the Squadron, telling me I was a fine fellow, joining a fine squadron full of other fine fellows, and he was sure I'd do them proud. I assured him I would.

In the pre-dinner chat, I met Vaughn and Tattersall, both pilots in B Flight with whom I will be sharing Hut Three. Ashton introduced me to them since he is also in Hut Three.

Ashton himself is a tall, gangling figure who looks rather awkward in his movements, but he's a decent fellow, and one of the squadron's most experienced observers.

"Bertie says I've to team up with you from tomorrow," he told me, referring to our Flight Commander by his first name. "We've to do two practice flights tomorrow. The first will be at oh nine hundred, then up again at fifteen hundred."

All I could do was nod and murmur that it would be good to team up with him. I really wanted to get stuck in to proper war flying, but Sibbald had insisted I needed more hours under my belt, so I had no option but to follow his orders.

"And you need to practise your landings," our surly Flight Commander growled at me, letting me know someone had ratted me out.

As for my other hut mates, Vaughn is an Irishman with a mop of dark hair and a deadpan way of joking. Everyone calls him Paddy.

"It's a lot shorter than my actual name," he told me. "Even I can't remember all the names my father gave me. I think he was drunk at the time he registered my birth."

I must admit my initial reaction to meeting Vaughn was one of confusion. I wasn't quite sure whether he was being serious half the time.

"It's a grand life in the Flying Corps," he assured me. "There's nothing quite like flying a B.E.2."

His tone and expression suggested he was in earnest, yet his words could, of course, be taken in different ways. Unsure of his true meaning, all I could do was nod and agree with him.

The fourth member of our Hut is Tattersall, universally known as "Dish". He laughed when I asked him how he had acquired this name.

"Tattersall," he explained. "All in tatters. Dishevelled. Dish."

That seemed rather convoluted, but it was typical of the Flying Corps. Most people in the squadron seemed to have some sort of nickname or casual name.

"And what should we call you?" Vaughn asked me.

"My first name is Arthur," I told him.

"You're from Scotland by your accent."

"Edinburgh," I told him.

"Well, we'll find a name for you before long. Most chaps soon get a nickname."

"If they last long enough," Tattersall said softly, providing a reminder of the dangers of war flying.

Dinner was held in the dining room of the Mess. We sat at a large table which had been created by pushing four smaller tables together to form a large rectangle. The Major sat at the head, from where he proposed the toast to the King. Then we sat and enjoyed a meal of chicken and vegetables, followed by prunes and custard. It was better than most meals I'd had at boarding school, so I tucked in, although Vaughn made some disparaging comments about the quality of the custard.

"It's lumpy," he complained.

"Just like your landings, then," said Watt, who is obviously another joker.

Vaughn threw a bread roll at him, earning him a sharp glare from the Major.

The conversation over dinner was relaxed, with some of the chaps exchanging comments about how the preparations for the Push were going. Everyone agreed it was going to be a huge effort.

The biggest news of the day came when the Major rose to give a short speech at the end of the meal. Once the waiters had been dismissed, he officially introduced me to the Squadron, then gave a short round-up of some administrative issues before turning to the question of duties.

"The offensive will begin any day now," he told us. "So it will be a hard time for a while yet. We need to keep flying at all times so, weather permitting, each crew will do at least two jobs every day. Three if there's enough daylight."

Everyone accepted that with smiles, and it was evident that these chaps were keen to do their bit to win the war. I'd heard some horror stories about front line squadrons where in-fighting and back-stabbing were commonplace, but Major Jones seemed to run a jolly friendly outfit, and I'm glad I've been posted here.

Then, though, came some sombre food for thought.

The C.O. told us, "Corps H.Q. has passed word that the Germans are preparing to meet the offensive by bringing in some of their most experienced fighting units."

He paused, letting his gaze rove around the table, then went on, "We hear that Baron von Richthofen and his unit have moved to Douai, which is not far north of here."

I could sense a rise in tension, but nobody said anything in response. Even I had heard of Manfred von Richthofen, though. He is Germany's foremost living fighter pilot, and he's shot down a lot of very good lads.

The Major assured us, "Corps tell me that our own scout squadrons will provide plenty of cover for us, so there is no need to be overly concerned. If you do happen to find yourselves being attacked by red Albatroses, get home as quickly as you can. Let our own single-seaters tackle them. Our job remains army cooperation, so I don't want anyone trying any heroics. By all means shoot at the Huns if they come close, but don't go looking for trouble."

There was a murmur of agreement, and then the Major said his farewells, leaving the rest of us to mull over the news.

"The Red Baron himself," Tattersall remarked. "That will make life interesting."

"And possibly very short," Vaughn put in. "They say he's shot down nearly thirty planes."

"Don't worry about it, Old Bean," grinned Normansby. "Like all Huns, he won't dare cross the Lines to chase us. As long as we see him coming, we can get away safely."

Chapman, one of C Flight's observers, suggested, "We could always fight back. I know the Major says he doesn't want any heroics, but running away doesn't seem right."

Sibbald overheard this, and he made a point of saying," By all means fight back if you can't get away in time, but the B.E.2c is no match for an Albatros. Even the old Fokker monoplanes shot down lots of B.E.s. We didn't get the name 'Fokker Fodder' for nothing, you know."

Chapman nodded, but I heard him mutter, "All the same, if the bloody Red Baron comes close to me, I'll give him a belly full of lead."

Sibbald, perhaps not hearing this, added, "Discretion is the better part of valour. Our job is to help the troops on the ground. We won't do that by tackling Hun scouts when the Flying Corps has other squadrons who are better equipped to do that."

Most of the squadron seemed to agree with this, although I'm sure Chapman was not alone in wanting to fight. What I learned from this is that my fellow squadron members are a plucky lot. The Major was right; this is indeed a fine squadron.

That all happened last night, of course. This morning, B Flight were up on the dawn job, and A flight were due out at nine ack emma. I was invited to their pre-flight briefing, so I joined the other crews in the office, all of us standing in our flying gear while Sibbald allocated tasks. He, Watt and Garrick were to do artillery shoots, while Sullivan and Normansby were tasked with taking photographs of the German trenches and rear areas.

"Kerr," Sibbald said to me. "You and Lieutenant Ashton will stay on this side of the Lines. I want you to rehearse combat manoeuvres this morning. I also want a report on how many other aircraft you see while you are up. Numbers, types, location, altitude and direction. Got that?"

"Yes, Skipper."

So, while the others went to do the real work of war, Ashton and I went up and flew among the clouds in safety, practising what to do if we were ever attacked.

The B.E.2 has no fixed machine gun. Instead, we have a portable Lewis gun which has a drum containing 47 bullets of standard .303 calibre in a circular drum on top of the gun. Between the two cockpits of our kite, I discovered a new attachment. A rotating spike jutted up from a base attached to the fuselage. On top of this spike was a notched quadrant of metal.

"It's called the Strange mount," Ashton informed me as he placed the Lewis gun on top of the odd-looking quadrant. "That's not because it looks strange, but because it was invented by Captain Louis Strange, one of the very first British pilots out here back at the start of the war."

Ashton turned in his cockpit, kneeling on his seat and holding the machine gun in position.

"This way," he explained, "I can shoot backwards and above. The gun moves on the ratchet, and the spike rotates to allow me a wide arc of fire over your head."

He went on, "If a Hun tries to get below us, I'll signal to you to bank the wings. That gives me a chance of shooting at him."

We went over the hand signals a couple of times.

Ashton told me, "The best thing you can do is keep dodging. Fling the kite around as much as you can, but don't bank too steeply because I won't be strapped in, and I don't fancy getting chucked out of the plane."

He then indicated two other metal attachments, one on either side of his cockpit.

"We call these Candlesticks," he explained. "The Lewis gun has a spike attached underneath, and it can slot into these mountings. That lets me shoot to the side."

"What if the enemy is in front of us?" I asked, knowing the Quirk's design meant that shooting forwards was impossible because of the propeller.

Ashton grinned, swinging the Lewis back onto the Strange mount, but reversing it so that the butt and trigger were closer to me, with the barrel pointing forwards.

"This way," he said, "You can use one hand to fire the gun ahead. It will stay fixed to the quadrant until I lift it off."

"But the propeller and wings are in front of me," I frowned.

"So am I," he said, his face serious.

"So what use is the gun?"

"You can't fire straight ahead without shooting off our own prop," he agreed. "But you can shoot upwards above the wings, and you can shoot obliquely to left and right, aiming between the wings."

"But I could hit our struts or bracing wires!" I protested.

"Yes, you could. Better aim well, then. But if it's a choice between that or being shot down, I'd rather risk you hitting our own kite."

I wasn't sure how to respond to that, but Ashton seemed very earnest. Having explained the use of the gun, he went over the various hand signals once again. When he was satisfied I knew how to respond to each gesture, we took off and tried them out for what seemed an age. Because of the engine noise, it's often difficult to make out what your companion is saying, so hand signals are important. In response to Ashton's gestures, I would turn the Quirk or dip one set of wings to allow him to swing the machine gun to defend us against attack from an imaginary opponent. It was very tiring, swinging the heavy machine around the sky, and I was sticky with sweat by the time we returned to the airfield for lunch.

"How many planes did you spot?" Sibbald asked me when he returned from his own flight.

I swallowed nervously. I'd completely forgotten about that.

"None," I admitted.

Sibbald looked at Ashton who said, "There were some F.E.2b's going out on a patrol near Arras. They were level with us. A flight of Sopwith Pups were up high over us on their way home, and there were a couple of Flights of Nieuports over the Lines at around twelve thousand feet. I also noticed a Hun two-seater way up high as we were coming back. I'm sure there were others around, but those were the only ones near us."

For a moment, I thought he was making all this up. I'd had no idea there were that many other planes near us, and certainly not a Hun.

Sibbald told me, "Seeing other aircraft is not easy. The sky is a big place, and you need to be able to spot them. You also need to learn how to recognise different types of machines from any angle. It's a knack, and it comes with practice. When you're out on an artillery job, your observer will be busy with the wireless, so you need to watch the sky. So go out again this afternoon and repeat the exercise."

So we did. This time, Ashton was kind to me, pointing out other aircraft as we stooged around behind the Lines. Sometimes he seemed to be pointing to empty sky, but I did catch sight of some tiny dots which could have been other aeroplanes. I did, though, see bursts of anti-aircraft fire which everyone in the R.F.C. calls Archie after some old music hall song which one of the first pilots used to sing whenever the Germans tried to shoot at him.

"Archibald, Certainly not!" went the refrain.

It was how the Flying Corps responded to everything the Germans did, treating it all as a great joke, but I must admit the sight of those black explosions suddenly appearing in the sky looked rather daunting.

When we returned to the airfield, Ashton explained, "The Hun Archie can be a nuisance, so you need to keep altering course and height if he starts having a go at you. That usually throws him off. The time to really worry is when he stops shooting at you."

"Oh? Why?"

"Because that usually means some Hun machines are coming for you. Their Archie won't risk hitting them."

I nodded, "That makes sense."

He said, "Sometimes our own Archie will warn us by putting a shell nearby. You can tell the difference because our shells burst into white smoke, while the Huns' are black."

He said it almost casually, as if we were discussing nothing more serious than an everyday routine, which I suppose it is. His confidence certainly made me feel a whole lot better about facing Archie.

That was my day, and I was exhausted when it was over. Sibbald, still muttering that I needed more practice, nevertheless told me that Ashton and I would be doing a photographic shoot at dawn the next morning, and that drove all thoughts of fatigue away.

"You're not ready yet," Sibbald told me, "but we have no choice. We need every pilot we can get."

Even the news that the squadron needed another replacement crew could not banish my feeling of delight that I would be taking part tomorrow, but most of the chaps were rather shocked that C Flight's commander, Captain North, had been shot down. Both he and his observer, Lieutenant South, were dead, their machine having crashed a mile or two behind the German Lines.

"They were jumped by a group of Albatroses," Potter said. "According to our Archie observers, it was probably von Richthofen's lot."

Vaughn sighed, "So North and South have gone west. Who will be next, I wonder?"

His comment was in bad taste, and I told him so, but he merely gave me an innocent look.

"The thing is," he said, "that it's usually the least experienced pilots who go first. If an old hand like Eddie North can be shot down, what chance do the rest of us have?"

"We are here to take chances," I told him. "This is war, not a game of cricket."

He seemed on the point of saying something more, but Dish Tattersall gave him a poke in the ribs and told him to stop winding me up.

I have decided to pay no attention to Vaughn. Everyone else treats him as if he's amusing, but I don't take to him at all.

But, as I said, who cares? Tomorrow, my war begins. At last, I'll be helping defeat the Boche.

Wednesday 4th April, 1917

What a day it has been! I feel as if I have crammed a lifetime into the past hours. I should really try to get some sleep now, but I am still too jazzed by everything that has happened, so I'll take some time to note everything down in this journal.

I'm in the hut, writing by the light of a single candle. I can hear Vaughn and Tattersall snoring nearby, and I can't disturb Ashton since his bed is empty.

But I'll come to that in the proper place. It's best to start with the dawn patrol.

Etherington woke me and Ashton when it was still dark. Groggily, we dressed in our flying kit and then trudged to the Mess for an early breakfast which comprised a cup of sweet tea, some toast and boiled eggs.

"Always bloody hard boiled," grumbled Sullivan as he cut the top off his egg. "It doesn't matter how early you get here, the eggs are never soft boiled."

"It's an ancient R.F.C. tradition, Old Bean," Normansby told him.

"Ancient?" queried Long, Beano's observer. "The R.F.C. has only been around for a few years."

"So have the eggs," Watt put in with a grin.

Laughing, Beano waggled his teaspoon at Long as he explained, "Notwithstanding the age of the eggs, Old Bean, the march of progress is so rapid, even last year's events seem like ancient history."

"My egg certainly tastes ancient," Sullivan grumbled.

As usual, the Mess waiters paid him no heed, and everyone's eggs were hard boiled.

After quickly devouring our breakfast, we went across to the hangars. It was still dark, so we used the faint glimmer of the lamps which hung inside the huge tents to guide us.

Our machines were lined up, ready to be started. I found a Corporal from the Photographic Unit waiting for me.

"Good morning, Sir," he said in greeting. "I've set the camera up for you."

He indicated a large, black, metal box attached to the starboard side of the plane, just beside my cockpit.

"It's the L type," he informed me. "The very latest. Have you used one before?"

"I've had some instruction," I replied, irritated at having to admit my lack of knowledge. "But I've never actually used one."

"That's no problem, Sir," he assured me. "It's very simple. The L is much easier to use than the older cameras."

At his bidding, I climbed into the cockpit while he stood beside the aeroplane and showed me the operation of the equipment.

"The camera contains eighteen glass plates, Sir," he said. "Each one is five inches by four. The camera is operated by those two levers on the top, but I've set up a Bowden cable for you. All you need to do is press the button. The first press will take a photograph, then the second will activate the second lever which moves that plate out of the way of the lens and puts another one in its place. So, just keep clicking the button until all the plates have been exposed. You'll hear the camera give a clunk when all the plates are exposed."

I held the Bowden cable in my left hand, nodding my understanding.

"That seems simple enough," I agreed.

"The lens is set to take oblique photographs today, Sir," he told me. "So you need to be about half a mile west of your designated target at around eight thousand feet. You should be able to take all eighteen shots in about a minute and a half."

Then he wished me luck and stepped away from the aeroplane as our Ack Emmas began the process of starting the engines.

Ashton had set the Lewis gun up on the Strange Mounting, and now he strapped himself into his wicker seat while I pressed switches and exchanged the routine calls with Dunlop.

"Switches off! Petrol on! Suck in! Contact!"

All the engines were started, the six Quirks coughing into life. We sat there, letting the engines warm to optimum temperature, and to ensure that the oil had fully circulated. This took about ten minutes, by which time the sky to the east was growing light. I could see several Ack Emmas milling around Beano's machine, and noticed his propeller was stationary. Engine problems, no doubt. The ground crew made several attempts to get the engine going, but Beano eventually gave the washout signal to Sibbald. The Flight Commander waved his acknowledgement. Now only five of us would be going up. Beano and Long were supposed to be doing artillery spotting this morning, so now Beano would need to hurry to the office and telephone the Battery to let them know he was unable to carry out that task. I expected there would be some heated conversations between the artillery officers and Wing, but engine failure was a fairly common occurrence, and there was really nothing to be done about it.

It was light enough to see now, and Sibbald led the way, trundling out to the field and taking off. The rest of us followed in line, Ashton and I being last given my lack of seniority in the Flight.

Once up, we headed east, but each of us flew on our own. The sector we covered had been divided among us, and we each had separate targets. Those doing artillery jobs would first need to locate their batteries and make contact via wireless, but Ashton and I were charged with taking photographs of the German trenches south of the Scarpe, so we continued eastwards while the others began circling over the artillery batteries.

Our B.E.2 clawed its way into the sky. Our airfield is about fifteen miles behind the Lines, and we had almost reached our appointed height by the time we arrived above the ruined town of Arras. I circled for a few minutes, climbing all the time. Then, when the altimeter showed we had at last reached eight thousand feet, I ventured across the Lines for the first time.

I will admit I was excited, my nerves tingling with anticipation as I made that fateful step. The sun was also ascending, lightening the earth below us, casting long shadows. These, I knew, would help the Intelligence teams who examine photographs because shadows show up features which might otherwise be missed. This was all right for them, but the low sun was a problem since we were heading straight at it, and even though it was a relatively dull day, the brightness was still sufficient to obscure our view of much of the sky.

"Beware the Hun in the sun!" our training posters warned. It is a favourite trick of the German flyers to place themselves with the sun behind them, rendering them invisible when they make an attack. I could see Ashton holding up one gloved thumb to blot out the sun's disc and so hopefully reveal any Hun machines which might be trying to use the sunlight as cover. Either they were not there, or he could not see them, for he gave no warning signal.

There were other planes around, some so close even I could notice them. A troop of F.E.2b's were bumbling across the Lines, with a flight of Spads above them. One of the Fee gunners waved as they crossed our path on their way to whatever target they were heading for. I wondered whether my friend, Greening, might be in one of those big two-seaters. His airfield was close to ours, so it was possible.

Higher up, I caught a glimpse of some Nieuports, reminding me that Vanders was also out here. The lithe Nieuports were always painted silver because they were French machines, and the manufacturers used a special kind of dope to coat the fabric skin. This made those little scout planes stand out among the usually drab, olive brown machines of the Royal Flying Corps.

It was as the Major had said; there were plenty of scout planes around to protect us. This would allow me to concentrate on my job. I just hoped I would not bungle the task of taking the photographs. There were a lot of clouds around, forcing me to go a bit lower than I wanted. In turn, this meant I would need to fly slightly further east in order to compensate for the camera's angled lens. The other factor was the wind, which was buffeting us around rather more than I liked, blowing from the west and pushing us ever eastwards. I'd need to allow for that while taking the pictures.

While I was busy working this out, a loud bang exploded in the sky some yards off to our right. I jumped in fright, causing the plane to dip alarmingly, and I saw Ashton raise his arms in annoyance. As I righted the machine, I heard another bang, and this time I saw the puff of black filth as a shell exploded above us and off to our left.

Archie!

I'd forgotten the Germans would object to our presence over the Lines. Cursing, I remembered what I'd been told and I adjusted our course slightly, also dropping a couple of hundred feet in altitude. The next bursts from the Hun gunners flowered well above us and off to our left.

"Archibald, certainly not!" I sang as I made another slight alteration in course and began to climb again.

By the time we reached our destination, I was quite enjoying my little tussle with Archie, but I noticed Ashton was sitting up alertly, twisting his head constantly as he scanned the sky for Hun aeroplanes.

Now I needed to take the photographs. The best thing about photo shoots is that, once the camera plates have been exposed, you need to get back to the airfield as quickly as possible. On an artillery job, you need to stay over the Lines for a couple of hours, but H.Q. want the photographs as soon as they can get them, so these jobs were relatively short unless you were told to photograph well behind the Lines. Today, for my first mission, I think Sibbald had decided to give me a relatively easy task.

As I manoeuvred the B.E.2, I noticed sunlight glinting on some other plane far above us. I waggled the wings to attract Ashton's attention. He squirmed round, looking up when I pointed, then grinned and gave me a thumbs up, indicating it was a friendly machine. How he could tell, I do not know, but I was pleased that I had at least managed to spot another aircraft in the sky before he had.

I flew south from the line of the river, then confused Archie by doing a 180 degree turn and heading north. Leaning out over the side of the cockpit, I peered down at the ground, comparing what I could see against the map I had strapped to my right thigh. For a moment or two, I worried that I was in the wrong place, but there was a village down there, a pile of rubble and the line of a road which I had marked as the start of our target area.

I levelled the plane, seized the Bowden cable and began pressing the buttons. Even over the vibration and roar of the engine I could feel the camera working. The shutter clicked loudly, then I felt rather than heard the plates being moved when I pressed the button a second time.

Click, click. Hold the plane steady. Watch for wind drift. Don't bank the wings when you look down.

Click, click.

And Archie exploded in fury around us, realising we were flying straight and level.

Damn, some of those shells were close.

Click, click.

How many was that? I had already lost count, and the ninety seconds suggested by the PU Corporal seemed to be lasting an age.

Click, click.

Another photograph taken, another plate exposed and automatically pulled out of the way to be replaced by a fresh one. This was certainly a lot easier than the old-fashioned cameras the R.F.C. had used until recently. Those devices had required an observer to stand up and manually move the plates for each exposure. This new technology made life a lot better.

Click, click.

The plane wobbled as a gust of wind coincided with a burst of Archie below our tail. I grabbed the stick, swearing loudly because I'd just taken a photograph which would be ruined. I levelled off and began again.

Click, click.

And so it went on until I felt no response when I pressed the button.

All eighteen plates had been exposed. How many of them would come out remained to be seen, but I had had enough. I swivelled the plane to the left, banking the wings and throwing Archie off target as I headed for home. I was tempted to put the nose down, but I had been warned that Hun machine guns on the ground can reach targets up to around five or six thousand feet, so I dared not go too low. Instead, I opened the throttle and the engine roared, the revs climbing to over eighteen hundred. If I pushed the B.E.2, even this old crate should be able to reach something close to seventy miles per hour, but the ground seemed to be moving dreadfully slowly beneath us. Then I recalled the wind which had gusted behind us on the way out, and I knew we were facing the uphill struggle against the prevailing westerly. I'd heard some old pilots claim that the first machines used by the R.F.C. were so slow that they sometimes stood perfectly still in the air when confronted with a strong wind. Some even claimed those old kites would fly backwards if the wind blew strongly enough.

We certainly struggled to cover the couple of miles which eventually took us to safety beyond our own balloon lines. Then I put the nose down and followed the road from Arras which would guide us home. I was annoyed with myself as I lined up our approach, for the Quirk seemed rather sluggish in its responses, but I put it down to the blustering wind, concentrating as hard as I could on getting down safely.

This time, I managed to put the Quirk on the ground with only a very small bounce. Dunlop and Green raced out to meet us, then we were back at the hangars. As soon as I cut the engine, the PU Corporal was at our side, taking a wrench to the nuts and bolts which held the camera in place.

"Any problems, Sir?" he asked as he rapidly loosened the black box from the plane.

"One or two might be a bit out of focus thanks to Archie," I told him. "It was rather bumpy for a while, and I had to go a bit lower than planned because of clouds. I hope I made the right adjustments to compensate."

"We'll soon find out, Sir," he told me, his expression serious as he worked at freeing the camera. Then he shoved his wrench into a pocket, grabbed the bulky camera in both arms, and dashed away.

"The Stickybacks are always in a hurry," Ashton told me as he pulled his helmet off.

"Stickybacks?" I frowned.

"The Photographic boys. You'll see. They develop the photos so quickly, they are still wet when they deliver them. We call them stickybacks."

"The photographs or the PU fellows?"

"Both," he grinned. "Well done today, by the way. Archie got a bit rough there for a moment or two."

"Sorry about the first one," I said as I climbed down from the cockpit to stand beside him.

"Everyone does that the first time," he told me. "Now, let's make our report. Then we can get a decent breakfast while the Ack Emmas refuel and patch the kite."

I wondered what he meant by patching the machine, but then I noticed Green examining the aircraft's tail and shaking his head with the air of a man who knew he faced a difficult task.

"What's wrong?" I asked him.

"That must have been a close one, Sir," he said, pointing to several ragged holes in the tail fins. "It's lucky your elevator and rudder controls weren't cut."

He was right. The tail unit was a bit of a mess, strips of canvas hanging loose, and a couple of wooden spars clearly damaged.

"How long will that take to mend?" I asked him.

"A couple of hours should do it, Sir," he told me resignedly.

"Good. Our next job is at one o'clock."

"We'll do our best to get her ready, Sir."

As Ashton and I strolled back to the office to make out our report, I realised that the background noise was louder than usual. It often takes a while for hearing to return fully to normal after a flight, but this time I had felt as if my ears were still being assailed. Then I realised it was the sound of our artillery.

Ashton had noticed it, too.

"The main bombardment has begun," he said, listening to the thundering rumble of the great guns which had now reached new heights and continued without any break at all. It was like a constant roll of a large, bass drum hammering away at our ears.

"How long will that go on for?" I asked him.

He shrugged, "It depends on what the Generals want. Some of them prefer a long bombardment of days or even weeks to smash the Hun trenches and destroy the barbed wire. Others think a short, lightning bombardment is enough to stun Jerry long enough for the troops to cross No Man's Land."

"But it means the Push is close?"

"It does," he confirmed, and I felt a surge of patriotic delight. I was taking part in the great assault which would end this long war, and that felt good.

Potter and the Major were in the office when we went in to give our report.

"Any trouble?" the Major asked.

"Only a bit of Archie, Sir," I replied.

"No sign of Hun machines?"

Ashton quickly put in, "No, Sir. There were plenty of Spads and Nieuports around, as well as some Pups up at around twenty thousand. I did see a group of three Halberstadts, but they stayed well on their side of the Lines."

The Major seemed relieved at that news, and I realised he was worried about the presence of von Richthofen's red Albatroses. We'd lost a Flight Commander yesterday, and the Major was concerned we might lose more crews.

By the time we'd made out our report, one of Potter's clerks had typed it up and we'd both signed it, the photographs had arrived, brought by the same PU Corporal who had overseen the installation and removal of our camera.

"Not bad, Sir," he said to me as he handed over the black and white photographs. As Ashton had said, the ink was still damp, so he handled them with care, gripping only the edges between his fingers.

"I've sent copies to VII Corps H.Q., Sir," he told the Major.

"Very good," the C.O. nodded.

I looked at the photographs with interest as Potter spread them on his desk. To be honest, I could make out little sense from the images, but I was pleased to see that most were in focus, with the dark, zig-zag lines of the trenches clearly visible against the grey of the mud.

"Well done, Kerr," the Major said. "Not bad at all for a first effort. Now both of you run along and have a rest before your next job."

The rest of A Flight returned safely. Beano's engine had been fixed, and he was raring to go on the next job, vowing to make up for missing the early mission.

"How's the bombardment going?" he asked Sibbald.

"The Huns are taking a real pasting," Sibbald told him. "I think this bombardment is even bigger than the one before the Somme last year."

"Poor devils," Beano murmured. "Rather them than our lads, though."

While we waited, C Flight's new commander arrived, along with a replacement observer. The Captain is called Bernard, and he seems frightfully keen, announcing he'd go up as soon as he could.

The news was not so good for B Flight, though. Brown and Ramage did not return from their job. At first, nobody was quite sure what had happened to them. Paddy Vaughn, though, had a theory.

"I could see them just to the south of us," he informed the Mess. "They were doing the usual figure of eight pattern, then their port wings just broke up. They went into a spinning dive straight away, and the whole wing assembly broke off as they fell."

"Archie?" someone asked.

Vaughn shook his head.

"I didn't see any Archie bursts. I think it was one of our own shells that hit them. It must have smashed through their wings on its way to the German trenches."

"It happens," sighed Unswood, B Flight's commander.

And that was their epitaph, although Vaughn made me think when he later said to me and Tattersall, "Can you imagine what that must have been like for them? They were probably alive all the way down, knowing they couldn't get out."

I tried not to think about that. It had never occurred to me that our planes were at risk from our own artillery shells, but I supposed the shells had to go somewhere close since they were aiming for the targets we were circling over.

There was, though, no time to contemplate the vagaries of war flying. Ashton and I ate another, more substantial, breakfast, then prepared for our second job of the day. This one, as I'll explain, was even more eventful than the first.

Late Morning & Afternoon, Wednesday, 4th April, 1917

Our second job was another photographic shoot, this time five miles over the Lines, looking for any signs that the Huns were bringing up reserve troops to meet our Push.

"That's the point of this offensive," Sibbald informed me when he delivered the op briefing. "The French are going to make their own attack a bit further south. The aim of our offensive is to draw German reserves away from where the real blow will fall."

"You mean our Push is just a diversion?" I gaped incredulously.

"More or less," he shrugged. "Although I expect the Generals will be more than pleased if they do make an actual breakthrough. The real trouble is that the Germans are not stupid, and they must know what we are planning. You can't hide an attack of this size, so they'll have seen the French preparations as well. Still, we need to know what the Huns are up to, so go and take your photographs in case they have dug some extra fortifications in the rear areas. It's not likely, but you never know."

"Why isn't it likely, Captain?" I enquired, feeling rather let down that our major Push was being classed as a mere diversionary attack.

He said, "Because the Germans retired to the Hindenburg Line just last month. It's already very strong, with several sets of trenches going back a few miles, but Corps H.Q. want to be certain there have been no additional strongpoints added further back. Your job is to bring back some evidence one way or the other."

With that, Ashton and I made preparations for the flight. We were delayed because patching up our tail unit had taken a lot longer than expected.

"The fresh dope's not quite dry yet, Sir," Green apologised when I asked him if the kite was ready. "Give it another hour or so."

After kicking our heels while the new coat of varnished dope dried, we eventually set off shortly after two o'clock. The rest of the Flight were already out on artillery shoots, directing the fire of the heavy batteries. They would not return until around four pip emma, but we would hopefully be back in less than ninety minutes. Then after refuelling, we'd be back out again for a third job, with perhaps a fourth one if the weather held. Of course, the other Flights were doing the same, so the airfield was a constant hive of activity, with aeroplanes coming and going all the time, and I felt a thrill of excitement at being a part of this smoothly functioning machine which was the Royal Flying Corps.

The wind was still blowing strongly from the west, pushing us towards the Lines more quickly than I wanted, for the B.E.2 needed time to reach our required altitude. This time, I went above the clouds, hoping to use them to conceal our presence from Archie until it was time to drop down and take our pictures. I was using the dashboard clock and compass to estimate our position, but I looked down whenever there was a break in the clouds, and then referred to the map. Fortunately, there were plenty of gaps in the cloud cover, and the dull line of the River Scarpe was a good guide, while the wide morass of the trench lines was unmistakable.

As we neared the Lines, Ashton banged a fist on the fuselage to attract my attention. He was pointing upwards towards the north and west.

Squinting, I saw the dark cross of another aircraft high above us. It was only a silhouette, but I guessed Ashton was telling me it was a Hun.

I cocked my head, wondering what he wanted me to do, but he simply kept watch on the Hun. It was on our side of the Lines, so I was fairly sure it was a two-seater, no doubt engaged in a similar mission to us, taking photographs of our build up for the offensive. I was tempted to go after it, but it was flying much higher than our poor old Quirk could ever hope to reach, so I kept heading eastwards.

Then Ashton pointed again, giving a thumbs up signal, and I twisted round to see three other aircraft pouncing on the lone machine. The Hun turned, diving steeply, but the three British scouts had managed to surprise it. Before long, the Hun tumbled down, a thin trail of smoke marking its vertical descent. I watched it for as long as I could, but then it vanished into a cloud.

Ashton was grinning broadly, pleased at witnessing this triumph. Hun two-seaters are notoriously difficult to bring down. They have machine guns to front and rear, and they generally fly high and fast, making them very difficult to catch.

This seemed a good omen, but soon it was our turn.

I gently pushed down the plane's nose, squirming between two clouds and dropping down near what I hoped was our target. While Ashton kept his eyes on the sky, I looked down, checking my map. Where were we? Had I come too far? Not far enough?

I circled, a manoeuvre which fooled Archie into sending his opening salvo well wide.

Damn! I had come too far, no doubt propelled by the strong wind. Below us was open countryside, green fields and trees. The area we needed to photograph was closer to the desolated ruin of the Lines.

I headed south-west for a few minutes until we were above the trenches of the German back areas, checked my location, then swung north and began taking photographs.

The Hindenburg Line is a mass of concrete strongpoints and well-constructed trenches, with several lines stretching back over three or four miles. Faced with a war on two Fronts, the Germans seem to have decided to fight a defensive war against us while they try to knock out the Russians who are in turmoil after the abdication of the Tsar. In accordance with this doctrine, they had built the Hindenburg Line, then retreated a few miles to take up these much stronger defensive positions. The question now was whether they had moved extra troops into reserve positions behind the newly dug defences.

I began the run, pressing the button and feeling the camera respond. Archie continued to bother us, so I dropped a little altitude in between shots, hoping to throw off his aim.

I still don't know whether that move saved our lives or put us in more danger. All I know is that there was a fearful explosion just above and behind us. Looking back, I can't quite work out how the shell got there without smashing through us, but I still don't know how close it was. Certainly close enough to be audible, and to spatter us with tiny fragments of shrapnel.

I felt a thump on my back, all along my shoulders, and another blow on the top of my head which momentarily knocked me senseless. I could hear rips and clangs as metal struck the plane and bounced off the Lewis gun. The tiny windshield in front of me splintered and cracked, but it held together even though it was speckled with several tiny fragments of metal. The plane wobbled, dropped into a shallow dive, then I pulled her back up and shook my head. I was aching all over, and I could barely move my arms because my back was so sore, and my head was throbbing in protest.

I had dropped the Bowden cable, so my first reaction was to fumble around for it. Once I had located it, I looked up to check on Ashton.

He was slumped sideways in the front cockpit, his head lolling over the side. I could not see his face, for he had twisted in the cockpit, but he was lying very still indeed. His flying helmet was askew, and I noticed that his goggles were no longer strapped around his head. Ashton had often pushed his goggles up when looking for Huns, and I guessed they had fallen off when he fell. He was not moving at all, and I feared the worst, but there was nothing I could do to help him even though he was only a few feet in front of me.

I let go of the cable again, banging my fist on the rim of my cockpit to attract his attention, but he did not respond at all.

I turned the kite around, avoiding another burst of Archie, then looked down, checking my position. I had no idea how many plates were left to be exposed, but I knew the mission was more important than Ashton's life. As long as I got back, that was, and the question was whether I could get home without an observer to watch the sky.

The B.E.2 seemed to be flying all right. I could see some tears in the fabric, but the controls still responded. That made up my mind. I checked my position, guessed at where I had been when the Archie had hit us, circled around for another run, and began taking photographs again.

It did not take long. There must have been only a handful of plates remaining in the camera. As soon as they were exposed, I turned for home.

Now the wind was my enemy. Ashton had still not moved, and my head and back were protesting, making every movement painful.

But I was still conscious, and still able to fly. I did my best to watch the sky for Hun machines, but if one had come along, I'm sure I would not have got back safely. Fortunately, the only aircraft I saw were British; a couple of Sopwith One and a Half Strutters, another B.E.2, and a Flight of Spads all passed me as I headed westwards.

I crossed the Lines after about fifteen minutes of battling against the wind, then followed the road from Arras, losing height all the time.

The airfield came in sight. Awkwardly, every movement causing ripples of agony, I pulled the Very pistol out of its holder, rammed in a red flare and fired it high into the air. The gun went off with a loud bang, sending the red trail arcing above and behind me, then I fired another one, and a third.

The signals warned people on the ground I was in trouble. Funnily enough, I carried off the best landing of my short career as I brought the Quirk down in a perfect three-pointer, the tail skid slowing my forward movement.

A crowd of Ack Emmas and officers ran out to greet us, clustering round as soon as I killed the engine.

"Bloody Hell!" someone exclaimed.

The Major quickly took control, ordering some men to lift Ashton out and carry him to the ambulance tender which had rushed across the field and was standing beside our plane, its engine still running.

"What about you, Kerr?" the Major asked. "Are you hurt?"

"Something hit me on the back and my head," I said, feeling too tired to climb out of the cockpit.

"Give him a hand, lads," the Major commanded. "Get him in the ambulance as well."

While this was happening, the PU Corporal was removing the camera.

I said to him, "I had to go back for a second run to finish the plates. I hope they come out OK."

He nodded, but now the Major was speaking to me again. "What happened?"

"Archie," I told him. "A shell burst right above us."

"Righto. Get along to the hospital and let them take a look at you. We'll get your report later."

I was bundled into the rear of the ambulance where Ashton was lying on a stretcher. The orderlies tried to make me lie down as well, but I refused, telling them my back was too sore. So I sat hunched on a bench, looking across at Ashton.

What I saw horrified me. His face was a mask of blood, and where his right eye should have been, all I could see was a mass of bloody pulp.

"Is he still alive?" I asked.

One of the men, wearing a Red Cross armband, replied, "He's still breathing, Sir. It looks like a piece of shrapnel hit him in the face. We'd better leave him for the doctors."

The tender bumped across the grass, jostling us around, then reached the road and raced along, horn blaring to warn other traffic to get out of our way.

"How far is the hospital?" I asked dully, gritting my teeth against the pain in my back while I clung to the bench seat to counter the bumpy ride.

"Not far, Sir. There's a chateau in the town of Barly, just a mile away. It's been converted into a hospital. They'll see you sorted."

I did not pay much attention to my surroundings when we arrived. I managed to stumble out of the tender while Ashton was lifted out. Then someone took my arm and guided me inside a large building which echoed around us.

"In here," a woman's voice said as she gently guided me into a small room leading off the main entrance hall.

The room contained a single bed, plus cabinets full of medicine. A couple of chairs and a shelf holding assorted medical equipment completed the furniture.

There was a young doctor there, a thin-faced fellow who looked barely old enough to have qualified as a medical expert.

"Good afternoon, " he said. "What happened to you?"

"Archie," I told him.

"Archie? You mean anti-aircraft fire?"

"Yes."

I was feeling very slow and dull-witted now, waves of pain making it difficult to concentrate.

"All right," the doctor said. "Let's take a look at you, then we can decide what to do with you. You're still walking and talking, so hopefully the damage isn't too bad. Let's start by getting your helmet and jacket off."

He and the nurse helped me remove my clothing. I'd been afraid to remove my helmet while in the ambulance, but it came away without the feared stickiness of blood. I could feel a very tender spot, but perhaps the damage was not as bad as I had feared. When I examined my helmet, I found a small tear in the leather. When I poked at it with a finger, the doctor decided to check my skull first.

"That's just a glancing blow," he informed me after a moment of prodding. "There's a tasty little lump, but the skin isn't broken, so I doubt it's too serious. Still, you might suffer concussion, so you'll need to take things easy for a while."

"The main problem is my back," I told him. "I feel like I've been kicked by a horse."

Once my jacket, tunic and shirt had been removed, he made me lie face down on the bed while he examined me, chatting away all the time.

"By George!" he said. "You're going to have some lovely bruises, but I don't think there's anything serious. You have several small pieces of metal stuck in your back, but your thick jacket and tunic absorbed most of the impact, I think. You must have been far enough from the blast that you only caught the outer effects. We'll soon pick out the splinters. A bit of iodine on the wounds and a bandage should be enough."

The nurse had been jotting down notes, referring to my identification tags for my personal details. Now she held a small, metal dish while the doctor used tweezers to pick out the splinters of shrapnel from my back. I heard them clatter into the bowl as he removed them from my aching flesh, each one sending more stabbing shards of pain through me as it was plucked out.

Of course, I dared not show I was feeling any pain, so I tried to think of something else to distract me.

"How's my friend?" I asked.

"My colleagues are looking after him," the doctor assured me. "You're both lucky the Push hasn't started yet. We're geared up for lots of casualties, but so far we're only seeing the usual daily numbers."

He continued to dig away, making me grit my teeth to avoid crying out in front of the nurse.

"This one will need a couple of stitches," he observed as he pulled another fragment clear. To me, it felt as if it were the size of a football, but it made only the faintest sound as it dropped into the dish.

Then he stitched the wound, bringing a hiss of pain as he pinched my flesh and drove the needle rapidly back and forth. It was over in an instant, but it was very painful.

"All done," he announced. "You've been very lucky. You've only got minor flesh wounds. I'll let the nurse bandage you up, then you can get back to your squadron."

"Thank you," I hissed, still aching.

"Just take it easy for a couple of days," he cautioned. "A couple of those fragments were deeper than I'd thought, so you'll be very sore and stiff for a while. I'd prescribe aspirin, but it's hard to come by, so we reserve it for more serious cases. Whisky will probably do the trick, I expect."

"I'll be sure to tell my C.O. that," I said, smiling weakly.

The doctor bade me farewell, then hurried off to check on other patients, leaving me with the nurse.

Indicating the metal dish she still held, she said, "Nine fragments all together. Do you want to keep them?"

"What on earth for?" I sighed, squeezing my eyes tightly shut to keep the tears away.

"Some boys like to have a keepsake," she told me.

"I've got the bruises," I muttered.

"Well, I suppose none of these scraps are big enough to turn into a proper memento," she said. "But I'd recommend shaking out your clothes to make sure there aren't any other pieces lurking around."

She put down the dish, then briskly set about cleaning me up, beginning with dabs of iodine which caused yet more stinging pain. Then she told me to sit up while she applied a gauze patch to the stitched wound, then wrapped a bandage around my shoulders and upper chest.

It was only then that I got a good look at her. She was surprisingly young, with her brown hair tied beneath her bonnet, her long dress and white apron covering a slender body which looked almost frail. Her eyes were blue, full of compassion, and she seemed pleased with herself, a faint smile playing around her lips.

"Thank you," I managed to say.

"It's a pleasure," she told me. "Compared to some of the injuries we see here, yours are nothing."

If she was trying to make me feel better, that did not help. She might consider the injuries to be very minor, but I still felt as if I'd been trampled by wild horses.

"Can I go now?" I asked, wincing at the pain in my back.

"Yes. Keep the bandages on for a week or so, then have one of your squadron's medical orderlies take out the stitches."

"Can't I come back here and let you do it?" I asked her hopefully.

She refused to meet my eyes as she replied, "I expect I'll be very busy in a week's time. The Push will have begun by then."

"I might come anyway," I said, not sure why I was being so bold. Perhaps it was an attempt to disguise the pain I was experiencing. "I could land my plane in the grounds, let you remove the stitches, then fly back again. I could even take you up for a spin if you wanted."

Now she smiled more broadly.

"I see there is not much wrong with you," she said.

"Thanks to you," I grinned. "What's your name? You know mine."

"I am Nurse Routledge," she told me, her tone formal.

"Your first name is Nurse?"

"Behave yourself," she told me. "Now, put on your clothes. They are a bit ragged, so I hope you can have them stitched."

"I'm sure my batman can handle that," I nodded.

She helped me dress because my arms were very stiff due to the combination of the bandages and the injuries to my back.

As I fastened my tunic, I asked, "What about my friend? How is he? Can you find out for me?"

"I'll go and check while you call your squadron," she nodded. "There's a telephone in the front office. I'll take you there."

With my flying jacket, helmet and goggles draped over one arm, I clumped my way after her, crossing the wide entrance hall to the tiny office where a male orderly was busy filling in paperwork.

"Second Lieutenant Kerr needs to telephone his squadron," Nurse Routledge informed him.

The man idly waved a hand at the telephone, then Nurse Routledge went off, her shoes clacking on the tiled floor of the entrance hall. I heard her climbing the wide staircase which led to the upper levels of the house. Then I picked up the telephone and began the tortuous task of being put through to the squadron. I could probably have walked back faster than the operator connected me, but I was eventually able to speak to Potter.

"Glad to hear you're not badly hurt," he said. "Wait there and I'll send a tender to collect you. What about Ashton?"

"I'm trying to find out," I told him.

I left the orderly to his reams of paper, and strolled out into the hallway. Peering out through the glass windows set in the main doors, I could see that the chateau's grounds were mostly comprised of woodland, with a grassy area in front of the house containing a large pond around which the gravel pathway formed a semi-circle.

"You won't be able to land a plane there, will you?" someone asked.

I turned around, seeing Nurse Routledge smiling at me, her expression suggesting she was mocking me.

"Probably not," I agreed. "My Fight Commander would tell you I can't land a plane properly anywhere."

"I can't understand how anyone can go up in one of those things," she said conversationally. "They're very dangerous, aren't they?"

"Not really," I told her. "Things have come a long way since the Wright brothers."

She considered that for a moment, then said, "Perhaps one day I'll take you up on your offer."

"Any time," I grinned. "But what about Lieutenant Ashton? How is he?"

Her expression gave nothing away as she told me, "He's being operated on just now. That's all I can tell you."

"Is it serious?" I pressed.

She gave a vague smile in response.

"He's in safe hands," she assured me.

"Can I see him?"

"Not just now, I'm afraid. I'm sorry."

I shrugged, "Well, thanks for patching me up."

"That's what we are here for," she told me. "But now I must get back to my duties. Sister will not be happy if she finds me chatting to you when you're all fixed up."

So saying, she turned and walked towards the staircase. I watched her go, admiring the way she walked, her long skirt swishing around her.

As she reached the foot of the staircase, she suddenly stopped and swung back to face me, one hand resting on the broad, wooden banister.

"Jennifer," she said.

"Sorry?"

"My name is Jennifer," she told me.

"That's an unusual name," I said. "It's very pretty."

"Thank you," she smiled. Then she turned and climbed the stairs, leaving me full of throbbing pain from my head and back, and a strange sensation of happiness.

Thursday 5th April, 1917

I had no flying duties today. Sibbald told me to obey the doctor's orders and take things easy.

"Your kite's a bit of a mess anyway," he said by way of explanation. "And since you can't fly, I've told Sergeant Stirling to give your engine an overhaul."

In truth, my back ached abominably, and the bump on my head felt very tender. However, I discovered that I had gained a certain respect among the other officers for bringing Ashton back and also for completing my mission.

"Corps H.Q. said the photographs were very helpful," Potter informed me. "As for poor Ashton, he's recovered consciousness, but he's lost his right eye. They're sending him back to Blighty."

"That's rotten luck," I said. "The fragments that hit me were all small and, according to the doctor, can't have had much force left by the time they reached us."

Potter sighed, "I don't suppose they need to be going very fast if they hit you in the eye."

That was true. I felt sorry for Ashton, but I knew there was not much I could have done, and even losing an eye is better than the fate that awaits so many out here. With luck, and in time, Ashton may well be able to return to service, although he'll never fly again, and perhaps that is the worst thing about his injury.

C Flight lost another crew today. Bernard led all six of them out on a bombing raid against a railway marshalling yard some ten miles behind the Lines. They had an escort of Nieuports, but a bunch of Albatroses attacked them on their way home, and Burns and Chapman were shot down. There seems little doubt they are dead. Another crew, Bates and Vickers, were also hit, but Bates managed to nurse his Quirk across the Lines before crashing into a shell hole. The two of them returned late in the evening, both nursing bumps and bruises, but otherwise unharmed.

"I'm glad to be back," Bates said with relief when he flopped into one of the armchairs in the anteroom. "The trenches are bloody awful. Mud and freezing water everywhere. We had to wade through some of them. God knows how the P.B.I. cope with that."

Everyone agreed that we had better living conditions than the Poor Bloody Infantry but, as Beano pointed out, we go over the top several times a day.

"I still wouldn't swap places with them," Bates insisted. He'd only arrived at the squadron that morning, having moved into Hut Three to take Ashton's bed, but already we'd discovered that he is quite outspoken.

Not having been anywhere near the trenches, I had nothing to offer to the conversation, but I was inclined to agree with Bates, and I certainly had no desire to get any first hand experience of life in the mud. Looking down on the hellish quagmire was more than enough for me.

But I am getting ahead of myself again. My own day was not entirely uneventful. Vaughn and Tattersall returned from their morning jobs just before lunchtime, and they suggested we go into Fosseux village to get a bite to eat.

"It will make a change from the Mess fare," Dish assured me.

So the three of us, clad in our greatcoats and caps, walked out the gate and down the narrow road to the village, shoulders hunched against the chill wind.

Fosseux is not much more than two lines of small cottages lining the cobbled road. Most of the houses have tiled roofs, but one or two still have thatched roofing. It's a squalid-looking little place, and I was not looking forward to finding out what type of establishment we would be eating in. As far as I could see, the village was a rural backwater, every household having a field at the back. Some people grow vegetables, others keep chickens, goats or even pigs, but Vaughn assured me that some residents have turned their living rooms into *estaminets* where we can get a bite to eat.

"Lucille is the best cook around," he declared, leading the way to a house with a brightly painted green door. There was a piece of cardboard in the tiny window proclaiming the establishment to be an *estaminet*.

Inside, the main room was small, containing four round, wooden tables which had been squeezed in close together. Only one was occupied, two staff officers with their red tabs on their collars sitting with a middle-aged man who wore a civilian suit. All three of them glanced up when we entered, the staff officers quickly averting their haughty gazes, while the civilian regarded us with some interest before returning to his conversation with the red tabs. Following Vaughn and Tattersall's lead, I did my best to ignore the three of them. Most front line officers detest the sight of red tabs, for the staff officers never go anywhere near danger, and are always to be found in the best accommodation. I recalled Potter telling me that Corps H.Q. was in a chateau just to the north of Fosseux, so I suppose it should not have been surprising that they were here.

After hanging up our caps and greatcoats, we took our seats at the table nearest the door. The room was rather chilly, the small fire under the chimney in the far wall failing to overcome the seeping cold from outside, but we soon relaxed when we were greeted by the hostess.

The lady in question was a middle-aged, rather plump woman who was helped by her teenage daughter. This girl was also plump and rather plain, but she had a smattering of English which she had no doubt learned from the troops who ate here. Vaughn, though, talked to her in what sounded to me like fluent French, and the girl's face lit up with delight as she chatted back to him.

I'd studied the language at school, of course, but I'd never been very good at it, and the rapid-fire exchange was completely incomprehensible to me. However, it did not take a knowledge of the language to realise that they were talking about me, for the girl regarded me with wide eyes.

"What did you say to her?" I asked Vaughn.

He grinned, "I told her you are a wounded aviator who is in need of some restoration."

"There was no need to do that," I mumbled, feeling a little embarrassed.

In halting English, the girl asked me, "You hurt head, yes?"

Feeling my cheeks begin to burn, I gave a brief nod to confirm this, then Vaughn rattled out another French sentence, and both of them started laughing.

"What's that all about?" I asked.

Vaughn chuckled, "I told her you'd bumped your head when you were hiding under a table during a Boche bombing raid."

"Thanks very much!" I protested.

"Well," he laughed, "we can't have you getting all the attention thanks to your war wounds."

Tattersall chuckled, "Paddy's jealous because he reckons you probably had your evil way with several nurses yesterday."

"Don't be daft!" I exclaimed.

"Then why are you blushing?" Vaughn demanded, peering at me with mock intensity.

"Because you're a couple of idiots who are just trying to embarrass me," I retorted.

They continued to pull my leg, and I continued to deny their accusations, but I must admit that their words conjured a mental image of Nurse Jennifer Routledge which was difficult to dispel.

Fortunately, the food arrived, and we moved off the subject of my nefarious dealings with what Vaughn insisted were dozens of nubile nurses.

I was, as usual, a little put out by Vaughn's sense of humour, but the food put me in a better frame of mind. We were served slices of lamb in a wonderful sauce, and it was certainly a lot better than the fare we were served in the Mess. It was accompanied by an earthy red wine, although Tattersall insisted we restrict ourselves to the one bottle.

"Paddy and I are flying again soon," he explained. "It's not a good idea to go up when you're blotto."

He shot Vaughn a knowing smile when he said this, and the Irishman said, "I only did it once."

"And you got yourself lost. You landed on a French airfield somewhere down south, didn't you?"

"It was a fine spot of navigation in dreadful weather," Vaughn insisted with mock pomposity. "I refute all allegations to the contrary."

Tattersall gave me a wink, then added, "You can have as much wine as you like, though, seeing as you've got the day off."

"I still don't want to get blotto," I replied, sipping at the dark liquid which, in my opinion, was rather ordinary.

I said, "I hope Sibbald lets me back on flying duty soon. I'm a bit sore, but I'm sure I can fly. I think he's overly cautious."

"He's survived a long time by being cautious," Vaughn countered. "He was at the Somme last year, you know. That's where he won his M.C."

"What did he do to earn that?" I asked, curious about my Flight Commander.

Vaughn shrugged, "He never says much about it. All I've heard him say is that he was the only survivor from the original members of his Flight when the gongs were being dished out after the campaign, so he got the medal."

Tattersall put in, "You should be thankful he looks out for you. I mean, look at our new hut mate. He arrived this morning, and Bernard has already taken him out on a mission."

At that time, we didn't know Bates had been brought down in No Man's Land, and I must admit I felt rather jealous that Bernard, C Flight's commander, was happy to throw his lads in at the deep end while Sibbald fussed over us like some officious nanny.

"Bernard understands we need to attack the enemy," I said. "That's what General Trenchard says. Aeroplanes are best used as offensive weapons."

"I certainly find the Quirk offensive," Vaughn muttered.

"You know what I mean," I argued, irritated by his flippancy. "We must take the war to the Huns. That's how we'll win."

"I'd agree with you if we had decent kites," Vaughn returned. "The Huns can run circles around us. Even our best scouts aren't a match for the Albatros."

"There's supposed to be a new machine coming out soon," Tattersall put in. "Albert Ball will be flying it. He'll show the Hun a thing or two."

Vaughn frowned, "The S.E.5a is built by the Royal Aircraft Factory. Have they ever produced a decent aeroplane?"

"Not so far," Tattersall admitted. "But there's a first time for everything."

"I wouldn't count on it," Vaughn snorted.

"The B.E.2 is a decent machine," I insisted.

"For joy rides and sightseeing, perhaps," Vaughn scoffed. "For war flying, it's bloody useless."

The chat continued in this vein for a while, with me arguing that British pluck and determination could overcome the Huns no matter what type of machine we flew, while Vaughn insisted that the Germans had quality and experience on their side.

"Our Generals believe the war will be won by attrition," he announced in a rather loud voice which I think was intended to be overheard by the red-tabbed staff officers. "And they seem to be applying the same logic to the air war. But throwing large numbers of antiquated machines at the Huns only gives the Red Baron and his cronies some shooting practice. Attrition won't work with odds like we face."

"But we are winning the air war," I insisted. "Apart from their two-seaters, the Huns never come over our side of the Lines."

Vaughn countered, "They never cross the Lines because they don't need to. They can wait for us to go to them, then pick us off as they please. As for their two-seaters, they dash across high up, take their photographs, then dive for home before our scouts can catch them. Compare that to our Quirks, which can't even climb above ten thousand, and are as slow as any kites out here."

Tattersall remained neutral, enjoying listening to us argue, but he did point out that our offensive spirit must have some effect on the ground troops.

"Imagine you're a Hun in the trenches," he said. "Every day you see R.F.C. kites flying overhead, dropping bombs or directing artillery fire on you. It must sap their morale."

"That's all very well," Vaughn argued. "But can you imagine the boost to their morale when they see the Red Baron shooting our kites down?"

"He's one of their heroes," admitted Tattersall. "But he's only shot down about thirty planes, hasn't he? In the overall scheme of things, that's not a huge number."

"It's a damn sight more than most pilots manage," Vaughn countered. "But I'm talking about morale, not absolute numbers. He could kill more of our troops if he joined the artillery, but he's worth a lot more to the Germans than his aerial victories."

He went on, "When the Push begins, we'll soon see how poor their morale is. But I expect it will be the artillery which does them more damage than the sight of us flying over their heads."

Even I could not argue with that. Artillery will win this war. Most men are killed or injured by artillery fire, and the bombardment our guns were dishing out even as we sat there enjoying our lamb, was a truly amazing thing. Even hearing the guns from a distance was awe-inspiring. I'd certainly hate to be on the receiving end of the gunfire.

I heard movement behind us, and the staff officers left their table, tugging on their greatcoats and heading for the door. Their civilian companion did likewise, then told them he'd catch them up.

Turning, he came to our table and smiled at us.

"I'm sorry to barge in," he said, "but I couldn't help overhearing some of your conversation. I take it you are from the airfield next door?"

"That's right," I said.

His smile broadened, and he held out his hand, insisting on shaking each of us in formal greeting.

"My name is Richardson," he told us. "Basil Richardson. You may have read some of my articles in The Times?"

"You're a journalist?" Vaughn asked a little warily.

"Indeed I am," Richardson confirmed. "I'm attached to VII Corps Headquarters. But I'd really like to find out more about the Flying Corps. Perhaps we can have a chat?"

"Not just now," Vaughn said hurriedly. "We need to get back. We have some flying jobs lined up."

Richardson's smile never wavered. Looking at me, he asked, "What about you? You're not flying today, are you?"

"He's Orderly Dog today," Vaughn said. "And he's late. So if you'll excuse us?"

Richardson continued to smile, but Vaughn called for the bill, and we settled up, assuring Lucille and her daughter that the food had been excellent. The reporter hung around hopefully, but eventually gave up when he saw us gather our coats and caps.

"Well," he said, "I'll have a word with the General. Perhaps he'll talk to your C.O. and arrange for me to visit you."

None of us made any reply, so he waved a hand in farewell, wishing us good luck, then he went to the door and set off in pursuit of his companions.

"Bloody reporters," Vaughn muttered darkly. "Keep away from him, young Kerr."

"Why? He has a job to do."

"His job is to tell the public at home what the Government and Army want him to tell them. He's not interested in truth."

"How do you know?" I asked.

"Because they're all the same," was all Vaughn would say.

His attitude mystified me, but much about Paddy Vaughn puzzled me. I noticed the reporter and the two staff officers walking further along the road, but we soon turned off and made our way back to the airfield, with Vaughn and Tattersall eyeing the sky with some concern.

"It's still like the middle of winter," Tattersall grumbled. "But it's not bad enough to cancel the flying and give us a day off."

They each had another mission to complete that afternoon, but I sat in the Mess, catching up on the newspapers which generally arrive here a day late. I found a few copies of The Times, and I looked for articles by Basil Richardson. I found a couple, reading them with interest now that I'd met the man. The reports were full of praise for our Army, applauding the knowledge and skill of our Generals, the pluck and bravery of our troops, and the certainty of our success. It all seemed perfectly normal to me, and I felt Vaughn had over-reacted.

With plenty of time on my hands, I browsed through the latest R.F.C. Communique which everyone refers to as Comic Cuts. It gives details of what the Flying Corps has achieved, naming pilots and observers who have accomplished something special. The Corps does not believe in glamourising scout pilots like the French and Germans do, because General Trenchard, the G.O.C., firmly believes that this detracts from the essential work of everyone else in the Corps. Still, Comic Cuts is where those of us in the Corps learned of the exploits of Captain Albert Ball, Britain's greatest fighter pilot. I'd love to meet him in person one day. Everyone says he is totally fearless, and he attacks the Huns whatever the odds or circumstances. At the moment, though, Ball is back in England, training on the new S.E.5a plane. His squadron are supposed to be coming out here soon. That will show the Red Baron a thing or two.

Between flights, Sibbald spoke to me, checking on my injuries. He made a point of pressing his fingers against the back of my shoulders, almost making me yell as he probed my bruised back, but I managed to keep a stiff upper lip and assure him I was perfectly capable of flying.

"All right," he conceded grudgingly. "Take your kite up for an engine test tomorrow morning. In the afternoon, you can do a job taking more photographs."

"Thanks," I nodded, delighted at the prospect of getting back into the war. "But what about an observer?"

"We've got a new lad arriving today, but I'll take him up with me. You can team up with Sergeant Turnbull. He's an experienced man."

I'd seen Turnbull at the Flight briefings and down at the hangars. Being a Sergeant, he was not permitted in the Officers' Mess, so I hadn't had a chance to talk to him, so I know nothing about him other than that he's a short, wiry fellow from Manchester. Tomorrow, I'll find out a lot more, I'm sure.

At dinner, after we'd heard Bates and Vickers recount their adventures in the mud, the C.O. gave us the usual little pep talk. This time, he had a special announcement which clearly displeased him, for he chewed his lips while considering how to pass on the information.

"I've heard from Corps H.Q.," he said in a low growl. "It seems they have a war correspondent from The Times who wants access to a front line squadron to do some interviews. Since we are the closest to H.Q., they've asked General Trenchard, the Flying Corps' G.O.C. for permission, and he's agreed the man can visit our squadron. He may be here as soon as tomorrow."

The Major paused, his keen eyes scanning us as he went on, "I'm sure I don't need to remind you to be careful in what you say to this man if he speaks to you. I want only positive things reported. We have a tough job to do, but there's no need to paint a black picture. Is that understood?"

I caught Vaughn's eye as we all murmured our agreement. He was frowning deeply.

"Do you have a problem with journalists?" I asked him when we returned to our hut.

"I've learned to distrust them," he admitted.

"Why?"

He took a deep breath, as if wondering how much to reveal. Tattersall and Bates were listening, so he knew this could not be a private conversation.

"I had a friend," he told me. "We were at school together. I met him back in Dublin when I went home on leave just after completing my training."

He hesitated, then plunged on, "I'd known him for years, but what I didn't know was that he had joined the Republicans."

"The I.R.A.?" I gasped.

Vaughn nodded, "He took part in the Easter rising last year. And what he told me about what happened was not how it was presented in the newspapers."

"And you believe him?" I challenged. "He's a rebel!"

"He is also my friend," Vaughn said, his expression as serious as I could recall. "I have no reason not to believe him. And what he said made me talk to others who witnessed the events."

"What sort of thing did he say?" Bates asked bluntly.

Vaughn shook his head sadly as he said, "I'll not go into details, but the way the British reacted to the rising was a lot more brutal than the newspapers reported."

"Rebels need to be treated harshly," I stated.

Vaughn gave me a strange look, a mixture of sadness and contempt, I think.

He said, "It made me think, that's all. As my friend said, all Ireland ever got out of being part of the Empire was famine and military occupation."

He held up one hand to stifle my protest, adding, "Those were his words, not mine. I'm here, remember. All I'm saying is that it made me think. That's all. So don't trust that journalist if he starts asking you questions."

Tattersall put in, "If you're right, then it doesn't matter what we say to him. He'll write it up the way he wants."

At that, Vaughn forced a smile.

"Yes, I suppose you are right," he admitted. "Personally, I'll not be talking to him at all, though."

This conversation worried me a little. As Vaughn said, he is here, and he must be a volunteer since there is no conscription in Ireland, but to learn that he has friends who are rebels, and that he might be harbouring some sympathy for them is rather shocking. I suppose I can't say too much since he is risking his life as much as the rest of us, as are thousands of other Irishmen, but his revelations mean I'll be very careful what I say to him in future.

Now I must stop writing and get some sleep. Tomorrow, the war begins again.

Friday 6th April, 1917

Today is Good Friday, although it was not so good for the squadron. We lost another crew today. Chillingford and his observer, Roberts, were shot down while on a photographic job some way behind the Lines. Their escort of D.H.2s also lost two pilots when a bunch of Albatroses pounced on them. Rumour has it that it was von Richthofen's mob again, although Sibbald did remind us that the Huns have other Albatros units in the area, so we should not assume that every Albatros was one of the Red Baron's mob.

"It doesn't really matter, does it?" Vaughn sighed. "Any Albatros can run rings around a Quirk. As for the D.H.2, it's an ancient pusher. It's not much better than a tiny bathtub with wings and an engine stuck on the back. It might have been good enough to tackle the old Fokker monoplanes, but it's no match for an Albatros."

Naturally, the loss of another of B Flight's crews upset both Vaughn and Tattersall.

"I've only been out here five weeks," Vaughn informed me. "But I'm already moving up the seniority. From being the newest recruit, I'm now Number Four in the Flight."

The odd thing is that, although his words were pessimistic, Vaughn's tone was light-hearted, and he seemed to be making a huge joke of the situation.

He went on, "If things carry on like this, I'll be a Flight Commander in a few days."

"And you'll get your own squadron after that?" Dish Tattersall grinned.

"Who knows?" Vaughn shrugged expansively. "I may end up in charge of the whole R.F.C. before too long. Just you wait and see."

Dish wagged a finger at him.

"Hold on!" he insisted. "I'm senior to you by at least three days. So you're behind me in the rankings. If you are going to rise so rapidly, that means I need to be shot down to make way for you."

"Not necessarily," Vaughn countered. "The Flying Corps recognises talent. I could simply overtake you through sheer skill and ability."

"You're more likely to get promoted just to get rid of you," Dish retorted with a laugh. "I've heard that happens. Officers who annoy their superiors are promoted to other units just to get them out of the way."

Bates, who had been listening to the banter with a bemused expression, put in, "I don't think that's really necessary, is it? I mean, if they want rid of us, all they need to do is keep sending us out in ancient kites."

"We'll get new machines eventually," Tattersall replied, his tone a little more serious.

"Maybe we should come up with some other ideas in the meantime," Vaughn suggested, his eyes glinting with mischief.

"Like what?" I asked him.

"Oh, something innovative."

He paused for a moment, then grinned, "I know! We could attach hand grenades to our wireless aerials. If a Hun comes along, we keep our aerials extended instead of reeling them in. The Boche pilot will fly into the wire, the grenades will explode and Voila!"

He raised his hand dramatically, then lowered it in a fluttering motion to suggest a falling aeroplane.

"Goodbye beastly Hun!" he declared.

Tattersall remained silent for a moment, then looked at Vaughn with a serious expression.

"You," he said slowly, "are an idiot."

"It's been said before," Vaughn admitted.

Both of them laughed aloud, then began swapping ever more extravagant suggestions as to how they could bring down an Albatros. They talked such nonsense that I left them to their pointless chat and decided to update my journal.

My day began with a test flight at just after seven this morning. Etherington had worked wonders with his needle and thread, patching up my old tunic and my flying jacket. He'd even managed to repair the slash on the top of my leather helmet, leaving only a faint line as a memento of my lucky escape.

My kite had also been patched up, and the engine given a complete overhaul. I trundled out onto the airfield, turned west to face the wind, and took off. Instead of immediately climbing, I held the Quirk down low, turning south-west and quickly reaching the town of Barly.

The chateau was easy to locate, sitting with its wooded grounds and large pond in front of the building. I saw other, smaller buildings behind the hospital, but I kept the chateau lined up as my target.

Pushing the throttle open, I banked the wings almost to the vertical and flew round the hospital in a complete circle at a height of less than fifty feet. I repeated the manoeuvre, then levelled off and went a bit higher. Looking down, I could see faces at some of the windows, so I waggled my wings and waved to them. I could not tell whether Nurse Jennifer Routledge was among the spectators, but I was fairly certain she would hear of my visit, and she'd know it was me.

Feeling a warm glow, I looked around, trying to decide what to do next. I was still fairly low, only at around two hundred feet, and I saw another chateau just ahead of me. Checking my bearings, I realised this must be the H.Q. of VII Corps. Lying just to the north of Fosseux, it was another rectangular block of decorated brickwork, with extensive grounds around it, and I noticed several horsemen cantering across a wide field beside the chateau. Even from my height, the red tabs on their uniforms were visible.

Feeling a bit of devilment come over me, I juggled the throttle to blip the engine as if I was in trouble, and I went even lower, heading directly above their heads, wings waggling and nose falling and rising as if I were struggling to maintain control. The horses scattered as I roared overhead, and I caught a glimpse of one of the riders shaking a fist at me.

Laughing, I continued on my way, still playing with the throttle.

I suppose what I was doing was foolish considering I was supposed to be testing the engine, but the haughty way those staff officers had ignored us in the *estaminet* yesterday had annoyed me, and it was nice to get a little revenge, even if the men on the horses were probably not the same ones I had seen the day before. In the eyes of most pilots, staff officers deserve anything we can throw their way.

Having had my fun, I took the Quirk into the upper sky, dodging my way around clouds. The engine was running really well, but the weather was not very good at all, and I flew through a couple of rain showers. That was most unpleasant as well as potentially dangerous, for visibility was greatly reduced, but no harm came to me.

Once back on the ground, I told Sergeant Stirling and Dunlop, who had overhauled the engine, that I'd had a little trouble at the start but that whatever had caused it had cleared by itself.

Dunlop frowned, but said he'd take another look at the petrol feed lines.

"It could be dirty fuel," he sighed.

I felt a little guilty at giving him unnecessary work, but it was as well I did because the Major accosted me in the Mess, telling me that a complaint had been made by Corps H.Q. about a low-flying B.E.2 with my squadron markings on it.

"I had a spot of engine trouble, Sir," I told him in my most innocent voice. "It soon cleared, but the Ack Emmas are checking the fuel lines at the moment. I do hope nobody was hurt."

"Just their pride, I think," the Major said. Then he grinned and winked at me as he added, "Or perhaps one of them got some mud on his uniform. That would never do. Still, don't do it again, Kerr. Or, at the very least, don't get caught doing it again."

"Understood, Sir," I grinned.

I went up again in the afternoon, this time with Sergeant Turnbull in the front cockpit. He was taciturn, but clearly very experienced, and he handled the Lewis gun with considerable aplomb. He did ask to go over the agreed hand signals, and seemed satisfied that I knew what I was doing. I must admit that I found him rather intimidating even though he is a small fellow, for his attitude was very much that of a veteran who had been ordered to take care of a tyro.

Sibbald had given us another photographic job near the Scarpe river. The bombardment had been going on for a couple of days now, so it seemed our Generals were going for the total obliteration of the German defences over a long period of time. What they needed were photographs to show how effective the bombardment had been so far.

Turnbull suggested, "It might be safer to go beyond the Lines and photograph from the eastern side, Sir."

"That would put us further into Hunland," I pointed out, thinking of the danger presented by the Red Baron.

"But it takes us out of the arc of fire of our own guns, Sir," Turnbull pointed out. "The artillery are chucking so many shells over, we might get hit if we stay on the western side of the Lines. We'll be in the direct line of fire."

"What about the German artillery?" I asked. "We'd be in their line of fire, wouldn't we?"

"Only if they were shooting, and they won't be."

"Why ever not?"

Patiently, Turnbull explained, "Because they know we can see their gun flashes if they fire. At the moment, they will be camouflaged and hidden, but as soon as they open fire, we can direct counter-battery fire on them. They'll be saving their ammo for when the Push begins. Once our boys are out in the open, the Huns will bombard them with everything they've got, but they'll sit tight until then."

He spoke with such authority that I decided to follow his advice. I stayed high up as we went over, then dropped down and flew directly south, clicking away with the Bowden cable to take our photographs. Turnbull, I noted, spent that entire time standing up in the front cockpit, constantly turning. Once or twice, he adjusted the position of the Lewis gun, moving it deftly from the Strange Mounting onto one of the candlestick mounts at the side of his cockpit, but he gave no warning signals, so I kept flying straight, doing my best to ignore Archie, and took my photographs.

I must admit I jumped a little when the first burst of Archie exploded close by, but I gritted my teeth, pushed memories of Ashton and my bruised back from my mind, and kept going.

Down below, the earth was a mass of explosions, one shell after another bursting among the German trenches, sending up great gouts of mud and creating even more devastation than there had been before. It was truly awesome, and I could not fathom how anyone could live through that pummelling barrage of high explosive. There were no trees, no buildings, only muddy earth, barbed wire and inter-linked shell craters. Surely nothing could live down there? Yet the bombardment continued, presaging the big Push which would surely end the war. Sibbald might claim it was a mere diversionary attack to allow the French to make the breakthrough, but I could not see how the Germans could possibly stop us. Our troops would simply walk across No Man's Land and take over the Hun trenches.

I completed the run, then headed for home. We returned without any incident of real note, making sure to hurry through the danger zone. I actually saw one of our shells tumbling end over end as it arced through the sky on its way to deliver death to the German infantry, and I offered up a prayer that we would not be struck by our own side.

Fortunately, we returned home safely. Turnbull merely shrugged when I mentioned seeing the shell whizz past us. When we gave our report, I discovered he had been more concerned with other things.

"There were five Huns hanging around up high," Turnbull revealed when we returned to the office. "But there were some Pups even higher, and a Flight of Spads nearby, so they kept well clear of us. They flew away when the Pups dived down on them."

"Was there a scrap?" Potter asked. "Were any of them shot down?"

"Not that I saw," Turnbull replied. "The Huns just flew off as soon as the Pups came down."

I hadn't seen any of that, so I contented myself with explaining why I had taken the photographs from behind the German Lines. Potter agreed that made sense, and the results were perfectly satisfactory. The Stickyback Corporal showed us the pictures, some of which included frozen images of exploding shells.

"The Huns must be terrified," Potter reflected when he saw the extent of the barrage and the damage it was doing to the German trenches. Some sections had collapsed, others had disappeared completely, replaced by shell craters.

"The wire hasn't been completely broken up yet, Sir," the Stickyback observed as he pointed to one picture which showed the barbed wire entanglements. "That lot must cover a depth of at least two hundred yards, and it will take a lot for it to be blown apart."

"I expect that means the barrage will continue for a few days," Potter guessed.

That, of course, was up to the Generals, but I felt very pleased with myself that my photographs would help the powers that be reach a decision.

The only other thing to mention today is that Basil Richardson, the Times reporter, was a guest at dinner. His presence rather muted the usual buzz of conversation, but nobody said anything out of turn, and Captain Bernard of C Flight regaled him with a few stories of his time at the Front. Bernard had been with another B.E.2 squadron for nearly six months. He had been due to go home after finishing his tour, but he'd taken a promotion to Captain in order to join our squadron, extending his time at the Front by another three months.

"We're going to win this war," he stated, addressing Richardson but also, I think, letting the rest of us know his thoughts. "And air war is going to play its part. We outnumber the Hun, and we'll keep attacking him until we wear him down."

Which, Vaughn quietly pointed out, was how a war of attrition worked.

"The winning side will be the one with the last man standing," he murmured.

"Or," Dish put in, "in our case, the last man flying."

"That will probably be Kerr," Vaughn said, nodding in my direction. "He survives direct hits by Archie, then swans around behind the Hun Lines with total impunity. Even the Red Baron hasn't dared come near him."

"So far," I rejoindered. "I've only been out here a week."

"A week is a long time out here," Vaughn said grimly.

As usual, I couldn't tell whether he was being serious. Not that I really care. I'm back in the war, and doing my job. That is all that matters. Bernard is right, air power is playing its part, and we are going to win.

Saturday 7th April, 1917

What a day! The news spread like wildfire, and many of us did not believe it at first. However, Richardson, the reporter, assured us it was true.

"It will be the headlines in the papers today," he assured us.

You see, America has declared war on Germany.

"About bloody time," said Unswood. "The Lusitania was sunk two years ago."

Richardson said, "Yes, and the U.S.A. warned the Germans they would not take kindly to further loss of American lives. But it's the Zimmerman cable that's done the damage. It was the last straw for President Wilson."

He went on to explain that the British Navy had intercepted a secret telegram from a German Foreign Minister named Zimmerman. He had been trying to persuade Mexico to join the war, promising them the recovery of Texas and other states if they helped keep the Americans out of the European conflict. In support of Mexico, Germany was going to unleash unrestricted submarine warfare off the eastern coast of the United States.

"It sounds like a daft idea," Potter frowned. "The Americans might be helping us with supplies, but they would probably have stayed out of the war if the Germans had left them alone."

Richardson explained, "But Germany is suffering because of our naval blockade, and they can't win a war on two fronts. They are gambling on us seeking peace if they can cut off the supplies of food the Americans are sending to Britain. If our people are starving, it doesn't matter what our armies are doing. We'd have no choice but to negotiate a treaty. From the German point of view, the only way to force us to stop the war is to cut off our supplies. That means they need to sink American ships, which would bring the Yanks into the conflict anyway. The point of persuading Mexico to join was to keep American troops occupied defending their own land instead of sending their army over here."

"But it hasn't worked?" asked Howden.

"No," Richardson confirmed. "The Mexicans took cold feet as soon as they discovered the Americans knew all about the plan. They are staying neutral."

With a knowing smile, he added, "Of course, some American Generals wanted a war with Mexico anyway because they thought they could seize the Mexican oilfields, but the Mexicans have destroyed them rather than risk an American invasion. And now the Yanks have a much bigger fight they can get involved with."

The politics did not concern us. What excited everyone was that, with the Americans joining the war, our ultimate victory is assured. This is a great relief, because the news from the east is not good, although the Russians are still fighting for the moment. The trouble, as Richardson pointed out, was that the Bolsheviks were making a lot of noise about taking Russia out of the war.

"That would pose a problem," Bernard agreed. "But with the Yanks on our side, we are bound to win."

That was obvious to everyone except Sibbald.

"A word of caution," he said. "The Americans will make a difference, but it will not affect us for a long time yet. As far as I know, they have a small army and no air force at all. So don't expect to see fleets of aeroplanes flying overhead soon. It will happen, but not for a while, so we are on our own for the moment."

The Major shot him a warning glance, flicking his eyes towards the reporter, but Sibbald was unrepentant.

"We'll win with America on our side," he insisted. "But it will be months before they get here."

Richardson, I saw, was mentally noting this down, just as he was listening intently to everyone else. The majority opinion was that Sibbald may be correct, but it was still fantastic news.

I said, "Of course, we might win the war before any Americans get here."

That brought a ripple of support.

Vaughn said, "There are already some Americans here. They are flying for the French in the Lafayette Escadrille."

"And a fine bunch of fellows they are," the Major said.

Despite our excitement, though, the war went on. Turnbull and I did three more photographic shoots today, still monitoring the progress of the barrage. Again, Archie was our main opponent, although our second mission was twice interrupted by the arrival of some Hun machines.

This was the first time I'd seen German aeroplanes relatively close, but Turnbull spotted them in time for us to dive westwards. Once across the Lines, we were safe from pursuit, for Hun scouts rarely come over to our side, preferring to defend their own territory.

We stooged around, using cloud cover to conceal us, then went back to complete our job when we thought the Huns had moved on. Unfortunately, they must have suspected we would do this, for they reappeared, diving down on us. Turnbull saw them coming, and I turned again in response to his warning, and we ran for safety once more. I saw their tracers flashing past us, but none of their bullets came close for they were firing at long range. Once again we hung around behind our balloon line, then went back twenty minutes later. The Huns only have enough fuel for around ninety minutes of flying, but the Quirk can stay up for over three hours, so we simply outlasted this lot, dashing back to take our final photographs, then heading for home before any more Huns arrived on the scene.

"They were Halberstadts," Turnbull said as we made our report. "There were only three of them, and they never got very close to us."

That, I knew, was down to Turnbull himself. He'd spotted the Huns as they tried to manoeuvre among the clouds to surprise us.

"Well done, Sergeant," I told him.

"Just doing my job, Sir," was his reply.

In the evening, we had more good news. Bobby St. James, who is B Flight's Deputy Leader, has been posted to Home Establishment. He himself was surprised, for there was an offensive about to begin, and he was annoyed that he would be missing it. Still, he's been out at the Front for over six months, so he is overdue going home.

"He'll get a nice, cushy job at a training school, or maybe on Home Defence," Vaughn opined. "Good for him."

Naturally, we held a binge in Bobby's honour. There were speeches after dinner, a great deal of larking about, then lots of alcohol was consumed. Beano Normansby turned out to be a decent piano player, although the piano itself is rather out of tune, a situation not helped by the amount of alcohol some of the lads poured into its innards.

Beano didn't seem to mind, and he rattled out plenty of music hall songs from all the favourites like Chu Chin Chow and Maid of the Mountains, then we had a sing-song, belting out some of the Flying Corps' traditional favourites. There were a couple of songs I didn't know, one of which stuck in my mind as terribly funny. It was a play on the old Nursery Rhyme, "Who Killed Cock Robin?", and I laughed aloud when I heard the older pilots bellow the line, "I, said the Hun, with my Spandau gun."

I can't remember the rest of it, for I'd had rather a lot to drink by that time.

Sibbald warned me, "Better stop drinking now. You're on the early show tomorrow. Having a hangover won't help."

I promised I'd stop, but Watt persuaded me to have another whisky, so I did.

Poor old Bobby St. James was in quite a state by the end of the evening. We had to carry him out to the tender which was taking him to the rail depot where he'd board a train for Calais and the Channel Crossing.

He kept trying to kiss everyone goodbye, but he was staggering around so much he kept missing people as he tried to hug them.

Eventually, we got him into the tender, sang a verse of "For He's A Jolly Good Fellow", then waved him off.

I have no recollection of how I got back to Hut Three and my bed, but I was still fully dressed and had an awful headache when Etherington woke me for the dawn patrol.

Sunday 8th April, 1917

Today was Easter Sunday, but I had no chance to attend a church Parade. Nursing a throbbing headache, I joined the rest of A Flight for the dawn patrol, all of us looking the worse for wear.

All except Sibbald, of course. He scowled at us, making some sarcastic comments about our chances of surviving the mission.

"Sore heads mean your reactions are slower, and your attention is distracted. I've seen too many lads fail to return after a binge, and I don't want to see it again. So go out there and prove me wrong."

We did our best, and it must have been good enough, for we all returned. Once again, Turnbull and I photographed the Hun trenches. Beano and Howden were doing the same a little further south, while the rest of the Flight were directing artillery fire on the German rear lines. Sibbald told us that he had spotted a Hun battery concealed in a wood. His new observer, Goldberg, had sent a wireless transmission which had called down heavy fire on it, destroying the German guns. Sibbald made it sound very routine, but the Major was delighted as this was a real feather in the squadron's collective cap.

Late in the morning, Sibbald called the pilots to the office where he briefed us on a special mission.

"There are a couple of balloons Corps want rid of," he told us.

Sullivan let out a groan.

"Balloon busting? That's a one-way mission."

Sibbald gave him his stare, silencing the protest.

"We're not making a direct attack," he explained. "This is a two-part job."

He had our full attention as he went on, "Our kites are being loaded up with bombs, so we won't be taking observers on this trip. We'll split into two groups of three. Watt, Kerr, you will be with me, and we'll target the northernmost balloon. Sullivan will lead Normansby and Garrick against the southern one."

I could see Sullivan frowning, and he seemed on the point of making another objection, but Sibbald continued, "We will meet up with a Flight of Nieuports from the squadron just to the south of here. Then we'll fly across the Lines as if we are on a bombing raid further over. While we do that, another Flight of Nieuports will make a low-level attack on the balloons using Le Prieur rockets and Buckingham bullets. With luck, they'll bring down both balloons."

"So what is our role?" Beano wanted to know.

Sibbald told us, "As soon as the Nieuports make their attack, we will alter course and dive on the balloon site. We'll drop our bombs in the hope of killing the ground crew. As some of you know, shooting down a balloon is usually only a temporary success. The Huns soon replace it. This way, we are hoping they won't have enough men to man replacement sausages."

He took out a large scale map, going over the details several times. The Major was there, nodding in approval, but leaving all the details to Sibbald.

"Good luck, lads," was all the C.O. said.

"We'll bloody need it," Sullivan muttered under his breath.

Sibbald didn't hear him, but I did.

"What do you mean?" I asked him.

"You'll find out," he growled before stomping off to the hangars.

I was puzzled by his remarks, but Sibbald took me aside and provided an explanation.

He said, "You've not gone near a Hun balloon before, so you need to know what to expect. Balloons have no way of defending themselves, but they are vital for the Huns who use them to direct their own artillery. So they have lots of other people defending them. There are usually several machine guns, plus Archie batteries, and they also chuck up Flaming Onions."

"What are they?" I asked.

"You'll recognise them when you see them. They are like long strings of flaming, green balls. They don't usually hit anything, but they can be scary, and if you are unlucky enough to be hit by one, chances are your kite will catch fire."

For want of anything better to say, I remarked, "It sounds nasty."

"It can be," Sibbald nodded dourly. "Balloons can be real bastards to bring down. But just stay close to me and drop your bombs when I let mine go. Got that?"

"Yes, Skipper."

He gave another nod, then strode towards our aeroplanes.

Racks of bombs had been attached beneath the kites. Sibbald and Sullivan would each carry two 112lbs bombs, one on either side of their undercart. The rest of us had ten 20lbs bombs in two racks, evenly placed with five bombs beneath each wing.

A Sergeant from the Armaments Section showed me the switches on a panel he had rigged inside my cockpit.

"It's dead easy, Sir," he assured me. "There are ten switches; one for each bomb. It's best to balance them out by dropping one from under each wing. If you release all the bombs from under one wing first, the poor old bus will be unbalanced."

"We're letting them all go at once," I told him.

"Then you shouldn't have a problem, Sir," he nodded. "Just swipe your hand down and hit all the switches at once. The bombs will arm themselves on the way down, so you don't need to worry about anything else."

"Got it," I confirmed.

Green and Dunlop wished me luck, then we started the engine, letting it warm for a few minutes. When everyone was ready, Sibbald led us out onto the airfield.

The kite felt odd with the extra weight, but the Quirk could handle it as long as there was no observer in the front cockpit. I saw Turnbull, Howden and the other observers watching us go. They knew how dangerous this mission was. Without them and their Lewis guns to protect us, we were as defenceless as the balloon observers we were trying to kill. If we ran into any Hun machines, all we could do was use our service revolvers which were no defence at all.

We bumped across the field and rose into the air, circling above the airfield until we met up at seven thousand feet. This took over twenty minutes, by which time a Flight of silver Nieuport scouts had joined us. There were five of them, looking dainty but deadly, each of them having a Lewis gun on the top wing to fire over the propeller. They waggled their wings joyfully when they joined us, then we set off on an easterly course with the Nieuports climbing above to watch over us.

It was another dull, horrid day for weather. Rain and sleet showers were in evidence, and Sibbald skirted some dark clouds, climbed to get over others, and led us on a twisting, turning route towards the Lines.

Archie greeted us as usual, filthy black explosions bursting all around us, but Sibbald dropped a few hundred feet in altitude, throwing off the gunners' aim.

I looked northwards. There, three or four miles behind the German rear trenches, hung two fat balloons. Elongated like the sausages which gave them their slang name, and with inflated tail fins to provide some balance, each had a wicker basket hung beneath it. From this vantage point, the observers could use binoculars to peer down at our trenches, and direct artillery fire on our troops. They could also watch for movement, reporting everything to their Generals via a telephone.

Some pilots develop a knack of shooting down balloons, but everything Sibbald had told me, plus Sullivan's obvious dread of going near these sausages, made me realise that these cumbersome slugs were not as defenceless as they appeared.

We were behind them now, and I wondered when we would turn. I could see no sign of the Nieuports who were supposed to be making the first attack, but Sibbald must have spotted them, for he waggled his wings, then turned back towards the balloons.

I flew on his right, just behind his tail, with Watt adopting a similar position on Sibbald's left. Behind us, Sullivan led a similar vic of three planes, while the five Nieuports were three thousand feet above us, watching for any Hun scouts.

We were only a couple of miles from the balloons, diving down towards them. As I watched, the two fat, sausage-like bags of gas began to descend as their tethering cables were reeled in by the ground crews. At the same time, I saw long lines of bright tracer bullets flash around the sky, and Archie began to give us his close attention.

Now I realised Sibbald had not told us the full story. We were attracting all the Germans' attention, while four more Nieuports were whizzing across No Man's Land, racing towards the balloons. They rose to meet the dropping balloons, and I saw the German observers take to their parachutes, leaping out of the baskets to avoid being burned if the attack succeeded. Their parachutes blossomed like pale flowers, the men dangling beneath them, while the balloons were rapidly hauled down.

Some of the Hun gunners switched their aim towards the Nieuports, but the little biplanes were close to the balloons now, so most of the Archie and machine guns continued to put up a tremendous barrage to block our way.

All hell broke loose, and I began to think this is what it must have been like to be a part of the Charge of the Light Brigade. Archie came up as heavy as I'd ever seen, some of the shots terribly close. Tracers from machine guns zipped around us, and I saw the Flaming Onions Sibbald had warned me of; long strings of evil-looking, sulphurous fire which sparkled and hissed as it flashed by our wings.

Streaks of fire came from the Nieuports as they released their rockets. I saw their own tracers now as they added machine gun fire with explosive Buckingham bullets to the rockets.

One balloon suddenly burst into flame, struck by a rocket. The gas ignited in a great flash, flames replacing what had been a balloon only a moment before.

Then the Nieuports were past the balloons and twisting away. I saw one roll onto its back and plummet into the ground where it smashed apart, scattering debris everywhere, but the others escaped, dodging and twisting at ground level to throw off the aim of the defenders.

One sausage was destroyed, but the other, the one Sibbald and I were to attack, was still more or less intact. It seemed to be losing its shape as if it had been punctured, but it was still there, and drawing ever closer to the ground.

Explosions rocked us as Archie filled the sky with hate. More holes appeared in my wings as bullets ripped through them.

The noise was deafening, audible over our roaring engines which were going flat out as we dived, the wind whistling in the wires as a mad accompaniment to the music of death.

We passed the southern site where the balloon had been shot down. Sullivan, Normansby and Garrick would drop their bombs on that spot, hopefully catching the crew out in the open. Sibbald led us on to the second balloon which now seemed to be on the ground.

I hunched low in my cockpit, peering through the tiny windshield, keeping my eyes fixed on Sibbald's tail. It is odd, but I managed to convince myself that the wood and canvas of the cockpit would somehow protect me from the bullets and high explosive that surrounded me.

That was a delusion, of course. From the corner of my eye, I saw Watt's plane suddenly drop away, its dive turning into a spin. He had been hit!

There was no time to watch him go. We were at less than one thousand feet now, and spinning was risky from that height in a Quirk. With a full bomb load, it was probably fatal, although I realised Watt must have been hit by the German ground fire. Perhaps he was already dead. For his sake, I hoped so.

God! We were all going to die. The Archie was horrendous, shredding our planes, while the machine guns sent raking fire all around us. One of my wings struts had a chunk ripped from its trailing edge, and more than one bullet whined off the engine cowling. A bracing wire snapped, flapping wildly, and I prayed the others would hold the wings together.

Then Sibbald dropped his bombs. It took me a moment to react, but I hit the switches using the edge of my hand to push them all at once. Instantly, I felt the plane lighten as the bombs dropped away.

Then we were twisting and diving, heading west, the Huns still trying desperately to bring us down. I don't think I have ever been so afraid in all my life. All I could do was try to follow Sibbald, but he was chucking his kite around like a madman, twisting, banking, diving and zooming, so I soon lost contact with him.

A burst of Archie just ahead of me made my plane wobble. Instinctively, I shoved the stick to the right, dodging the smoke, and then I yanked it back to the left, tramping on the rudder for all I was worth.

I have little recollection of the next few minutes. What I do recall is a wave of relief when I suddenly flew into a heavy downpour of rain. Normally, I'd have dreaded such an occurrence, but this time the rain helped mask me from the ground fire.

I continued to dodge and weave, paying little attention to anything. My compass was spinning like a top, providing no clue as to which direction I was flying in, and the rain concealed the sun, so I could have been heading deep into Hunland for all I knew.

No! There were shell craters beneath me, and trenches too, zig-zag lines cut into the mud. Faintly, I saw faces peering up at me as I passed overhead at less than one hundred feet, but whether they were British or German, I could not tell. Nobody seemed to be shooting at me, though, which was a good sign.

I considered climbing for some height, but that might put me inside the cloud which was chucking down all this water, so I kept on, hoping that it was just another localised squall.

When I did emerge from the rain, I found myself over open countryside, with green fields and trees. A farm passed beneath me, and a narrow lane came into view, a French peasant driving a horse-drawn wagon along it. He did not look up as I roared over his head, simply continuing on his way as if the war was none of his concern. Even his horse ignored me, simply plodding on as if low-flying aeroplanes were run of the mill happenings.

My compass had now stopped whirling, so I knew I was flying roughly south-west. That was good. I must be on our side of the Lines.

But where?

I pulled the stick back, trying to gain some height in order to identify landmarks. As I did so, I looked around, almost throwing the kite into a spin when I saw another aeroplane beside me.

It was a Nieuport, and the pilot was waving to me.

Sighing in relief, I waved back. Then he waggled his wings and gestured for me to follow him.

As we flew on, I saw a long, straight road which I guessed was the main route from Doullens to Arras. It was the road I had travelled on in the tender which had taken me from Candas to my squadron, and it was still busy with military traffic.

Then an airfield came in sight. I followed the Nieuport into the circuit, checking for other aeroplanes and making sure the wind was still coming from the west. I knew roughly where I was now, so I suppose I should have flown back to my own base, but I was wet, cold and still anxious after the beating we had taken, and I could see scraps of canvas fluttering from my wings. The loose bracing wire was also a concern, so I decided it would be safer to put down and let someone carry out some basic repairs.

I followed the silver Nieuport down, rumbling over to the hangars and cutting the engine with considerable relief.

There were several other Nieuports there, pilots and ground crew gathering in the way they do after a mission has been completed.

I took a deep breath, then climbed out of my cockpit, adopting an air of insouciance, or as close to it as I could manage in the circumstances.

"Hello, chaps," I said to the gathered scout pilots as I took off my flying helmet. "That was some fun, wasn't it?"

The pilot I had followed in was a Second Lieutenant like me, and he offered me a handshake.

"Bloody well done," he grinned. "Was it you who got that second sausage?"

I blinked in surprise.

"I'm not sure," I replied. "I didn't see what happened after I dropped my eggs on them."

At that moment, another pilot came up, a broad smile of welcome on his handsome face.

"Kerr? Is it really you? I wondered if you were on that job."

"Vanders? Hello. Good to see you. Were you one of our escorts?"

"Yes," he nodded. "What a show that was!"

He made some brief introductions, although I confess I can't really recall the names of the other pilots. All of them were, though, full of praise for me and my fellow Quirk pilots. It seemed Sibbald and I had blown up the second balloon with our bombs. Or, at least, it had burst into flames shortly after we'd dropped our eggs, so the Nieuport boys were happy to give us the credit.

"I didn't see much of it," Vanders told me as he led me to the Mess. "We tangled with a bunch of Albatroses, so I was rather busy."

"Did you get any?" I asked him.

He pulled a face.

"I'm afraid not. I popped off a few shots at one, but they are bloody hard to hit. Chalmers got one, but we lost one of our lads, so it was evens."

In the Mess, the Nieuport boys plied me with drinks. I did manage to find time to telephone my squadron and tell them I was safe. I promised Potter I'd fly back once my kite had been patched up a little.

"Don't get too blotto while it's being repaired," he chuckled.

The scout pilots were a good bunch, but Vanders had some bad news for me.

"Greening went west," he told me over a glass of whisky.

"Greening? How?"

He told me, "I heard about it from another chap I know in his Fee squadron. Apparently, poor Greening flew into some clouds while trying to find his way home. The people on the ground could hear him, but the clouds were so low he couldn't see the airfield. When he did come out into clear air, he was down to two hundred feet and in a vertical side-slip. He went straight in."

"Poor Greening," I sympathised, remembering the happy-go-lucky fellow who had learned to fly alongside us. All that training, and he had lasted barely a week at the Front.

There was no need for Vanders to explain further. In an F.E.2b, the crew had very little chance of surviving a crash like that. The enormous engine was behind them, and would crush them to death.

"That's the trouble with clouds," Vanders reflected. "You can think you are flying straight and level, but you are really climbing or falling. Or you can feel as if you are banking while you are actually flying straight."

"I've never flown into a cloud," I admitted.

"Try to keep it that way," Vanders advised.

"So how are you finding the Nieuport?" I asked him.

"It's a lovely kite," he told me. "But war flying isn't as easy as I'd thought. I seem to be having trouble spotting the Huns."

"You and me both," I said, telling him about my total failure to spot any other aircraft during one of my training flights.

"They tell me I'll get the hang of it soon," He sighed. "I certainly hope so. We need every advantage we can get. Those new D.III Albatroses are good. We can match them in a turn, and can just about keep up with them in a climb, but they are much faster than us on the level or in a dive."

"And they've got two machine guns," I pointed out.

"That too. I must say I don't envy you flying a Quirk up against them."

"I haven't come close to any of them yet," I confessed. "We're told to scarper if they turn up. It's up to you scout boys to deal with them."

"And we are!" Vanders assured me. "Once I've found my feet, I'll knock a few of them down."

"You haven't had any luck yet?" I asked.

"Not yet," he admitted with a rueful smile. "But the squadron is doing its bit."

"I know. And I'm sure you'll bag a Hun soon."

He gave me a smile of thanks, then shook his head.

"It's odd," he said. "Some fellows seem to have the knack. There's another Nieuport squadron a little way further north. They've got a new lad who has already bagged a few Huns even though he's only been out here a week or so. His name is Bishop. He's a Canadian. Watch out for his name in Comic Cuts."

I sensed some envy in Vanders's words, although I suspected it was more that he was annoyed at himself for not being able to emulate this new Canadian pilot.

It was strange to see Vanders so uncertain of himself. All through training he'd been the confident one, the pilot who could handle any plane in any situation. Yet here he was a novice, and his lack of success seemed to be haunting him.

"It's early days," I told him. "My Flight Commander reckons nobody should even cross the Lines until they've got fifty hours under their belt."

"He may have a point," Vanders nodded. "I've already noticed that it's the new boys who don't last long. We've lost a couple of lads who have only been out here a short time."

It was interesting to see things from a different perspective, and the scout pilots were certainly a more raucous lot than my own comrades in the B.E.2 squadron. They did seem to have a lot of sympathy for those of us who did the drudgery.

"I wouldn't fancy your job," one of them told me. "I think you all deserve medals just for crossing the Lines in a Quirk."

"I'll tell General Trenchard the next time I see him," I joked.

I made my excuses before it got dark. Vanders offered to put me up for the night, but I thought of Sibbald's reaction to that and I insisted I needed to fly back home.

The Ack Emmas had repaired the bracing wires and stitched up the worst holes in my wings, but my poor old Quirk was still a bit of a mess.

"We counted forty-six holes, Sir," one of the mechanics informed me. "And two of them went right through your front cockpit. It's just as well you didn't have an observer with you."

I examined the holes in question. Right enough, two bullets had smashed through the floor of the front cockpit. If Turnbull had been standing in his usual position, he'd have received some nasty wounds to his legs or posterior. Or possibly worse. From my point of view, though, I had been just as lucky, for the main petrol tank is situated underneath the seat inside the front cockpit. A few inches of a difference and I'd have very possibly gone down in flames.

"And there's another hole right behind your seat, Sir," the mechanic said cheerfully, pointing out how close I had come to being hit.

"A miss is as good as a mile," I responded. "It's all in a day's work for us."

I hoped my display of sang froid impressed the Nieuport pilots. Somehow, it made me feel better that they were rather in awe of what I had to put up with.

I settled in, ran through the start up, waved my farewells, and flew back to Fosseux, arriving just as the sun was nearing the horizon. My landing was rather rough, although I put the blame on the whisky I'd consumed at Vanders's squadron.

Sibbald greeted me with a curt nod as he said, "I'm glad you're back. Well done."

That, it seemed, was all the praise I was going to get. The Major, though, was more effusive. He was delighted that we had destroyed one of the balloons, and he told me I would officially be credited with a half share in the victory.

"It's not often we get a chance of that sort of thing," he beamed.

Then he clapped me on the back, making me wince because he'd caught me where it still hurt from my earlier wounds.

I was pleased to learn that everyone else had got back. We'd lost Watt, and the others had returned with kites full of holes, but nobody had been injured, although Beano's engine had been emitting a trail of smoke all the way home and had conked out just as he was lining up his approach, forcing him to do a dead stick landing.

"I need a new engine anyway," he declared. "That one has been nothing but trouble. I hope they replace it."

"It got you home," Sibbald pointed out.

"It's still a rotten engine," Beano insisted.

Richardson, the journalist, asked lots of questions which we answered as vaguely as we could.

"It was just another job," Sibbald told him.

Even this answer seemed to please Richardson, since it would allow him to write about our bravery in the face of danger.

Once the reporter had gone to write up his notes, Sibbald said to us, "Well done, lads. It's a pity about Watt, but it could have been a lot worse."

"Not that I'd want to try it again," Garrick said softly. "It was pretty rough."

Which was the last anyone mentioned of our dive into danger. We had done the job, and now we must prepare for the next one.

Monday 9th April, 1917

The entire squadron was up with the dawn. This was not because we were all on the early show, but because we were woken by the most tremendous noise any of us had ever heard. From the east came a booming, rolling, continuous reverberating thunder which lasted around half an hour.

"It's the Canadians," Sibbald told us, although I have no idea how he knew. "They are attacking Vimy Ridge, and they're putting in a lightning barrage."

"Good luck to them," said Unswood. "The Huns have been up on that ridge since the early days of the war. The French tried twice to take it, and our lot tried as well. The whole place is like a fortress."

Other guns were blazing away as well, and we all knew this signalled the start of the Push. This sent a thrill of excitement through the entire squadron, for we knew we were about to witness history. C Flight, who were on the early job, came back with tales of murderous destruction being wrought on the German trenches.

"There's a bloody snow storm as well," grumbled Bates. "We could hardly see a thing."

"How's the offensive going?" I asked him.

"I can only speak for our sector," he replied. "The P.B.I. are breaking through the first line of trenches, but it's slow going."

B Flight were up next, then it was our turn.

Sibbald said, "The artillery has a planned schedule today. Their barrage will creep forwards so as to stay just ahead of our infantry. So they don't need much wireless direction this morning. I'll do the wireless work, but the rest of you need to be in close support. The biggest problem our artillery have is that they can't tell how far our troops have advanced. Your job today is to go down low over the battlefield and find out where our infantry are, then go back and drop messages to the artillery lads. In turn, they will relay the information to Corps H.Q. by telephone. As soon as you've dropped your message, head back and repeat the exercise for as long as you have fuel. Is that clear?"

We all nodded, but I asked, "Can't we use wireless transmissions?"

"You'll be too low," was Sibbald's response. "You need to be agile, and you can't be that when your aerial is trailing out behind you."

I had to take his word for that, although I wasn't convinced that a Quirk was agile at the best of times. Sensibly, I held my tongue on that point, and we all filed out, making our way across the airfield to the hangars.

There, I discovered that a klaxon had been attached to the underside of our B.E.2.

Turnbull explained, "I'll use that to attract the attention of the infantry, Sir. They'll be busy with what's in front of them, and it will be noisy. Once we find out where they are, I'll write a note, shove it in a despatch bag, then you fly back to the battery and we drop the note."

It all sounded very simple, but I soon discovered it was not nearly as easy as Turnbull had made out. The clouds were low, with showers of sleet and snow making life difficult. The ground was white where shells and the tramping of thousands of booted feet had not turned it to muddy slush, and shells were exploding all over the place. We were, I quickly learned, in as much danger from our own artillery as from anything else. Added to that, the German guns had broken cover and were now sending in a counter-barrage, hoping to catch our troops in the open as they advanced.

With the dirty line of the Scarpe on our left, Turnbull and I flew at just above ground level, risking machine gun and rifle fire as well as the tumbling artillery shells which were exploding in huge gouts of earth, flinging up mud and splinters of rock, any one of which could have brought us down. In fact, I noticed a B.E.2 lying crumpled in a crater, its wings smashed, its tail high in the air. I checked the lettering on its side, and recognised it as belonging to Harvie of B Flight. There was no sign of him or his observer, so I hoped they had managed to get out in one piece.

Men were below us, too, struggling their way through the horrendous landscape. They plodded at little more than walking pace, many of them hunched against the storm of weather and bullets. Some crawled from crater to crater, while far too many simply lay there, unmoving.

I had no option but to ignore the huge amount of metal flying all around us. Using a Bowden cable, Turnbull sounded the klaxon as we flew over what had been the German front line, and some soldiers waved at us. They were supposed to lay out strips of white cloth, or let off white flares to confirm their position, but none of them did so. There was no doubt, though, that they were British troops, for we flew so low we could make out their khaki uniforms and dish-like steel helmets.

Up ahead, a wall of explosions showed that our artillery had moved on, but it was soon apparent that it was too far ahead of our troops who had become bogged down trying to take the German second line trenches.

A Whack! Whack! of bullets punched holes in the rear of our fuselage, and I saw Turnbull heave the Lewis gun onto the side candlestick mounting. He signalled for me to bank right, so I tilted the plane and he pulled the trigger, sending several short bursts against some target on the ground.

I pulled the Quirk into a tight circle, and looked down to see a couple of Germans in the ruins of what must have been a machine gun post. The wreckage of what seemed to be wicker defences were strewn across the snowy dip, but there was enough whiteness on the ground to show up their grey uniforms. One of them was lying on his back, flopping around wildly, and I guessed Turnbull had hit him. The other, though, was hunched determinedly over his machine gun and was watching us, waiting for us to come back into his sights.

The problem with an aeroplane is that you cannot stop. We were coming round in a circle which would very soon bring us within his field of fire, so I levelled off and reversed bank, swinging the kite around so as to come at him from behind once again.

By the time I had completed this manoeuvre, the German gunner had heaved his machine gun around and was already popping off a stream of bullets in our direction. Turnbull fired back, but we were a couple of hundred yards away, so his aim was off. Then, however, I saw an explosion fling the gunner across the crater, then British troops scrambled into the dip. One of them must have used the time provided by our arrival to get close enough to the nest to fling in a hand grenade. That had taken some guts, I am sure.

We waved to the soldiers as we flew over their heads, but only one waved back, raising his rifle in salute.

Turnbull gestured for us to return to the artillery lines. I was very happy to do so, for I saw more holes appear in our wings, and drifting smoke was obscuring much of the ground, so I was terrified I'd fly straight into a crump hole.

Turnbull scribbled away at his notepad, stuffed it into a weighted bag, then changed the drum on the Lewis gun, giving him a full quota of ammunition for our next jaunt over the Lines.

I passed over our own trenches where another wave of troops was already hauling themselves out into that morning's No Man's Land and setting off to support the attack. I could not imagine how they were feeling, trudging across that cratered quagmire in the face of sleet, snow, bullets and shells. As far as I was concerned, every one of them deserved a medal simply for climbing out of the trench and going over the top.

Moments later, we flew over the field artillery, then we reached the heavy guns, the great howitzers which could hurl enormous shells several miles. We dropped our message bag, then flew back into the hell and repeated the exercise several times.

We flew two more missions that day, and I was exhausted both physically and mentally by the end of it. The strain of flying at low level, with every German in the vicinity shooting at you, and with our own artillery lobbing shells which could hit us at any time, was enough to sap anyone's strength.

On our second flight, we had to make a run for it. Turnbull had, I was pleased to discover, been watching the sky as well as the ground. He suddenly gave the signal for hostile aircraft, gesturing that I should turn and run westwards. He turned to kneel on his seat, gripping the Lewis gun and aiming it back over my head.

"Keep dodging!" he yelled, the words just audible over the racket around us.

I was so low, all I could do was twist and weave. The Lewis gun blazed into life again, the noise extremely loud since it was only a foot or so in front of me. Turnbull, his face impassive, swung it, fired a short burst, adjusted his aim, fired again, and kept repeating the drill as calmly as if he were on a practice range. Even the wild gyrations of the Quirk as I banked steeply and swung it all over the place did not seem to put him off.

I had no idea what he was shooting at, and I did not really want to know. I saw some tracers flash past us, missing our starboard wingtips by a yard or so. Instead of dodging away from them, my next move was a sliding turn to the right, and I glanced left to see another line of the sparkling tracer bullets whizz past us on that side.

I dodged right again, hoping to fool the Hun, then swung left, but Turnbull put up his gun and waved at me that we were safe.

I'd had enough. Our fuel was running low, for we'd already been out for nearly three hours, and low level jinking at full throttle can burn through a lot of petrol, so I gave him the washout sign. He nodded, and we went home.

"It was an Albatros," he told me when we landed. "One of the older D.II types. Still very dangerous, of course. I didn't think any of them would dare come down that low above the trenches, but he was either very brave or very stupid."

"Did you hit him?" I asked.

Turnbull shook his head.

"I just wanted him to know we weren't defenceless. He gave up once he realised he wasn't going to get an easy kill. Well done dodging around like that, Sir."

I suppose I should have been delighted to receive such praise from a veteran like Sergeant Turnbull, but I was too worn out to fully appreciate his compliment.

I think everyone felt the same, for the Mess was very quiet that evening. It had been a rough day for the squadron. Harvie had returned safely, but his observer, Ainslie, had been badly wounded. Harvie had been left with no option but to leave him at a Casualty Clearing Station.

"It didn't look good," Harvie admitted. "He took a bullet in the stomach, and another one smashed his thigh."

Ainslie was not the only casualty we suffered. Garrick and Long were missing, while C Flight had lost Parker and Vickers, both of whom were definitely dead. They had been flying low and had been brought down by machine gun fire from the ground. Their fuel tank must have ruptured, because the plane had been seen to burst into flames when it struck the ground.

Sibbald had been chased by three Albatroses but had managed to get into a cloud to escape. Being Sibbald, he thought nothing of this, simply explaining that he'd stayed concealed for a while, then come back out of the cloud. He made it sound very simple.

Watt's replacement has arrived. He's a Canadian named MacCallum. Like all Canadians, he is a big fellow, broad-shouldered and apparently in glowing good health. I don't know what they feed them on in Canada, but every one of them from that province seems to be bigger and healthier than anyone from the British Isles.

Naturally, Sibbald did not allow him to cross the Lines today. He grumbled at MacCallum's paltry thirty-one hours of flying time, and insisted the big Canadian spend the day on practice flights.

"He does that to everyone," I told MacCallum.

The big Canadian grumbled a bit, but sighed, "I suppose it's only for a day. But I hope the war isn't over by the time he lets me cross the Lines."

"I reckon it will go on for a few days yet," I told him with all the implied knowledge of a veteran.

"That's good," he grinned. "I want to do my bit."

He is frightfully keen, and he must think he's come to a very dull squadron, for we all went off to bed early, exhaustion our excuse. I've stayed up to write this journal, but I need to stop now and get some sleep. I expect tomorrow will bring more of the same, and I must admit that is not a happy prospect. But then, this is the assault which will win the war, and we must all face hardships if we are to defeat the Boche.

Tuesday 10th April, 1917

Garrick and Long turned up during the night, having come down near our own starting trenches.

"I don't know what hit us," Garrick said. "It could have been a machine gun on the ground, or perhaps just engine failure. All I know is that the engine gave a loud bang and just stopped. We were too low to do anything other than come down in a crump hole."

"The salvage team are going to be busy today," Beano remarked. "That's two kites down in No Man's Land."

We did not envy the squadron's salvage team. Their job was to pull back anything they could recover from a crashed plane. Even a wreck could provide spare parts to repair other machines, and engines were so valuable, many risks were taken in order to recover them. Only if a crash site was behind German lines did the scavengers of the salvage team stay at home.

"I hope we don't give them any more business today," I said.

MacCallum was sent back to Candas to collect a new B.E.2, so Garrick and Long used his plane. Like me and Turnbull, they were given wireless duties today, with Sibbald, Sullivan and Beano doing the low, close contact work.

"The attack seems to be going well in most places," the Major told us. "Incredibly, the Canadians have captured Vimy Ridge already. Nobody thought they had a hope in Hell, but they've done it. Unfortunately, the troops on either side of them have run into some problems. VII Corps is pushing on well, and only a little behind schedule, so it's our job to help them make the vital breakthrough."

We learned that the Canadians had exploded several mines beneath the Hun trenches on Vimy Ridge. This sequence of massive explosions, allied to the incredible bombardment, had so stunned the Germans that the Canadians had been able to climb the ridge and take control.

In other parts of the sector, miles and miles of tunnels had been dug beneath the city of Arras. This complex contained stores, hospitals, miniature railway tracks and plenty of space for our troops to remain out of sight until the offensive began. Yesterday, they had burst out and moved forwards, driving hard at the Huns, many of whom surrendered.

It was going well, but the breakthrough had not yet materialised.

"This is the hard bit, Sir," Turnbull informed me.

"What do you mean?" I asked. "If we've captured their trenches, there must be open ground we can exploit."

"Oh, there is, Sir," he nodded grimly. "The problem is getting there. Our cavalry could make the most of it, but they need to cross several miles of muddy craters, with the Hun artillery shelling them all the way. Horses ain't so good at crossing that sort of terrain at the best of times. Added to that, our own guns won't have the range to hit the Germans until they are moved up as well. That can take a long time. Only our biggest howitzers can trouble the Boche rear areas, and so our troops who are in the new front line will be under heavy bombardment, and also facing counter-attacks when the Germans bring up their reserves."

It sounded rather depressing, but our job was to cover those open areas and watch for the German reserve troops coming up. We were also to seek out Hun artillery, and direct our own big guns to hit them.

This was my first time on wireless duty, and I was surprised Sibbald had not given the task to a more experienced pilot, but I think he was giving me a break from the low flying. Garrick, too, had been spared that horror after his crash yesterday. He was sporting a black eye and had lost a tooth when his kite came down, but he was determined to keep flying.

"This is going to win the war," he declared. "I'm not going to let anyone say I am slacking."

"That's the spirit, Old Bean!" grinned Normansby, slapping him on the back.

So off we went.

Turnbull had a map which was divided into four large squares, each of which was further divided into thirty-six smaller squares. These small areas represented a one thousand yard area of ground. Using the numbers and letters on the map, he could direct fire onto any target, then correct the aim by using a clock code, with twelve o'clock oriented to the north.

Our wireless was, of necessity, a small thing. It was a Type 52 Sterling, powered by a six volt accumulator, and has a range of about ten miles. We were operating at its extreme range today.

Turnbull would tap out Morse signals to our assigned battery. In the R.F.C., each of us is required to pass a Morse test and be able to send signals at a minimum of eight words per minute. Trained wireless operators usually manage at least twenty words per minute, but the Flying Corps recognises that we need to learn lots of other skills as well. Besides, most transmissions use code letters, so messages can be relayed using only a few signals.

What I hadn't realised until Turnbull told me was that the artillery batteries had R.F.C. personnel assigned to them. When he sent a message from our wireless, it was another Flying Corps man who would receive it and pass the message to the commander of the battery.

"Those chaps earn their money, Sir," Turnbull told me. "They are a lot closer to the Front than we are."

Our first duty was to find the battery and send a recognition signal. I flew to the designated spot and began circling while Turnbull tapped out the letter R several times.

Dot-Dash-Dot.

R stood for, "Are you receiving me?"

We were circling above a small, wooden hut beside which stood a tall aerial pole. A man emerged, carrying a bundle which he threw to the ground, quickly spreading it out to reveal a large patch of white linen in the shape of a T. That was the confirmation that he had heard us. Of course, there are lots of aeroplanes sending wireless transmissions at any one time, and even with the limited range of our sets, the wireless operators could be overwhelmed by the sheer volume of signals and, in the early days of this technology, they often could not tell which aeroplane was sending which message. As usual, the boffins had come up with a solution, and the sets were equipped with what they termed clapper boards which altered the pitch of our signal so the operator could distinguish our messages from those of other planes.

As we circled, I admired the battery of four howitzers. They were enormous, with a 9.2 inch calibre. Each gun was so huge it had to be split into three separate parts before it could be moved. And setting one up could take three or four days even in optimal conditions. Moving these great guns forward to support our advancing infantry was simply not possible. At the moment, though, they still had just enough range to reach the limit of where our infantry had got to.

Howitzers have an old history. In the Middle Ages, cannons were used to fire solid balls in a straight line. Even in the days of Napoleon and Wellington, most cannons had retained this feature. They could be used against men on a battlefield, and they could bombard the stone walls of a fortress, but a howitzer was designed to lob its shell high into the air, sending it over defensive walls to drop inside a town or city. Nowadays, the practice remains the same except that the howitzers fire their shells thousands of feet up into the air, over our own trenches, then down onto the enemy.

And these huge guns, the largest the British Army had ever used, could hurl a 280 lbs projectile of high explosive as far as seven or eight miles.

With our signal acknowledged, I set off for the new Front, climbing up to around four thousand feet. To go any higher was impossible because of the clouds which were still sending down sharp showers of rain, sleet and snow.

I could see other Quirks lower down, doing the close contact job we had done yesterday. They scuttled around, blaring their klaxons, identifying our troops and reporting back. We, on the other hand, went further, seeking targets for the mighty howitzers.

I began my figure of eight patrol, a pattern designed to allow Turnbull to keep our assigned sector in view at all times. He paid out the aerial again, winding it loose through a hole in the floor of his cockpit. This long length of wire would trail one hundred and twenty feet behind us, adding drag to the Quirk's already legendary inability to perform quick manoeuvres.

Turnbull watched the ground while I maintained our pattern and watched the sky for signs of Huns. I saw a Flight of Spads, and another of ancient F.E.8 pusher planes which, although they were single-seaters with a forward firing machine gun, were almost as outclassed as our own B.E.2c. I was sure there must be other planes around, but the combination of the many clouds and my own inexperience meant that they remained invisible to me.

Turnbull gestured to me to alter course slightly. I was happy to do so since it helped throw off the occasional Archie burst. Our advance had pushed the Germans back a bit, and their Archie batteries had clearly been affected, for they threw very few shells up at us. Still, maintaining a steady, predictable course was to invite danger, so I followed Turnbull's pointed finger.

Down below was a patch of woodland. Then it belched fire and smoke, and I knew it was the site of a Hun artillery battery. More flashes appeared from beneath the dense foliage which I suddenly realised was probably only vegetation on top of camouflage nets. Few trees were showing signs of greenery despite it being April, for the weather had remained stubbornly cold.

Turnbull began tapping out coordinates using his map grid. Then he sent Dash-dash-dot for "G", the signal to open fire.

We waited, circling at a discreet distance until a massive explosion rocked the earth some fifty yards short of the wood. Fired by dead reckoning using a map reference, it had been a damned good first shot.

Turnbull would now refer to the circular clock face, sending a note of how far and in which direction the aim had been off. After a minute or so, we saw a section of the woodland erupt as another of the massive shells found the target.

Now Turnbull gleefully tapped out "BF" to order the entire battery to fire. The lead gunner had found the target, and all four howitzers would use the same range and direction. Of course, some would be less accurate than others because the gun barrels became worn with use, and these guns had been hammering out shells for the better part of a fortnight in the run up to the Push, but we grinned at one another as the explosives rained down on the Hun battery. Earth and trees were flung high into the air as the shells burst all around the German guns. In minutes, the woodland became a tangled mess of shattered tree stumps and distorted metal. I even caught sight of some mangled bodies lying twisted amidst the carnage.

This was why we were here! This was us helping to win the war. That German battery would no longer hurl death and destruction against our advancing troops.

Turnbull gestured at me, pointing to the sky, and I guiltily resumed my search of the heavens. I had been so excited about finding and destroying the guns that I had forgotten to keep watch. Fortunately, no hostile aircraft were in the vicinity. I did see some tiny dots whirling around far off to the east, and I stared as one of them suddenly flared into bright light and fell, trailing dark smoke. Someone had been shot down in flames. Ours or theirs? I could not tell.

We continued our patrol, Turnbull having signalled to the battery to cease fire once we were satisfied the target had been destroyed.

And then we found the most glorious thing possible. There, advancing in a series of tightly-packed lines, was an entire regiment of German soldiers. These must be some of the reserves who would be making a counter-attack against the positions our troops had recently taken.

Turnbull gave me a quizzical look as if debating something. He mouthed something which I could not catch, then I realised what he was asking.

"Zone Call?" he was shouting.

This was a big decision, certainly not one anyone would make lightly, least of all a sergeant. But he was right. Over a thousand German troops were out in the open, heading towards the battle lines. They could throw back our entire advance.

I nodded, giving Turnbull the thumbs up and yelling, "Zone Call!" at the top of my voice.

Nodding, he returned his attention to the wireless set, tapping out "LL" and giving the map coordinates.

I edged away from the target. Turnbull would have needed to allow for where the advancing soldiers would be by the time our batteries responded, then adding on more time to allow for the flight of the shells.

He had judged it perfectly.

A Zone Call is an instruction for all batteries to fire. This meant that not only the single battery of howitzers we were assigned to, but any other battery which could reach the target we had signalled. The top brass could get really tetchy if someone called in LL without justification, for each battery already had important targets to aim for, but this was simply too good an opportunity to miss.

Shells rained down on the Germans, flinging men in all directions and turning the grassy meadow they were crossing into so many muddy craters. In a downpour of death, our guns shattered the regiment, most of whom scattered, vainly trying to escape the deluge of high explosive. Many did not make it, for the guns were inexorable, and Turnbull was sending adjustment signals.

It was a horrible yet fascinating sight, and I struggled to remember I was supposed to be watching the sky. I looked up, twisting my head in all directions. My heart skipped a beat when I saw, through a gap in the clouds, some biplanes several thousand feet above us, but even I could tell from their straight, rectangular wings and dove-shaped tails that they were Spads.

My relief was short-lived, though. Movement caught my eye, and I saw five shapes diving down from high above the Spads, tearing past them and coming down on us.

Huns!

Frantically, I waggled the wings, giving Turnbull the HA signal.

He tapped out a rapid "MQ" to order the guns to stop firing, then "CI" to signal we were returning to our landing ground.

The big question was whether we would make it, for the Huns were dropping on us with alarming speed. They had already scattered the Spads, one of which was fluttering downwards, clearly in trouble. But the Albatroses had not tarried to fight the Spads. After diving through them, they were coming for us because they knew we could do more damage to the German troops on the ground.

While Turnbull desperately spun the handle to reel in our aerial, I was already diving westwards, pushing the throttle open and giving the Quirk its toughest test yet.

I had recognised the Huns as Albatroses, the deadliest of them all. These were the new type, the D.III, which had copied the highly successful French Nieuport and had a narrow lower wing with a V-shaped strut connecting this to the larger top wing. This design gave the aircraft greater manoeuvrability than the older D.II type, and the powerful Mercedes engine, combined with the two Spandau machine guns which fired through the propeller thanks to their highly efficient interrupter gear, made these the most feared aeroplanes on the Western Front. With their rounded snouts, smooth bodies and spade-shaped tails, they reminded me of a pack of sharks.

And they were hunting me.

I turned to look back. The Spads, having recovered from the initial attack, were coming down after the Huns, but the Albatroses had left them well behind. Already I could see the sparks of the muzzle flashes as the lead Albatros began firing at us.

Turnbull was still winding in the aerial, but he finished at last, then sprang to his Lewis gun. He rattled off a short burst in response to the attack, while I tramped on the rudder, yawing and swinging the plane to throw off the enemy's aim.

It was futile, I knew. Hard as I tried, I could not turn the B.E.2 into a fighting machine. It was simply too slow and clumsy to evade the sleek killers who were chasing us. The Albatroses, aided by the speed they had gained in their dive, were travelling at around forty miles per hour faster than we could manage, and the lead plane sent a stream of bullets which whizzed all around us. Somehow, nothing vital was hit, although splinters flew from one of our struts, and holes appeared in the top wing dangerously close to the gravity tank which held our reserve supply of petrol.

The Albatros zoomed past us, climbing steeply, then turned for another attack, sliding in behind us.

It was a heart-stopping few moments. I could hear the rat-tat-tat of the Hun's machine guns, and I could see more holes appear in our wings. My back began to sweat in anticipation of being struck by a bullet, but Turnbull was calmly firing back, concentrating his fire in short bursts while I continued to swerve and slide as best as I could to throw off the enemy pilot's aim.

Then, as I skidded the Quirk to the left, I heard a series of metallic sounds as several bullets smashed into our engine. The R.A.F.'s note rose alarmingly, and oil began to fly out in great gobbets, some of them striking Turnbull on the back.

The revs dropped, and so did our speed. I think that saved us, for the German's next burst missed us, although not by much. Whoever he was, he was a damned good shot, and I knew his next burst would finish us.

I remember thinking that I didn't mind dying as long as we didn't catch fire and burn all the way down, but Turnbull was suddenly punching the air in delight, pointing upwards.

I was still battling to control the damaged Quirk, but I looked up to see another group of planes join the fight. And what planes! Half a dozen Sopwith Triplanes had dropped out of the cloud cover and dived on the Huns.

The Triplane is a superb design, its three sets of wings connected by single struts on left and right. It can turn more tightly than an Albatros and can climb like a lift. It is the one British aeroplane which can match the Albatros in a fight. Its only real disadvantage is that it has only one machine gun.

Even so, the Huns did not hang around to argue. With the Spads coming down behind them, and the Triplanes tumbling from in front of them, the Germans decided that discretion was their best option. Outnumbered and at a lower altitude than the British scouts, they were very much at a disadvantage, so they used their superior speed in a dive to twist away, putting their noses down and heading towards the east. The Triplanes set off in pursuit, but I did not watch the chase, for I had other concerns.

I was trembling and sweating profusely, and I began to look for a place to put the Quirk down. Yet we were already crossing the area which had formed the rear trenches of the German Lines, so all that confronted me was miles of shell holes.

I throttled back, nursing the engine which, miraculously, continued to run. It was knocking and grinding terribly, and the temperature gauge was in the red, but the propeller was still turning.

Gripping the stick tightly, I pressed on, praying that no other Huns would find us limping homewards.

The engine finally gave up with a splutter as we passed over Arras at less than one thousand feet. Here, though, there were fields. I chose the largest one I could see, and glided down. I'd practised dead stick landings during my training, but this was the first time I'd needed to put that practice to the test.

There were cows in the field, but they had clustered in the far corner, so I had a relatively easy landing. We hardly bounced at all, and the tail skid dragged us to a smooth enough halt.

Turnbull let out a sigh of relief. Whipping off his goggles and helmet, he asked me, "Do you know who that was?"

"What? Who?"

"The Hun. I think it was the man himself."

I blinked at him.

"The Red Baron?"

"I think so. The plane looked all red from its nose to its tail. Wings and everything. All red except the black crosses."

I could only grin back at him like a fool. To me, everything had happened so quickly I had barely paid attention to the colour of our foe.

"I wonder if he'll claim us as a victory?" I mused.

Turnbull shook his head.

"The Germans don't count kills unless they see the crash. And we didn't crash."

"No," I agreed. "But the kite might still end up wrecked if those cows come over and take an interest."

Fortunately, the farm's owner, a rangy, grey-haired Frenchman with a stubbled chin, soon arrived on the scene with his two young daughters. They herded the cows into the next field, and the farmer even lent Turnbull his bike so the Sergeant could pedal his way to the nearest Army base and find a telephone.

"The salvage team will be happy they don't need to go too far to collect us," was his parting shot.

I kept guard on the plane until a lorry arrived to collect the kite, and a tender turned up to whisk Turnbull and me back to the airfield.

"Remember to bring the clock," Turnbull advised.

I dutifully removed the dashboard clock from the plane. These timepieces were much in demand, so there was always a row if you left one where it could be filched.

I was the toast of the Mess this evening, even though I only had Turnbull's word for it that we had encountered the Red Baron and lived to tell the tale.

"We were bloody lucky," I kept telling everyone. "If those Triplanes hadn't arrived, we'd have gone west without any doubt."

Unfortunately, C Flight had lost another crew. Arnold, one of the new boys, and his observer, Sergeant Overton, had gone down behind the German Lines. Our Archie had seen them being attacked by a bunch of Albatroses. They could not confirm their fate, but Arnold and Sergeant Overton were either dead or prisoners. It was a shame, but there was nothing we could do about it, so everyone concentrated on the good news.

"You did a damned fine job with that Zone Call," the Major beamed. "Very well done."

Vaughn may or may not have been jealous when he said to me later, "You'll get a gong if you carry on like this, young lad. You destroy enemy regiments, and you face down Germany's greatest fighter pilot. You must have a guardian angel watching over you."

"Perhaps he's got some lucky charm or other," Dish suggested, his words slightly slurred by the whisky he had consumed.

Swigging at a beer, Normansby said, "Whatever he has, Old Bean, I'd like some of it. I got a massive Archie splinter in my main spar today, and a row of bullet holes just behind my cockpit. This close contact stuff is enough to give you nightmares."

I think most of us privately agreed with him, but I did not care. I had survived a moment of real danger, but I had achieved much more than that. The work Turnbull and I did today had made a difference. Perhaps Vaughn was right and I would get a medal of some sort. That was a nice thought, and I'll try to dream about it tonight. Better that than think about how close I came to being shot down.

And tomorrow, we will do it all again.

Wednesday 11th April, 1917

I hope I am able to update this journal properly. I am writing from memory now, since I had no opportunity to record daily entries for a couple of days, and my memory of everything that happened is still a bit jumbled. However, I thought it would be better to set my thoughts down in writing while they are still relatively fresh in case I get out of the habit of recording events.

Anyway, Wednesday morning was routine enough. A Flight was up to full strength, MacCallum being permitted to do a photographic shoot, while Turnbull and I did another close contact patrol, flying low over the shifting front lines, sounding our klaxon and scribbling messages which we would drop near Divisional and Corps H.Q. to let the commanding officers know what was happening. We were in a brand new B.E.2c, freshly delivered from Candas the previous evening. Dunlop and Green had given it a thorough going over during the night, and it was in good condition, the engine giving full revs and the rigging adjusted to perfection. I'd taken the kite up on a quick test early in the morning, and then Turnbull had joined me for the patrol.

Down on the ground, things were fairly chaotic. The infantry had pushed forwards, but were now meeting strong resistance. Some of the chaps in the Mess had been of the opinion that the German reserve troops had been held too far back, allowing our advance to push on, but now the Germans were counter-attacking with vigour. Our infantry were suffering because our artillery had not yet been able to come up to support them, and the Front was now beyond the range of even our biggest guns.

The close contact work was as terrifying as I remembered from our previous experience. Bullets and explosions rocked us constantly, and I returned damp with sweat despite the continuing bitterly cold weather, and with the pristine canvas of our lovely new Quirk punctured by several bullet holes.

"We have a bombing mission this afternoon," Sibbald informed me once we returned from the morning job.

Unfortunately, Garrick and Long would not be with us. They had been shot down again, ground fire probably claiming them, and this time there seemed little chance they had survived. Sullivan had seen them going in, the plane rolling onto its back before diving into the earth with engine full on.

"Garrick must have been hit," Sullivan guessed.

This was a blow, but one brighter bit of news came when Potter informed us that he had heard that Arnold, who had been shot down a couple of days ago, was alive. He and Sergeant Overton were prisoners. Overton had been wounded, but both men were said to be in fair shape.

"You know the odd thing," Vaughn mused after we'd heard this. "Lots of chaps are taken prisoner. I mean, we spend most of every flight over enemy territory, and there's always the risk of engine failure over and above being shot at by Archie and various Hun machines."

"Not to mention ground machine guns," Tattersall put in. "One of those buggers nearly got me this morning. He put a row of bullets through our fuselage just behind my seat."

"Yes, those too," Vaughn agreed.

"So what is odd about that?" I frowned, not following his train of thought.

"It's this," he explained, his mood apparently serious although it was still hard for me to tell whether he was pulling my leg. "The powers that be don't trust us with parachutes. They think we would use them as an excuse to jump out of our planes at the first sign of danger."

"That's rot!" Tattersall exclaimed.

"What is?" Vaughn challenged. "That we would do it if we could, or that the G.O.C. thinks we would?"

"That anyone thinks we would," Tattersall said, shaking his head at Vaughn's pedantry.

"Exactly!" agreed Vaughn. "And we already have the proof of that."

"We do?" I asked, still unsure of his point.

He nodded, "Of course we do. I mean, what could be simpler than crossing the Lines, cutting power, then landing in a nice, flat field. You set fire to your kite as per instructions, and nobody can ever prove you weren't telling the truth when you said you had engine trouble."

I stared at him for a long moment.

"Nobody would ever do that," I insisted.

"I agree," he smiled, "although you can never rule anything out completely. But I've never met any pilot I thought would be capable of it."

Tattersall said, "So your argument is that we should be given parachutes because we've already proved we don't try to dodge our duty?"

"That's right," Vaughn nodded.

"Parachutes are bulky things," I pointed out.

"The ones used by the balloonatics are," he agreed. "But there are smaller, more compact models which would easily fit in a cockpit."

"If you say so," I grunted, uncertain whether to believe him or not. "But I'm not sure I'd want to jump out of a plane at ten thousand feet and hope that the bloody thing opened."

"Better that than sit in a burning plane or watch the earth rushing up to meet you with no chance of escape," he countered. "Besides, the balloon fellows regularly use parachutes. They open more often than not. In fact, I don't recall ever hearing of one failing to open."

With one of his usual sly grins, he added, "Although I'm sure the powers that be would hush it up if one of the parachutes failed."

"You don't know that!" I objected.

Dish Tattersall chuckled, "He's trying to distract you, Kerr."

"What do you mean?" I scowled angrily, casting a dark look at Vaughn who was grinning at me, his eyes full of mischief.

Dish said, "We were talking about the feasibility and psychology of parachutes. Whether they are reliable is another matter. So, getting back to the original point, the reason the balloon observers have parachutes is because they can't defend themselves against an attack."

Vaughn had an answer ready for this.

His eyebrows arching as if in astonishment, he asked, "Do you really think a Lewis gun with a very restricted arc of fire is much defence against an Albatros?"

To which, Tattersall and I were obliged to concede he had a point.

"It's better than nothing," was all the response I could make.

As usual, Vaughn's argument unsettled me slightly, but I had occasion to remember this conversation that afternoon.

Sibbald led our Flight of five Quirks, each of us with bombs beneath our wings. As before, we had no observers and no machine guns to defend ourselves. Our target was a railway junction some ten miles beyond the fighting zone.

"The Boche are bringing in supplies by train," Sibbald explained at the briefing. "Food and ammunition, plus some extra troops. Our job is to destroy the track if possible."

He then went on to explain how we could accomplish this.

"There's a trick to hitting railway lines," he told us. "You don't fly along the line of the track because the bombs are likely to miss unless you go so low you'll be hit by the blast of your own bombs exploding. Nor do you fly across the track, because it's a narrow target from up high."

"So what do we do, Old Bean?" asked Normansby.

"You fly across the track diagonally," Sibbald told us. "Release your bombs in a rapid string, one after the other. It improves the chances of one hitting the track, and it only takes one hit to disrupt rail traffic. With ten bombs each, we have enough for two runs, dropping five each time. Just remember to alternate between left and right wings or you'll unbalance your bus."

So off we went, our Quirks waddling across the airfield like pregnant ducks, then heaving up into the air and setting off to the east.

Corps had arranged an escort of F.E.2b's plus some Sopwith Pups providing high cover. I wasn't hugely impressed by the lumbering F.E.2's although they did at least have machine guns. The big pushers were strong machines which could carry two or three guns, although I didn't envy the gunners. Sitting in the exposed front cockpit, each gunner had a wonderful field of fire because there was nothing in front of him. He could swivel his gun in all directions except behind. Some of the pilots also had a machine gun attached to the outside of their cockpit. This could fire straight ahead, although they needed to be careful not to hit their own gunner if he was jumping around in the front.

The most dangerous part, though, was when they were attacked from behind. Because the crew sat in what looked like a layered bathtub, with the pilot up high and the gunner in front and lower down, everything else was behind them. The wings, engine, propeller and twin-boomed tail all blocked their view. Some genius had come up with the idea of mounting a third machine gun pointing back and up over the pilot's head. All the gunner needed to do was stand up, turn round, then climb up to the gun, balancing his feet on the rim of his cockpit. It may have sounded simple when the plane was on the ground, but doing it in a sixty mile per hour wind, with the plane moving all the time, it was a desperate manoeuvre. The gunner risked being thrown off the kite if the pilot banked or turned too sharply, sending him tumbling to earth.

The F.E.2 is also a slow bus, but it was fast enough to keep up with our laden Quirks.

So five of us crossed the Lines, with six F.E.'s in close attendance, while five Pups followed us high above.

We reached the target unmolested by anything worse than a severe barrage of hate from Archie, then Sibbald led us in a bombing run while the Fees circled protectively above us.

There was a signal box at the junction, but no station or unloading point. Fortunately, there were no ground defences either. Our target was a Vee of railway tracks where two lines came together before a single line continued towards the front.

I don't think I'd ever been so far over the Lines before, and I could hardly believe we had reached this place without being attacked, but we did not hang around congratulating ourselves. Dropping to around fifteen hundred feet, Sibbald led the way, with the rest of us following in single file.

MacCallum was second in line, then me, followed by Beano and, finally, Sullivan.

I watched as the first two planes dropped a string of bombs. Showers of earth burst upwards as the bombs landed, all of them close to the juncture of the tracks, but none of them hitting anything vital. One of MacCallum's bombs did go through the roof of the signal box, more or less destroying the building when it went off, so that was a success, but the track remained intact.

It was my turn. I flew across the junction at an angle as Sibbald had advised, flicking the switches to drop one bomb after another. I released four before the tracks vanished beneath my nose, so I hauled the Quirk into a circle to follow Sibbald and MacCallum in a second run.

I looked down as I turned, noting that all my bombs had done was create more craters beside the track. I had missed.

Beano, though, scored a direct hit with one bomb, transforming a huge timber sleeper into matchwood and buckling the metal track of one of the two approaching lines.

Sullivan missed, and then Sibbald was going round for his second attempt. This time, he dropped a bomb slap bang on the junction of all three sections of line, with another bomb falling so close to the single track that it lifted the rails.

MacCallum's second run produced no results, then I let all six of my bombs go almost all at once. As I circled away, I saw that I had missed again, although I'd hit the edge of the raised earth beneath the tracks, causing a minor landslip. That would weaken the track, I was sure.

Beano scored another hit, and Sullivan did some minor damage, then we were climbing for height and heading home.

Our good fortune could not last, of course. We were a couple of miles from where I thought the new Front was, when a solitary biplane came from the south to take a look at us. Sibbald spotted it first, waggling his wings and pointing high to his left.

I could not see it at first, but then I caught a glimpse of movement and knew it was a Hun.

But on his own?

It was a Halberstadt, one of their older models still in action. It's actually a lovely plane to look at, with flared wingtips, a rounded nose, and a fuselage which tapers away almost to nothing before flaring out in a curved tail. It looks almost too fragile to be a fighting machine, certainly a lot less imposing than the fearsome Albatros, but it's still dangerous enough even if it does carry only a single machine gun.

But one plane?

He flew above us, clearly taking a closer look. I could make out the huge, black Maltese crosses on the underside of his lower wings as he passed over us, and I thought he'd decided to leave us alone. There were eleven of us, with five Pups higher up, and only a madman would contemplate such odds, even if the five Quirks had no machine guns.

The Halberstadt was painted green and purple, the sun highlighting its shading as he turned and flew back over us.

I wondered what the Pups were doing. Why had they not come down to chase him away? Perhaps they thought he was trying to lure them into a trap? Or perhaps they thought the Fees could keep a solitary Halberstadt at bay.

That seemed sensible, for surely he could do nothing against us.

Then he rolled onto his back, the move almost lazy, gathering speed as he dived down.

I confess I was mesmerised. He came down through the Flight of F.E.2's, dodging and weaving, turning and banking with astonishing skill and speed. It was almost as if he was playing with them. The gunners stood up, blazing away at him, but he danced around them, diving and zooming, occasionally squirting off bursts of fire to distract them.

I kept looking around, expecting to see other Huns joining the attack, but there was only this one machine.

Twisting to look behind me, I saw him continue to toy with the cumbersome Fees. They were too slow and heavy to match his turns, and none of them seemed capable of holding him in their sights as he dodged between them. They split apart, turning all ways as they vainly tried to catch him, but he was far too clever for them, never giving them a clear shot.

And then I realised what he had done, for he suddenly banked steeply and came after us. He had been playing with the Fees in order to slow them down, letting us get ahead, and now he outstripped them easily as he dived after us.

This pilot, I realised, was no novice. He was clever and skilful, and he had expertly removed our escort through sheer flying ability. I doubt that the Pups could have stopped him even if they had come down from their lofty vantage point. They were coming now, but far too late, and the Halberstadt was closing on us fast.

Sibbald fired off a red flare, warning us to scatter. We dodged, banking and turning in an attempt to make him pass us thanks to his faster speed.

It did not work. I heard his machine gun firing as I swerved to my left, and I felt the impact as bullets smashed into my lovely new Quirk. His shooting was incredibly accurate, for his bullets slammed into my engine. Several tore through the front cockpit, and some struck my dashboard, my instruments exploding, showering tiny splinters of glass and wood all over me. I still don't know how he missed me, but I suspect the bullets which tore through my instrument panel were the final ones of his burst. The bullets stopped, and then the Halberstadt roared past me, his wheels missing my top wings by only a couple of feet.

I had no time to congratulate myself on my narrow escape, for I could smell petrol. The stink was so strong, I suspected my main tank, sited beneath the seat in the front cockpit, might have been punctured, but I could see that the gravity tank had definitely been holed. This emergency reserve of fuel was fastened beneath the upper wing, just above the engine, and I could see a faint stream of bluish vapour streaking back above my head.

Fire! The airman's greatest fear now threatened to kill me. If that escaping fuel came in contact with hot metal, it would ignite, burning me to a crisp.

I needed to put down, and in a hurry.

The Hun's bullets had obviously done even more damage, because my engine was coughing and spluttering. Then there was a loud bang, a puff of dark, oily smoke, and the engine stopped dead.

In the silence, I could hear the buzz of other engines and the rattle of machine guns. Looking frantically around, I dreaded the sight of the Hun coming back to finish me off, but he had clearly decided I was as good as dead anyway, for he was now aiming at Sullivan who was frantically trying to dodge a stream of bullets.

The escorting Fees were closing again, some of the gunners taking long range shots at the Hun, and the Pups were still diving down.

The Hun pilot must have been aware of everything, for he broke off his attack at the perfect moment, leaving Sullivan limping homewards with bullet holes everywhere. The Halberstadt rolled again, diving away to stay well clear of the Pups. I could almost imagine the pilot putting a thumb to his nose and waggling his fingers as he headed for home. He deserved his triumph, for he had made fools of us all, and he'd shot me down, even if I hadn't quite hit the ground yet.

That would not be long in happening. I scanned the land below me, searching for a spot to put down. We were close to the battlefield, for the earth was more craters than fields here, so I just kept pointing the kite to the west and began praying.

This was when I remembered Vaughn's remarks about a parachute. At that moment, with petrol streaming out above my head, and the prospect of crashing into a shell hole which might bring hot metal into contact with the fuel, I began to think it would be nice to have the option of a parachute.

I saw artillery shells exploding ahead of me, only about half a mile away. Oddly, this encouraged me, for it meant that I was close to the fighting, which meant I was close to British troops on the ground. Perhaps I had a chance to avoid being captured.

But there was nowhere to land safely, and I was convinced I was about to kill myself by trying to crash land in the midst of a battle.

Then I saw a road.

Or what was left of a road. It was a narrow stretch of cobbles running roughly east to west, with some wrecked buildings on either side. One or two had been completely obliterated apart from the lower sections of wall, while others still stood, albeit with roofs caved in, or with great holes blown in their sides.

Even as I watched, another shell exploded close to the road, telling me this was very much a live war zone.

Yet I had no choice. I was too low now to land anywhere else. Besides, the terrain ahead, while still showing some clumps of greenery, was as cratered and pitted as No Man's Land.

I was coming down in a fast glide, desperate to prevent the Quirk stalling. I aimed for the roadway, grateful that the controls still responded, and I tried not to look out over the side of the cockpit in case I saw German troops.

My attempt at playing the part of an ostrich did me no good, for the Germans certainly saw me. I distinctly heard the crack of rifles, and a bullet tore a chunk out of one of my interplane struts just in front of the forward cockpit, adding to the damage already wreaked by the Halberstadt.

I was low down now. The ground rushed up to meet me. I was going too fast, I knew, but fear of the petrol catching fire, perhaps ignited by the heat of a bullet from the ground, made me desperate.

At the last moment, I pulled the stick back, pulling the nose up and trying to flop the kite onto the cobbles.

We hit, bounced, hit again, and then the tail skid was scraping loudly along the cobbled road. Normally, it would dig into the grass of the airfield and slow me, but now it seemed to have no effect, for the Quirk kept going, speeding along the road at nearly forty miles per hour, with wrecked buildings passing me on either side, and bullets whining about my ears.

It seemed to take an age, but the Quirk began to slow, then was down to walking pace, and almost stopped. I had kept my head down, hunching my shoulders to make myself as small as possible, but I took a look over the side when I felt the plane was about to stop.

On the ground, the nose of the B.E.2c points upwards, obscuring the view directly in front, but I could see between the wings on either side, and what I saw was another shell crater. The road vanished, replaced by a dip in the ground where some German gunner had scored a direct hit on the cobbles. Without brakes, there was nothing I could do except cling on and hope for the best. With luck, I'd stop just short.

My luck did not hold. With almost comical slowness, the wheels reached the edge of the crump hole, and the kite began to tip, the weight of the engine dragging it down.

Even as I felt the tail rising into the air, and as gravity flung me forwards, the seat belt almost cutting me in half, I caught sight of some startled faces as men leaped aside. My crater was already occupied!

I heard the sound of splintering wood as the propeller snapped, felt a jolt as the nose dug into the mud, and then I was hanging there, almost vertical.

And the petrol from the gravity tank was now dripping towards the front of the plane where the hot exhaust pipes were located.

"Hands up, Fritz!" shouted an angry voice.

I unclipped my belt, grabbed the edges of the cockpit and flung myself out, scrabbling desperately for the earth just below the rim of the crater. I hit hard, slipped, then slid down into a puddle of muddy water. I could hear bullets buzzing overhead, and others whacking into the fabric of my poor old Quirk. Or poor new Quirk, for I'd crashed a brand new kite.

Gasping for breath, I ripped off my goggles and helmet. And looked up into the muddy face of a soldier who held a rifle with a very long and very sharp bayonet held inches from my throat.

"I said Hands UP!" he growled.

"I'm British, you idiot!" I snapped back.

He frowned, but other men were scuttling across the crater, coming towards me, and one of them was a sergeant.

"That's one of our aeroplanes, Alf," he told the man with the bayonet.

"Not for much longer," I told him. "Can't you smell the petrol? The whole thing could blow up at any moment. We need to get away from here."

The Sergeant looked from me to the plane, sniffed, then nodded.

"Everybody back!" he barked. "Into the next crump hole."

As if with an afterthought, he said to the man he had named Alf, "Give the gentleman a hand."

Alf reluctantly grabbed one of my muddy, sodden arms, hauling me up, then all of us, six men in total, scrambled out of the far side of the hole, staying low to the ground. We crawled and rolled our way into another shell hole some twenty yards from where my Quirk had crashed. That didn't seem far enough, but the soldiers weren't going to go any further.

"Stand to!" shouted the Sergeant. "Get that Lewis gun ready."

I was dazed, confused and felt totally lost. Explosions were still going off nearby, and I looked up to see a burst as high as a house go off some forty yards to our left. Screams sounded in its aftermath.

"Someone's caught a packet," observed one of the soldiers as he flung himself to the eastern rim of the crater and poked his rifle over the edge. Another rifleman copied his example, while a third soldier rammed a Lewis gun into position. The fourth man held spare drums for the Lewis, and all of the men were festooned with spare ammunition pouches, gas masks and several grenades.

The Sergeant was about to say something to me when another man arrived, sliding in from our right. It was an officer, a Second Lieutenant to judge by the single pip on the sleeve of his filthy tunic. He was holding a bulky revolver in his right hand, and he waved it in my direction.

"Is that your plane?" he snapped at me, his grimy young face displaying an angry expression.

"Yes," I confirmed, wondering who else he thought it might belong to.

"You need to move it!" he told me peremptorily. "It's blocking our view of the road. We need a clear line of fire."

I almost laughed at the absurdity of his demand, but I recalled that very few people have any great understanding of how aeroplanes work, so I simply said, "I can't move it. The engine is ruined, and the fuel tank is leaking."

The Sergeant put in, "I can vouch for the petrol leak, Sir. The gentleman said it was likely to blow up at any moment, so I ordered the lads to fall back."

I suspect the officer was about to order the squad forwards again, but fate intervened because the Quirk, as if on cue, suddenly went up in flames with a soft whoomph!

I think we all ducked, even though there was not much of an explosion, simply a ball of fire which consumed the kite and lit up the area around us, issuing a wave of heat which made my face tingle. A cloud of oily smoke drifted upwards as the flames destroyed what was left of my Quirk.

The Lieutenant glared at me.

"How do I know you're not a German spy?" he demanded.

"That's what I said," muttered the man named Alf.

"Because I'm British!" I retorted, growing weary of this ignorant young man. Looking at him more closely, I don't think he was much older than me, possibly no more than nineteen or twenty years old, and I thought I detected a glimmer of fear in his eyes.

I went on, "If you'd checked the roundels painted on the wings, you'd know I'm with the Flying Corps. Besides, if I was a Hun trying to get behind our Lines, don't you think I'd have crashed somewhere a lot safer than this?"

The Lieutenant did not look convinced, so I asked him, "Where is your Commanding Officer?"

"I have no idea," he admitted. "Dead, possibly."

That perhaps explained his fear, for he and his men were out here at the apex of the advance, and shells were still exploding all around us. I could feel the earth trembling beneath me, and the noise was truly terrifying.

"I need to get back to my squadron," I told him.

I could see he was in a dilemma.

"I can't spare anyone to take you back," he said, pursing his lips. "So you'll need to take your chances."

Then one of the soldiers yelled something which sounded to me like, "minnie wafers!"

Everyone dived to the ground. I was already crouching, trying to keep my head below the level of the crater, so a shove from the Sergeant was enough to bowl me over, sending me sprawling into the mud once again.

And all hell broke loose around us.

Wednesday 11th April, 1917 – Evening

A barrage of shells struck the earth, hurling debris high into the air. The noise was almost constant as bomb after bomb exploded, drowning out all other sound. I grovelled on the muddy floor of the crater, my hands over my head, trying to press myself into the earth like a worm.

I have no idea how long this lasted, but I heard a shout from somewhere nearby.

"Here they come!"

"Stand to!" the officer yelled, his voice almost breaking into a falsetto as he scrambled to his feet.

I pushed myself up onto my knees, looking around to see if there was any way of escaping, but shells were still dropping everywhere.

"Trench mortars," the Sergeant told me calmly. "Best stay here, Sir."

Then I ducked as a loud bang sounded just behind us, and a blast of air buffeted me. I was spattered with gobbets of mud, and I flinched in case I had been struck by anything more deadly.

I was lucky, but the soldier manning the Lewis gun was less fortunate. He and his mate who held the spare drums were closer to the edge of the crater, having taken a position from where they could shoot past the still burning wreckage of my B.E.2. I heard the soft, sickening slap of metal striking flesh. The soldier holding the Lewis slumped forwards, then slowly began to slide down the inner edge of the hole. His companion let out a gasp of pain, and I saw him drop his spare drums as he clamped a hand to his left arm.

"Someone grab the Lewis!" the Sergeant yelled as he tugged the body of the machine gunner over, checking to see if the man was still alive. From the sightless way his eyes gazed up, I was sure he was dead.

I was closest, and I knew how to use a Lewis, so I slithered over, grabbing the gun and flinging myself hard against the rim of the crater. My gloved hands, sticky with mud, found the trigger, and I waited.

There! Figures in dark grey uniforms were darting along the road, moving from one piece of cover to another. They held rifles, and one in the rear had a large, bulky container on his back.

"Flame thrower!" the Sergeant hissed when he flung himself down beside me. "Get that one first, lads. But wait until they are closer."

He shot me an enquiring look.

"Do you know how to use that thing, Sir?"

"Yes."

That was true, although I'd never fired one in anger. Now was going to be my first time, but I didn't think it would be sensible to tell him that. I was determined to do something to hit back at the Huns who were trying to kill me. Looking back now, I can see that was quite an irrational thought since the Germans were trying to kill all of us, but being shot down and then having mortar bombs land all around me made it feel rather personal.

"Hold them off!" the officer commanded. "I'm going to check the flank sections."

So saying, he threw himself up, wriggled over the rim of the hole, and crawled away.

"Mister Morris is a fine young officer, Sir," the Sergeant told me. "We're safe enough here, I think. It's the flanks we need to worry about. The Jerries are coming down the road because the buildings give them some cover, but there will be others moving up on either side. Just stay calm until I give the word. That lot will need to step out into the road at some point."

He was correct. The barrage of what I now knew were minenwerfer shells had stopped, and the German troops were rushing towards us, crouching low, rifles and grenades at the ready. It was hard to judge their numbers, but I reckoned there must have been at least fifty of them heading directly for us, and I could hear rifle fire from left and right, confirming that others were pushing forwards on our flanks.

"Now!" the Sergeant barked.

I pulled the trigger, aiming for the man with the flame thrower pack. Two of his mates were in front of him, but one of them spun around and fell to the road, his limbs flailing, and my next burst took my main target in the chest. My old instructors would have been proud of me, for it was the most accurate shooting I'd ever done with a Lewis gun.

Feeling grimly satisfied, I began scything the barrel from left to right, shooting off short, rapid bursts, while the Sergeant and his two remaining Privates fired their rifles. One of them, possibly Alf, tossed a grenade which fell short but which made the Germans dive for cover.

One of them threw a grenade of his own, but it fell into the hole in front of us where my Quirk was still burning, the explosion loud but doing no damage. Under its cover, though, the surviving Germans made a forward rush.

I fired again and again, and I'm pretty sure I hit at least one of them. Two more Huns were downed by the riflemen, and the Sergeant hurled several grenades, one after another, scattering the attackers. I also heard the heavier chatter of a Vickers machine gun from somewhere to our left, and this scything fire was the last straw for the surviving Germans. They turned and scuttled back towards their own trenches.

"They've had enough for now," the Sergeant said.

I watched as the remaining Germans scurried away, dodging behind walls to stay out of sight. I tried to shoot one of them as he ran, but the hammer clicked on an empty chamber. I had shot off an entire drum of bullets.

I felt a tap on my arm, and I turned to see a soldier handing me a spare drum for the Lewis gun. The man had a bloody field dressing wrapped around his arm, but he was grinning at me.

"Good shooting, Sir, but you'll need more ammo before they come back."

I replaced the drum, then settled in, waiting for the next attack. I did see a few grey shapes skulking at the far end of the street around one hundred and fifty yards away, and I sent a couple of short bursts in their direction in order to discourage them, but they came no closer. I could still hear firing from our left and right, but eventually Second Lieutenant Morris came scrambling back into our little den, his face pale but revealing his relief.

"Well done, lads!" he told us. "We've seen them off. And the Second Company is almost here."

Then he looked at me and nodded.

"Thanks for your help," he said.

"It was a pleasure," I assured him. "And an honour to fight beside you."

That pleased them all. They were, I learned, from the Seventh Battalion, the King's Royal Rifle Corps, and they were now leading the attack, but Morris admitted they could probably go no further.

"The Jerries have brought up their reserve troops," he explained. "Our artillery is too far back, so we're in for a pasting. That was just a probing attack to see if we were dug in. The real assault will come soon."

That thought horrified me, and I wondered how they could survive a heavier attack. Surely there was something to be done?

"What about the cavalry?" I asked.

That brought a bout of derisive laughter from the quartet of soldiers, but Morris said, "There's been no sign of them. Too far back to get through the mud, I expect."

The Sergeant added glumly, "And the tanks either broke down or were hit by artillery fire."

It was as Turnbull had told me.

I said, "I really do need to get back to my squadron. They need every pilot just now."

Morris nodded, "Fitchett can take you. He needs to get that arm seen to."

I said farewell to Alf, his pal and the Sergeant. This latter gave me a smart salute and offered his hand which I shook gladly. He also offered me a drink from his water canteen which I accepted gratefully.

"Glad to have met you, Sir," he told me.

And then Fitchett, rifle slung over his back, his left arm dangling uselessly and oozing blood, led me out of the crater and into another hell.

An intermittent bombardment was beginning again, shells falling randomly all along the front as far as I could see to either side. I desperately wanted to hunker down in a shell hole and wait until it was safe to move, but Fitchett pressed on. Weighed down by rifle, gas mask, entrenching tool, water bottle and assorted other equipment, he still seemed able to move more quickly than I could. My fug boots were not ideal for walking at the best of times, and in these horrendous conditions, they felt clumsy and awkward as they quickly became encased in a layer of mud. Not only that, my heavy flying gear, designed to keep me warm in the air, was too bulky for this sort of walking, and I was soon sweating profusely. I unfastened the front of my jacket, but I dared not remove the valuable protective clothing, so I sweated and gasped along in Fitchett's wake. I even put my flying helmet back on because it provided a sense of protection even though I knew the leather would not stop a fragment of shrapnel, but going bare-headed in that maelstrom of explosions felt very unsafe indeed. I suppose I could have taken a steel helmet from one of the dead we passed, but the sight of their twisted, mangled and gory bodies deterred me.

It was an exhausting, nerve-shredding journey. We slid into shell craters, clawed our way up the other side, dodged between holes, ploughed through the remnants of bushes and hedges, and all the while the German artillery were lobbing shells in our direction.

"They're hoping to catch our reserves coming up," Fitchett explained. "But they're firing blind. Anyway, most of our lads will wait until dark before they move forwards."

It was a horrible feeling, stumbling along, half falling all the time, every step a battle against the cloying, sucking mud, and knowing that at any moment a shell could land right next to us, blowing us to Kingdom Come.

One almost did. Without warning, Fitchett, who was walking ahead of me, spun round, waving his good arm and urging me to drop to the ground.

"Whizz Bang!" he shouted.

I dropped, lying prone on the muddy earth, once again putting my hands over my head.

How Fitchett could have heard one shell amidst the barrage, I do not know, but he did, and I was grateful when I heard it too. There was the whistling approach of the Whizz, then the deafening Bang as the shell exploded barely thirty yards from us. The blast rocked us, shaking the ground we lay on, and earth pattered down all around us. I was sure some fragment of shrapnel would kill me there and then, but Fitchett was already urging me to my feet.

"Missed us by a mile!" he declared cheerfully.

A few minutes later, after crawling up a steep rise, we encountered more British troops. They were digging trenches on the crest of the rise, picks and shovels being shared between three-man teams. At any one time, one of each section was hacking at the earth with all his might. After a couple of minutes, he would pass his implement to another man who would take up the routine in turn. This system allowed the work to take place at astonishing speed, and I could see that defensive positions would be ready very soon despite the German bombardment.

We slid down into a sap the soldiers had dug towards the German trenches, following the narrow trench back until I discovered we were in what had formerly been the German third line of defences. I had photographed these trenches several times, but I had never fully realised just how strong they were. Our own artillery had pounded them, and many sections had caved in, but those were only surface damages. I saw concrete strongpoints where machine guns had been sited, and other holes protected by wicker baskets full of earth. Steps led beneath the earth to concrete-lined bunkers where, according to Fitchett, the Germans had lived in safety and luxury.

"Some of the lads even found a four-poster bed in one of them," he assured me.

I could not begin to imagine how difficult it must have been for our troops to break through these defences. It must have been a nightmare, yet it seemed our artillery had done its job, for Fitchett told me that many of the Germans had surrendered without a fight.

"They had two weeks of hell being bombarded," he informed me. "Some of them hadn't eaten anything but rats for days because they couldn't bring up food supplies."

Not all the Germans had surrendered, though. Even as we made our slow way back through the crowded trench, work parties were flinging dead bodies over the parapet, or shoving them into freshly dug holes in the side of the trench. It was grisly work, and I averted my eyes whenever I could.

After another ten minutes of hard slog, we reached a main trench where a group of officers was gathered. One was a Colonel, a small, thin fellow with a dark moustache. His steel helmet was covered by a piece of khaki cloth to prevent the metal reflecting sunlight and so giving away his position. He wore what must once have been a well-tailored uniform, but he had obviously endured similar hardships to his men, for he was streaked with mud all over. Despite this, and even with the bombardment continuing, he was issuing orders in short, crisp sentences, pointing and often referring to a folded map he held in his left hand. He glanced up at our approach, then stared at me, signalling me over. Not that I could have done anything else, for the only way back was to pass him.

I threw a salute.

"Second Lieutenant Arthur Kerr, Sir. Royal Flying Corps. My plane came down a little way ahead. I met some of your men who were holding off a German attack."

The Colonel glanced at my guide.

"Fitchett, isn't it?" he asked.

"Yes, Sir. Got wounded, Sir. Mister Morris sent me back with this officer."

"Mister Morris is still up ahead?" the Colonel demanded.

"Yes, Sir. We couldn't get into the village, Sir. The Jerries are at the other end and sent in a small attack. Mister Morris reckons more will come."

"Mister Morris is probably right," the Colonel growled darkly.

He turned, fixing his eagle gaze on a Captain.

"Send a runner forwards. Tell Morris to bring his men back. They are to wait until nightfall if possible, but they can't stay out there."

The Colonel then told Fitchett, "There's a C.C.S. a mile or so back, set up in the German second lines. Get yourself there as soon as you can."

"Yes, Sir."

"And you," the Colonel said to me, "had better get out of here. You have no gas mask, do you?"

"No, Sir. We don't carry them in our aeroplanes."

"Then you'd best get away as quickly as you can. We've pushed forward this far, but the Division to the south of us has got bogged down, and we've got the Boche threatening our flanks. Once they bring up all their reserves, we're going to have a fight on our hands, and no doubt they'll drop gas shells as a little warm up."

That was more than enough encouragement for me to say farewell. I saluted again, then eased past the officers and followed Fitchett along a maze of winding communication trenches. Many had partly collapsed, others were ankle deep in muddy water, and all were crowded with British troops who were moving forwards. There were men carrying rifles, men carrying machine guns, men with mortars, and men with digging tools. There were engineers laying telephone cables, and pioneers digging new trenches and laying duckboards. It was frantic, chaotic, yet at the same time very efficient.

It was dark by the time we reached the Casualty Clearing Station. Here I said farewell to Fitchett, wishing him all the best from his Blighty wound which, if he was lucky, would see him sent home without being disfigured. For myself, I had to find somewhere to rest. I was absolutely exhausted, as well as hungry and thirsty. The constant flow of men did not cease with nightfall. If anything, it became busier, but I could not find my way in the dark, so I found a small recess where I settled on a low step. The place stank of faeces and rotting meat, and more than one rat scurried across my legs during the night. I'm not sure how much sleep I got. Probably very little, for shells continued to explode at intermittent intervals, and star shells would burst high above us, illuminating the earth with bright, deathly pale light. After an eternity of discomfort and noise, though, the dawn arrived, and it was time to continue my trek.

Thursday 12th April, 1917

In the morning, I resumed my journey, grateful that there had been no gas attack during the night. This time, I tagged onto the end of a column of wounded who were heading back. There were several stretcher cases among the walking wounded, and they were a pitiable sight to see, but following them made my way easier, for other soldiers stepped aside for them.

The journey was still dreadful. We waded through waterlogged trenches, scrambled around collapsed earth walls, and negotiated the hundreds of corpses, both human and animal. Horses and mules lay among the dead of both sides, with enormous rats feasting on them. The soldiers, I quickly discovered, detested the rats even more than they hated the Germans, and I can't say I blame them. At one point, a rat leaped from the top of the trench I was walking along, landed on my head, then sprang off, reaching the opposite side. It gave me such a fright, I yelped, causing some amusement among the men around me.

I still wondered at the strength of the German defences, and at the bravery of our lads who had stormed through them. As I kept moving, I caught sight of great fields of barbed wire which stood several feet high and was massed as much as two or three hundred feet in width. Channels had been blown in this seemingly impassable barrier by our artillery, but there were still several bodies tangled and trapped on the dreadful spikes, dangling obscenely like ragged scarecrows.

I saw a couple of wrecked tanks as well. These land leviathans looked rather pathetic stuck in the mud at odd angles, some with great holes blown in them where the German artillery had caught them exposed. Most, I was told by some disgusted soldiers, broke down long before they ever reached the German trenches.

I managed to scrounge some water from an officer of a Highland battalion, but I missed out on the morning rations. How I longed for even a hard boiled egg in the Mess!

I ploughed on, asking directions when I could. Some of the trenches now had wooden walkways stretched across them so men could walk more easily along these makeshift routes, but walking in the open in daylight was still dangerous. Shells continued to fall, so most men remained in the trenches where, despite the filth, it was safer.

Eventually, I reached what had formerly been No Man's Land. A new stretch of ground was already taking that name a few miles to the east, but this patch of desolation was now being reclaimed by British troops. The engineers and pioneers were creating pathways, and some field artillery guns were being hauled towards the new battle lines. The big guns, though, would be a long time in coming forward. Those huge howitzers took hours to dismantle, and were so large and heavy that moving them through this muddy hell would be a nightmare.

Horses and mules were much in evidence now, pulling guns or laden with supplies. Like the men, they floundered everywhere, and I knew they would suffer as many casualties as the soldiers.

The worst torment of all, though, was that I could hear, and sometimes see, aeroplanes flying above me. That was where I wanted to be. Red Baron or no, flying was infinitely more preferable to living down here in the mud. But some of those aeroplanes presented another sort of danger. We were some way back from the new battle zone, but the Huns had plenty of two-seater reconnaissance machines who could spot what was happening here. This could easily result in the Germans concentrating more artillery fire here rather than on our new fortifications. To counter this, the pioneers were erecting canvas screens painted green, black and cream to conceal our movements, or draping netting across the top of the communication trenches to mask them from view. As far as I was concerned, I wished they could mask the entire scene from my view, for I have never experienced such muck, filth and grisly sights in my life. Bodies with limbs blown away or with their inner organs on view as a result of being ripped apart by shell fire were all over the place. Most were Germans, victims of the horrendous artillery bombardment I and my fellow pilots had guided, yet the sight of them appalled me, enemies or not.

At last, some time after mid-day, I found a Divisional H.Q. established in a crude dug out. Here, they had telephones. The Royal Engineers were laying new cables to forward areas, but I'd not come across a working telephone during my long walk. The tiny bunker was full of officers, all of them talking, some shouting down telephones, but I managed to attract the attention of a weary-looking Captain who arranged a cup of hot, sweet tea and some hard tack biscuits while he had someone try to reach my squadron.

"We're rather busy," he told me, "but we'll do our best to get through when we get a moment."

It took over an hour, but eventually I was talking to Potter. He said he would have a tender sent out to Arras if I could get there. According to the Captain I'd spoken to, Arras was about four miles from this bunker.

Four miles! In my condition, that sounded as difficult as a marathon, but there was nothing else for it but to make the long walk.

Once again I waited until I could join a column of wounded men being taken back to safety. Men from the Medical Corps were straining and struggling to carry several stretchers, but at least they were heading in the direction of Arras, so I ploughed my way behind them. The men lying on the stretchers looked in terrible shape, but I must confess that the exhausted faces of the bearers meant that they looked little better. Still, following close behind them did make my travel easier, for, as I'd discovered yesterday, everyone made way for the wounded men.

It still took me all afternoon, sloshing through muddy, water-filled trenches, sometimes with the freezing water reaching my thighs. Then, when I thought I would need to give up, we arrived at the entrance to a tunnel which led us deep underground. This had been one of the jumping off points for the initial assault. Thousands of our troops had sheltered beneath the ground in these tunnels, emerging to launch the first wave of attacks on the German trenches. There was electric light and, best of all, an internal pulley-operated railway on a narrow gauge track. Flat wagons were still being used to ferry supplies forward and take wounded men back. I climbed aboard, staying close to the wounded men, and although I received a few strange looks, nobody challenged my right to be there.

The train moved off, taking us more than a mile through a warren of tunnels, and then I was nearly home. I plodded up out of the tunnels, coming out into the old town square of Arras. It took half an hour to locate the tender, but I was never so glad to see anyone as I was to recognise the driver as belonging to our squadron.

"Hello, Sir," he beamed. "Glad you made it."

I was too tired to do much more than grunt a response. Filthy, exhausted and hungry, I climbed into the front seat beside him, leaned back and fell asleep.

Friday 13th April, 1917

I was welcomed back with some hearty cheers and a few slaps on the back which served to reawaken the pain from my earlier wounds, but I did little more than speak briefly to the Major, fill out a written report, then stagger off to Hut Three for some sleep.

This morning, I learned the bad news about what had happened in my absence. Dish Tattersall is dead, he and his observer, Downey, having been shot down by the Red Baron's Albatroses.

Vaughn told me, "They are diving down from a great height, outrunning our own scout patrols, and hitting us as hard as they can. C Flight lost Edwards and Barnes, but we think they managed to get down safely on the other side of the Lines. I expect they are prisoners by now."

"It's been a rough couple of days," I observed.

Vaughn shot me a mocking look.

"But you survived. Two days in a row you get shot down, and you walked away from both without a scratch. That's not normal, my lad."

He reached out a hand and rubbed his palm over my hair.

"What are you doing?" I protested as I tried to duck away.

"Whatever it is you've got, I want some of it to rub off on me," he declared, his mood apparently jovial, although I could tell he was doing his best to conceal his grief at Dish's death.

Vaughn became sombre again as he said, "This means I'm now the Deputy Flight Leader of B Flight. Can you believe that?"

"Will you get a promotion?" I asked.

He shook his head.

"I doubt it. There are people like Beano who are senior to me. More likely he'll get put up to full Lieutenant and switch places with me."

For the moment, though, Vaughn is acting as Deputy Flight Commander, a position he has attained thanks to the death of his good friend, Dish. I'm a bit worried about how he is taking it, for he seems very morose, and I found him sitting alone in the hut, just staring into space.

"I'll miss him," he admitted softly.

Of course, life goes on. Our new hut mate is an observer from C Flight named Armstrong. He's a quiet fellow, but obviously very clever, and rather bookish. He brought several books with him, and he's lined them up on a shelf in his cubicle. I must admit I'd never heard of most of them, and I noticed one or two were written in French. It turns out Armstrong's mother is French, and he's fluent in the language.

Sibbald let me rest and recover during the morning, but I told him I was available to fly in the afternoon.

"Good," he nodded, his face grave. "It's mostly close contact work or photo shoots just now until our artillery takes up new positions."

"Fine," I said.

He gave me a serious look as he asked, "I assume it was a bit rough out there?"

"Yes," I agreed.

His mouth twitched in a faint smile as he told me, "I must admit I'm glad I got out of the trenches and took up flying."

"You started in the infantry?" I asked, hoping to learn a bit more about my enigmatic Flight Leader.

"Back in '14," he confirmed. "I was one of the Old Contemptibles. Saw my first action at Mons and Le Cateau, then spent several months in the trenches. It's not something I'd care to do again."

"Even with the Red Baron hunting us?" I asked.

"Even then," he said. "Not that he's the only Hun we need to worry about. That fellow in the Halberstadt who shot you down is very dangerous."

"Do you know who he is?"

"I have no idea. I've seen him before, of course. That green and purple colour scheme is quite distinctive. He's a wonderful pilot, whoever he is."

"And a damned good shot, too," I said. "He only had a few seconds to fire at me, but he knocked out my engine with one burst."

"You were lucky," Sibbald remarked drily. "He was probably aiming for you."

And that was all the conversation we had, for it was quickly back to duty.

Sergeant Turnbull was a little more effusive, telling me how pleased he was that I had got back safely.

"Everyone thinks you have a guardian angel looking after you, Sir," he told me.

Dunlop and Green agreed, telling me how proud they were to be servicing my kite.

"We've got another brand new one, Sir," Dunlop informed me.

"I'll try not to crash this one," I smiled. "But these things do come in threes, don't they? So far, I've only wrecked two machines."

After a quick test flight to put the new Quirk through its paces, Turnbull and I set off on another photographic mission, this time heading out over the new Lines where the Third Army's advance had stalled. VII Corps had done well, forcing a way through three sets of German trenches, but now the Huns are fighting back, and, as I'd witnessed at first hand, our troops were becoming bogged down again. Even where units like those of young Morris had managed to advance, they were being forced to withdraw because the units beside them had become stuck, leaving them exposed to flanking attacks.

It was yet another dull, blustery day. We went out as quickly as we could, heading directly for our target area which was, I realised, more or less where I'd crashed on Wednesday. I tried to find my burned out Quirk, but although I located the village, there was no obvious sign of my crash. I wondered how Morris and his men were getting on, then tried not to think about what they were going through.

Archie was back with a vengeance, the Germans having stabilised their new positions, so we were bracketed by his filthy explosions, some of which were close enough to rock our wings. I took the photographs as quickly as I could, then turned and hurried back to our airfield. Turnbull said he'd seen some Albatroses up high, but they had been further north, and had dived down on a flight of F.E.2's."

"I think they shot down a couple," he said grimly.

As far as our squadron is concerned, Friday the Thirteenth was actually one of our better days despite its ill omened reputation. Fitzgerald, an observer in C Flight, received a slight wound in his arm when a bullet grazed him during a close contact patrol, but the medics bandaged him up, and he insists he is able to continue flying.

MacCallum, our Canadian pilot, suffered engine failure during another close contact patrol, but he was already on his way back, and he managed to land safely enough. The salvage team went out with a recovery lorry and brought him back.

"It's a pity the plane is all right," he grumbled. "That engine is a real dud."

Looking at me, he added, "I should have done what you did and come down nearer the Front. Then I could have burned the ruddy thing."

"I wouldn't recommend it," I told him, although I couldn't help feeling pleased that tales of my exploits were being spoken of.

The only other news of note is that the French have, at last, begun their own offensive. Whether our attack succeeded in drawing any Germans away from the French sector seems doubtful. Sibbald is adamant that it didn't.

"The Huns are stretched enough on the Western Front," he said. "They knew a French attack was coming, and they aren't stupid enough to weaken their Lines in a sector where an attack is brewing."

I was prepared to accept Sibbald's argument because of his experience, but Sullivan was not convinced.

He said, "Still, the French might break through. Our boys have had some success."

"We've taken Vimy Ridge, and we've advanced a few miles," Sibbald pointed out, sounding like a schoolteacher showing a class where they had gone wrong. "We've moved the Lines a bit, but we haven't made the breakthrough. As usual, the cavalry were too slow to get forward, and the artillery is floundering in the mud as they try to get the guns closer to the new Lines."

The way he spoke sounded almost defeatist, and Bernard, who is as gung ho as anyone in the squadron, told him not to be so negative.

"The French will break through this time," Bernard declared.

Sibbald was not at all put out by Bernard's challenge. He merely smiled, nodded, and said, "We'll see soon enough, I expect."

Later, when we left the Mess to head back to our huts, we discovered that it had begun to snow.

Saturday 14th April, 1917

This morning, A Flight carried out another bombing raid. We had been ordered to destroy a narrow bridge across one of the tributaries to the Scarpe, and each of us had two of the large, 112lbs bombs slung beside our undercarts.

Six of us went out, our latest recruit being a chap named Ford. He and MacCallum followed Sibbald, while Beano and I formed the second section behind Sullivan.

Our escort this time was a Flight of Nieuports, and I wondered whether Vanders was among them. I reminded myself I should have written to him, but I never seemed to find the time. I shall rectify that as soon as I can.

We crossed the new Lines at around eight thousand feet, skirting our way through a maze of clouds, but we never reached the target. Half a dozen Albatroses dived down on us when we were three or four miles over. Four of them tackled the Nieuports, while two came after us. Even as they did so, five more appeared ahead of us, and they immediately dived to block our way ahead.

Sibbald did not hesitate. He fired a Very signal as soon as he saw the Huns coming for us, and he dumped his bombs with no regard for what lay beneath us. We all followed his example, then we turned as sharply as we dared, putting our noses down and heading for home.

There was no way of maintaining our formation. It was a case of every man for himself. If we had been carrying observers with machine guns, sticking together would have been the best option, but we were defenceless, so we scattered. Sibbald had drummed into us that the best way to escape the Huns was to get close to the ground and keep dodging, so we all ran for it. I heard the clatter of machine guns, and I saw tracers zipping past me, but this time no bullets struck my plane. I got to ground level and kept skidding the Quirk from side to side as I raced for home with the engine roaring. At low level, you really appreciate how fast you are travelling, for everything whizzes past you, just beneath your wings. I was doing nearly seventy miles per hour as I zipped over mud, shattered trees and ruined buildings. It was actually quite exciting, for you never have that impression of speed when you are higher up.

After a while, I realised nobody was shooting at me, so I relaxed a little. Once across the Lines, I headed straight for home.

We drifted back in ones and twos, but Ford was missing.

"One of the Huns got him," Sullivan reported grimly. "I think he must have been hit in the back, because his kite jerked, then flopped and went down in a spin."

MacCallum had limped in with a coughing engine and wings peppered with bullet holes, but he was unhurt.

"That Hun must have been a rotten shot," he declared. "I can't believe he missed me."

Sibbald made out his report, then warned us there would be another job that afternoon. In the Mess, though, Sullivan was not happy.

"We should have pressed on," he complained. "The Huns couldn't have shot us all down. Instead, we turned and ran like cowards."

I must admit that I hadn't felt particularly brave during our flight, but at the time, all I had felt was a desperate desire to get away from the deadly Albatroses.

Beano, loyally supporting Sibbald, said, "But most of us got back in one piece, and now we can go back and try again. If we'd pressed on, there was no guarantee we would have hit the bridge, and we could have lost a lot more than one pilot. I mean, it's hard enough to manoeuvre a Quirk, but when it's loaded with bombs, dodging Hun bullets is almost impossible. We'd have been sitting ducks."

Sullivan remained unconvinced, but he ceased his grumbling when Sibbald came into the Mess. I think our Flight Leader knew what we'd been discussing, for he gave us all an appraising look, but he did not say anything.

Later, we were visited by a Liaison Officer from the Field Artillery. He met us in the office, spreading out a map on Potter's desk as he pointed out our new targets.

"We've pushed a few batteries of eighteen-pounders forward, but we need to find the Hun batteries so we can try to knock them out. Our F.O.O.'s are doing their best, but we haven't had much luck so far."

I tried to think of those Forward Observation Officers who would be on the ground, inching as far towards the Huns as they could, armed with binoculars, maps and a wireless or telephone. I did not envy them their job, but I suppose they would not envy us either, for we would need to fly up and down behind the German Lines searching for the enemy guns, with every Hun in the air and on the ground shooting at us.

We agreed call signs with the Liaison Officer, then Sibbald divided the various sectors up, allocating each crew to a specific part of the front.

"The Huns are getting their act together now," he told us. "Our boys in the trenches will be taking a pasting, so let's see if we can help them."

It was another unpleasant flight, with low clouds, lots of rain showers and plenty of Archie to make life difficult. We made contact with the batteries, then went in hunt of targets.

They were not hard to find, for the flashes from their muzzles gave them away, but directing our own guns onto them was horribly difficult thanks to the Archie fire and the presence of Hun scouts. Turnbull and I witnessed a scrap between some Pups and Albatroses which resulted in one Pup going down in a vertical dive, and we saw a Big Ack being shot down by another group of the deadly hunters. We managed to call down some artillery fire on one German battery, but we could not hang around the target area because more Albatroses were nosing around in the clouds above us. Once again, I felt that chill of fear, combined with not a little shame in running away, but when we returned home, we discovered that Sullivan had been shot down. He'd lingered over a target and been caught by a group of Huns who had sent him down in flames. He and his observer, Howden, were definitely dead.

This meant that Beano was now Deputy Flight Leader. Vaughn's prediction that he would be transferred to B Flight would not now happen, for the next most senior pilot in A Flight is me, and C Flight are not much better. Appleby is still there, but the rest of them, apart from Bernard, are all relative newcomers to the squadron.

"You and I are veterans now," Vaughn told me wryly.

That is a sobering thought. I've been out since the start of the month, only two weeks ago, and I am already one of the most experienced pilots in the squadron.

Beano, naturally, had a solution for us.

"Eat, drink and be merry," he told us in the Mess. "For tomorrow we fly!"

He did his best to start a binge, and a few of the chaps soon became more blotto than was good for them. I did join in at the start, but every time I took a drink, I seemed to see Sibbald's disapproving face in my mind's eye, so I went to bed early.

Bates had also decided to give the binge a miss. He was sitting on his cot, writing a letter home, and that reminded me I should pen a note to Vanders. I did that before settling down to write this, telling him about my recent adventure in the trenches.

"It was dreadful," I told him, "but I'm honestly no longer sure it's any worse than what we are going through."

I almost tore the letter up, for I worried it might give him the impression I had the wind up about flying. Things are very tough, but I will not shirk my duty. If I must die for King and Country, then so be it. I added a bit to my letter to Vanders to explain that, then urged him to write back and let me know he is all right.

And now I must get some sleep, for Sibbald has informed us that we are going back to bomb that bridge again tomorrow.

Sunday 15th April, 1917

There was no flying today. The clouds were so low, nobody dared take off. The Major spoke to Brigade H.Q. and they agreed that the forecast suggested the entire day would be a washout.

"A day off!" beamed Vaughn. "I shall spend it sleeping the sleep of the redeemed."

I think he was serious, for he went back to bed after eating a late and leisurely breakfast with the rest of us.

We had two new pilots arrive today. They are called Maycroft and Falconer. Sibbald was his usual gruff self with them, bemoaning the fact that the weather was too bad for them to earn some extra flying time.

Our new observer is another Sergeant, so I haven't met him yet, for he obviously cannot come into the Officers' Mess. Nominally, his arrival brings A Flight up to full strength, but Sibbald told Beano, MacCallum and me that we would need to bear the brunt of the flying for a day or two until the new lads gained some more air time.

"Right you are, Old Bean," said Normansby.

He's been told that he has been promoted to full Lieutenant, albeit on an Acting Temporary basis, so he's well pleased with himself, and we all know he deserves it.

Beano then suggested that we take a tender into Barly.

"What on earth for?" I asked.

He grinned salaciously as he lowered his voice to whisper, "Why, to visit a house of ill repute, of course."

I blinked at him.

"A brothel?"

"Absolutely, Old Bean. There's one just for officers, you know. The Other Ranks have their own establishment."

I gaped at him.

"You mean the Army runs them?"

"It's better than allowing free rein," he nodded. "The girls are examined by the Medical Corps on a regular basis."

Sibbald, who had overheard our conversation, put in, "That doesn't stop V.D. spreading, you know."

"It's a risk I'm willing to take," Beano grinned. "What about it, Kerr? Are you game? Appleby and Marston are going."

I shook my head.

"Some other time," I mumbled, feeling my face redden.

Lowering his voice again, and sounding serious, Normansby said, "There might not be another time, Old Bean."

I know he was right, but I held to my decision.

"It's your loss," Beano shrugged.

I watched the three of them pile into a tender, then I went back to the hut and pulled on my greatcoat.

"Going somewhere?" Bates asked.

"Just for a walk."

"Fancy some company?" he enquired. "I could do with getting out of here."

"If you like. What about you, Vaughn?"

Vaughn mumbled a reply from beneath his blankets, waving a weary hand to shoo us out.

So the two of us set off at a slow stroll, heading into Fosseux. It was not a pleasant walk, for not only was the weather miserable, with rain and sleet spattering down from the low ceiling of clouds, the road was busy with traffic. Flying may have stopped for the day, but the war continued. Lorries and tenders rumbled past us, as did the occasional staff car with its red-tabbed occupants looking very superior when everyone else moved out of their way.

"Smug bastards," muttered Bates. "Is it true you attacked some of them in your Quirk?"

"Hardly," I replied. "I flew low over their chateau grounds because of engine trouble, and some of them were out exercising their horses. I think one or two got a fright, that's all."

"That's not the story doing the rounds," Bates informed me. "I heard you'd chased some of them across the field with your kite just off the ground."

"That's nonsense!" I assured him, although it was nice to learn that I seemed to be gaining a little notoriety within the squadron.

We had reached the village by this time. I was debating which way to go when a figure in a long trench coat, and with a trilby hat pulled down low, dodged between a couple of lorries and crossed the road ahead of us.

"Mister Kerr, isn't it?" he called in greeting.

It was Richardson, the journalist.

"Hello," I said guardedly.

I introduced Bates to him, then told him we were just out for a walk.

"Do you mind if I join you?" he asked.

"Actually, we were just going to head back to the airfield," I told him, wary of being lured into a position where I might say something I should not.

Richardson's smile was as smooth as ever.

"Let me treat you to a beer in the *estaminet*," he said. "Or a cup of coffee, although I doubt it would be the real stuff."

I would have preferred to decline, but Bates was not eager to go back to the airfield, so he accepted on our behalf before I could object.

The *estaminet* was busy, but one of the tables was free. Richardson ordered three bottles of beer and a plate of sandwiches.

"My treat," he assured us.

"Thank you," I said.

He grinned, "I can claim it on expenses."

"You can?"

"Of course. As long as you give me some gossip I can use in an article."

"We don't gossip," I told him.

"Then talk shop," he invited. "I like to hear genuine opinions about aeroplanes. Just how good are the German Albatroses, for example?"

"Why do you want to know?" I asked him. "I read some of your stuff after you spent that time with us. You must have been writing about a different squadron."

I knew that was unfair. We had all been at pains to present a positive picture when Richardson had been in the Mess, and what he had written had more or less reflected that, even if some of the glowing descriptions of our squadron members had been barely recognisable. In any event, my criticism made no impact on him.

"I can't write the whole truth," he confided. "You should know that. The public at home needs to hear stories of gallantry and plucky success. They want to know we are winning. If I wrote anything that contradicted the official line, it simply wouldn't be published."

"So you do write propaganda?" I challenged.

"That's a difficult word to define," he shrugged. "If you want real propaganda, read the stuff being churned out by the likes of Rudyard Kipling and John Buchan. Buchan is part of the official propaganda unit, you know."

I nodded. I'd read some of Buchan's fiction, and his short stories were always full of heroic British agents overcoming the dastardly Huns. They were exciting tales, but I could not equate them with the reality of our daily lives.

"So why do you want to know the dark side of the truth?" I asked Richardson.

"Because I'd like it to come out once the war is over. To do that, I want some genuine voices to tell me what they are experiencing."

Then, his face growing serious, he added softly, "And, if you don't mind me saying so, the chances are that most of you won't be around to tell me."

Bates laughed, "Thanks for your vote of confidence."

Richardson smiled back, but there was no humour in the expression.

He said, "I don't mean anything against you personally, but I know things are bad. I hear things at Corps H.Q., you know."

"What sort of things?" Bates asked.

Richardson told us, "Things about the losses the Flying Corps is suffering. Did you know that they always plan to lose about a third of their planes, and crews, of course, every month? And this month, they've reached that already. Things are very bad. What I haven't been able to find out is why."

"That's easy," said Bates. "Our planes are outclassed. The B.E.2 was designed before the war, and it's no match for the Hun machines."

I put in, "It's just a temporary thing, though. It happens. Sometimes we have the advantage, other times the Huns do. They took control last year with their Fokker monoplanes because they had an interrupter gear which let them shoot through their propeller. Then we gained the upper hand when the D.H.2 and F.E.2b came along. Now the Huns have brought out the Albatros, the pendulum has swung back again, but it will be our turn soon enough."

"I bloody hope so," muttered Bates.

"As I see it," Richardson prompted, "the tactics have a bearing on it too. If your machines are outclassed, why stay on the offensive. General Trenchard insists you always attack, and that you keep going over the Lines no matter the cost."

I recalled that I'd had a similar discussion with Vaughn a few days ago, but I decided I wasn't going to say too much to Richardson. I didn't really trust him even though he was obviously trying to appear friendly.

All I said was, "We are at war, and there's a ground offensive going on. Sacrifices must be made if we are to help our ground troops make a breakthrough."

"That's a quote I shall use," the journalist told me.

"As long as you don't mention my name," I told him. "I don't want to be in your newspaper."

He smiled again.

"It strikes me," he reflected, "that the war in the air is being fought much like the war on the ground. It's simply attrition. The Generals throw men at the enemy in the hope that the slight changes in tactics they have come up with will break the deadlock. Up in the air, we're just flinging you boys at the Hun in the hope of overwhelming him with numbers."

"Like I said," I told him, "we are at war. What sort of soldiers would we be if we sat at home and didn't dare go out?"

"A fair point," he conceded. "But I rather fear your bravery is taken for granted by some of those in command. Do you know I heard the G.O.C. complained that one of his Generals couldn't have been trying hard enough because his Division only suffered ten thousand casualties?"

He spread his hands in a gesture of dismay as he added, "I mean, that's ten thousand lives ruined, but it's still not enough to satisfy the men who are supposed to be trying to win this war. Some of them have no empathy with ordinary soldiers at all, you know."

"And what do you expect us to do about it?" I challenged.

"Ah, that's a good question," he admitted. "Quite frankly, I expect you will just carry on. Unlike our French allies, the British troops tend not to let conditions get them down too much."

Bates frowned, "What do you mean?"

Richardson's voice was barely more than a whisper as he told us, "I've heard some other reports too. Not that I can publish them, for it's being kept very quiet. But word has it that morale among the French troops is at rock bottom. There are concerns in our own High Command that, if General Nivelle's offensive does not succeed, there could be trouble brewing."

"What sort of trouble?" Bates frowned.

Richardson gave another shrug.

"Who knows? But the French have suffered horribly in the past two and a half years. As I said, morale is low, and it seems this offensive is not helping matters. General Nivelle promised the French Government and our own Prime Minister that he could win the war, but he's just throwing men into the mincing machine like every other commander. After the losses they suffered at Verdun last year, some of the French troops have almost had enough."

"You mean they've actually mutinied?" Bates hissed in astonishment.

"No," Richardson said quickly. "It hasn't gone that far yet. But it may do if things do not improve."

"Surely they won't do that!" Bates exclaimed. "The penalty for mutiny is death."

"I know," Richardson nodded. "And so do the French *poilus*. But consider what would happen if the French Generals did have to deal with a mutiny. They'd shoot the ringleaders, and the rest of the troops would go back into the Lines. But could the Generals ever trust them again?"

Bates and I exchanged horrified glances, then I said to Richardson, "This is all hypothetical. You are talking as if the offensive has already failed. That's defeatist talk."

"Perhaps it is," Richardson sighed. "Or it might be realistic to consider the possibility."

He took a gulp of beer before adding, "But even if my worst fears come true, I still won't be able to write about it. The whole thing would be hushed up, that's for certain."

I could not tell whether his apparent depression was genuine or a ruse to get us to open up our own concerns, so I decided to err on the side of caution.

I asked him, "So why are you telling us?"

He sat back in his chair, his expression that of a tired, defeated man.

"I honestly don't know," he confessed. "But the more I see of this conflict, the less confident I am that the stalemate can ever be broken. And I feel that I need to tell someone, I suppose. You chaps are educated, and you also know the score about what is happening in the air just now."

I took a deep breath, then said softly, "It doesn't matter. There's nothing we can do except our duty."

Richardson gave a sad nod.

"I know," he said. "And that's the worst thing of all. It's an epitaph for a whole generation."

I had had enough. I quickly finished my beer, then told him, "It's time we were getting back. Thank you for the beer."

"Any time," he said. "And get in touch if you ever feel like talking. You'll find me at Corps H.Q., or in here."

On the way back to the airfield, Bates said, "He's an odd sort of fellow."

I shrugged, "I expect he came out here with some idea of what the war would be like, and he's found out it's a much dirtier business. If he is forced to write propaganda instead of genuine news, it's probably getting him down."

Bates gave a soft, mocking laugh.

"We all came out with ideas of what it would be like, didn't we?"

I could not disagree. What shocked me was that it had been only a little over two weeks since Greening, Vanders and I had arrived at Candas with dreams of winning the war. It had not taken long for those dreams to be shattered.

We returned in a sombre mood, having agreed to keep Richardson's fears over the morale of the French troops to ourselves.

"He was just speculating," I asserted. The French are fighting for their homeland. They won't rest until the Huns have been driven off their land."

Bates nodded thoughtfully.

"It won't alter our job whatever happens," he said stoically. "We'll still need to keep flying."

Back in the Mess, Sibbald pulled me aside.

"We've to go back and bomb that bridge as soon as the weather clears up," he informed me.

"I thought so," I replied.

Looking grim, he said, "And I've been told in no uncertain terms that we are not to turn back no matter the odds. The G.O.C. himself has given the order."

I looked into Sibbald's eyes, but I could not read anything except determination. I knew, though, that he must have been reprimanded for turning back yesterday. He must have been hurting, but he did not let it show.

Personally, I remain in two minds about the situation. The R.F.C. has a policy of always being on the offensive no matter what. I agree with this, and I know chaps like Bernard are in wholehearted agreement, yet I also know from experience that Sibbald's more cautious approach keeps us alive in the face of challenging odds.

The fact was, though, that we had turned tail and fled, and that did not sit well with me even though, at the time, all I had wanted was to get away in one piece. That, I now tell myself, was a result of being shot down twice in the previous couple of days. This time, I will not turn back.

Monday 16th April, 1917

Well, we went back to bomb the bridge. Sibbald led the two new pilots, Maycroft and Falconer, while MacCallum and I were with Beano. Our escort were, thankfully, a Flight of Triplanes, the only kites the Huns are afraid of, so we were in good spirits as we crossed the Lines.

Sibbald kept us up in the clouds, leading us on a twisting route rather than taking a more direct flight lower down where Archie could see us clearly. For a long time, I feared he would not find a suitable gap in the cloud cover, for they formed an almost unbroken patch over the target, but fortunately he located a narrow break, saving us the danger of flying down through the clouds themselves. That was quite a relief, I can tell you.

We dropped into clear air only a mile or two from our target, and I instantly saw why Corps H.Q. wanted this bridge destroyed. There were Huns on the road, some of them on the bridge itself, a long column of grey-uniformed men with rifles on their shoulders and packs on their backs. They also had machine guns being wheeled along on little trolleys, and mules laden with baggage.

They saw us coming, and they instantly scattered into the fields, some of them turning to shoot at us.

We were now very low down because the clouds were, in all honesty, not a great deal higher than they had been the day before, most of them barely a thousand feet up. In normal circumstances, the Major would probably have washed out all flying today, but we had been given no choice in the matter.

I'd heard a few whispers in the Mess, notably from C Flight, that some people thought Sibbald's nerve had gone.

"It happens," I heard Bernard saying. "A chap can only take so much, then he can't hack it any longer."

I'd pretended I hadn't heard this, but I must admit I had wondered whether it was a correct assessment. Sibbald had been out since 1914, and he'd been flying over the Somme last year. He'd seen a lot of action, and maybe it had taken its toll.

But he'd won the M.C., a medal most soldiers can only dream of, and if Bernard had seen him this morning, he'd have changed his tune.

As I said, we were down low, below one thousand feet, but Sibbald went even lower, approaching the bridge at an angle, adopting the same strategy as we'd used against the railway track. Maycroft and Falconer stuck with him, running the gauntlet of the rifle fire, and Beano led me and MacCallum after them.

The bridge was a small thing, barely fifty feet from one end to the other, a stone-built hump crossing a narrow stream. Hitting such a small target was not going to be easy, and perhaps that is partly why Sibbald took his section so low. He knew how difficult it is to hit such a small target, and he wanted to be sure.

The only good thing about flying low over a regiment of enemy soldiers is that most of them aim directly at our aeroplanes, forgetting that we are moving. Most bullets miss, or sometimes catch the rear part of our fuselages, because the shooters take no account of our speed. Even so, some were better shots than others, and I gathered a collection of holes in my wings. I also heard one bullet whine off the cowling of my engine.

Of course, dropping bombs is just as tricky as hitting a moving target. There is no point in releasing your eggs when you are directly above the thing you are aiming for, because your momentum is transferred to the bombs when you let them go, so the trick is to judge when to drop them so they arc down and hit the target.

To my horror, Sibbald dived even lower, dropping his bombs from only a couple of hundred feet. Not knowing any better, Maycroft and Falconer followed, each of them releasing their two bombs when Sibbald let his go.

The bridge vanished as the bombs landed all around it. Great spouts of water shot high in the air, and I saw the three Quirks being buffeted by the blast which also threw masonry and men high into the air amidst the fountains of water.

We ourselves almost flew into the debris thrown up by the bombs, but Beano was not as reckless as Sibbald, maintaining a slightly higher altitude. Even so, it was horribly low, and I could distinctly hear the crackle of the rifles being aimed at us.

We dropped our eggs from about five hundred feet up, creating another huge fountain of water and masonry. Even as I hit the switches to drop the two huge bombs, though, I knew it was unnecessary. Sibbald's section had done the job. The bridge was no longer there, a huge chunk in the centre having been blown away. We dumped our bombs anyway, adding to the confusion, then roared away, sticking close to the ground until we were clear of the German regiment's bullets.

I thought we'd escaped unharmed, but MacCallumn's plane suddenly dipped, a trail of grey smoke streaming out below him. He'd been hit! One of the bullets must have found his petrol tank.

I watched in horrified fascination as he aimed for a narrow field of ploughed earth. He was travelling too fast for a safe landing, but he cut his engine and pulled up the nose to kill some of his speed.

It was a valiant attempt, but he was too low and flying too fast to make any sort of safe landing. His wheels struck the earth, caught in a furrow, and his plane somersaulted, the tail whipping up and over as the nose dug into the freshly ploughed earth.

And then it exploded in a ball of flame, chunks of wood and metal, along with scraps of canvas, being flung out in all directions as the fuel erupted into an inferno.

Poor MacCallum! I hope he didn't suffer too much. Perhaps he broke his neck when the Quirk went over, but I rather fear he was still alive when the petrol tank blew up.

We climbed as fast as we could, although that is not fast in a B.E.2c, but the clouds were low enough that Sibbald was able to lead us into relative safety. He did waggle his wings to signal hostile aircraft, and he pointed to a fast-moving group of small dots high above us. Fortunately, our escort of Tripes was still with us, flying above and behind us. The Huns must have seen them, for they left us alone.

Back at the airfield, Sibbald gave his report in short, terse sentences.

"Well done," the Major said. "Corps will be pleased, and so will R.F.C. Headquarters."

Sibbald merely nodded and asked whether a replacement pilot had been requested.

"I'll fill in the forms now," Potter replied gravely.

In fact, he had more forms to fill in, because C Flight lost a crew as well. Lawrence and Noone were shot down by an Albatros, although they did manage to reach the ground and get out safely. The last anyone saw of them, they were stranded well behind the Hun Lines, so they are almost certainly prisoners by now.

"A better fate than poor MacCallum," was Vaughn's comment, and I could not disagree with him.

Vaughn got rather drunk this evening. I warned him against it, but he has not been the same since Dish was killed, and he seems to be taking solace in whisky and gin.

"Bates said you met that journalist fellow again," he said to me as he swilled his glass thoughtfully.

"Yes."

"And he said the French have a mutiny on their hands?"

I frowned, annoyed that Bates had broken his promise of silence on that subject.

"That's not what Richardson said," I told Vaughn. "He was merely commenting on what might happen if the offensive does not succeed. It's a lot of rot if you ask me. I think he was just spinning us a yarn to try to get us to divulge our own problems."

"Maybe so," Vaughn sighed. "But the French have suffered a lot. They've lost hundreds of thousands of men already, and this offensive isn't really going to plan so far."

"We'll make a breakthrough soon," I insisted.

"Not if the French troops decide they've had enough," Vaughn argued. "What happens if they really do decide to stop fighting? The Huns could march right through them, then swing around to encircle us."

"That won't happen," I insisted. "There hasn't been any trouble, so don't go spreading false rumours of defeat."

He gave me a look of mock indignation as he said, "Me? I wouldn't dream of such a thing."

"Yes you bloody would!" I retorted, jabbing a finger at his chest to reinforce my point.

Vaughn held up his hands in surrender.

"Fat lot of good it would do me if I did blab," he said. "I'd be up before a Court Martial before you know it. That's one thing you British are good at; killing your own troops to keep them in line."

"That's outrageous!" I almost shouted, feeling my temper rising.

"Is it? Why not ask your journalist friend to check the records. Hundreds of men have been executed for cowardice, even though many of them had been through hell at the Front. But that's not the point."

"Then what is the point?" I challenged.

"It's that, even if that journalist's fears do turn out to be accurate, you can be sure the British High Command would keep it quiet. They don't want the peasants getting any notions above themselves. That's how they maintain power, you know; by convincing people to stay quiet and do as they are told."

"It's called Army discipline," I retorted. "You can't fight a war without it."

"Indeed you can't," he agreed. "And it must be enforced rigorously. I'll bet you anything you like that the Army will shoot anyone who tries to start any sort of trouble."

"That's an easy claim to make," I sneered. "If news is going to be hushed up, how will we know what's happened?"

To which, Vaughn merely knocked back his whisky and called for another.

A short while later, Sibbald came over to tell me he was making some changes within the Flight.

"The new lads need experienced observers," he told me. "And our new observers need experienced pilots. So I'm going to pair you up with Goldberg."

It was quite a shock to realise that I was now one of A Flight's more experienced pilots, but I merely nodded my agreement. It would be a shame to part with Sergeant Turnbull, but Goldberg had been with us for a week or so, and was shaping up well, having flown with Sibbald several times. He was a tall fellow with thin features and a serious expression which belied a wicked sense of dry humour. He seems a decent sort.

I knew without being told that Sibbald would take the newest observer and pair Sergeant Turnbull with one of the new pilots. That seemed to be his way. I know Bernard prefers C Flight to have experienced crews flying together, but that does mean new pilots are paired with inexperienced observers. Given how hard it is for newcomers to spot hostile aircraft, that does strike me as risky, but I suppose it is in keeping with Bernard's style of leadership. He isn't afraid to take risks, and doesn't think twice about throwing his lads in at the deep end. It does leave them vulnerable, though. Even now, after more than two weeks, I'm still struggling to spot other planes before someone else points them out to me. I just hope Goldberg has learned the knack quickly.

Tuesday 17th April, 1917

It rained all day today. I feel guilty now, but when I awoke to hear it drumming on the roof of the hut, I breathed a sigh of relief. Etherington had not come to wake me for the dawn show because the Major had washed out all flying. Even the dripping leaks through the roof of the hut could not spoil the joy of a day off.

Of course, I then recalled Morris and his men out there in the front line, and I knew they would be suffering in the downpour. Trenches already waterlogged would become even worse places to live and fight. To make matters worse for them, although no aeroplane could fly in such filthy weather, the artillery could still send explosive shells, and machine gun teams, snipers and trench mortar squads could still function.

For us, though, the rain meant we had no duties, and I think every one of the pilots and observers was grateful. In normal times, aircrew are usually allocated a day's rest every week, but with the Push on, and with casualties so high, nobody can be given that luxury, and most of us had been in the air every day for the past few weeks.

The Ack Emmas continued to work on our aircraft, but they did so under cover, because the low-hanging clouds were sending down a veritable deluge.

We spent the day in the Mess, listening to gramophone records, playing cards or chess, and reading.

Vaughn looked up from the latest edition of Comic Cuts to say, "This fellow Bishop of Sixty Squadron is making a bit of a name for himself, isn't he? He's only been out here a few weeks, and he's already knocked down half a dozen Huns."

"Good for him," said Bates. "But I bet he couldn't do it in a Quirk."

I think we were all in agreement about that. It's actually quite nice that the Flying Corps does not officially recognise the Ace system used by the Germans and the French. Their leading air fighters are lionised by the Press, while ours are little known outside of the R.F.C. itself. General Trenchard believes it is we in the two-seaters who do the valuable work, and I think we all appreciate that. It's all very well for men with a talent for air fighting to be esteemed by their colleagues, and we certainly appreciate their skill as it helps keep us safe, but for such men to be seen to be doing more valuable work than the rest of us would, I think, be a source of resentment. Still, it was nice to know that at least one British pilot was able to hold his own against the likes of the Red Baron.

Beano tried to rouse interest in arranging a tender to go to Barly or even Arras, but nobody was tempted, not even by the thought of the lascivious girls Beano assured us were waiting just for us.

"It's not worth getting soaked for," said Goldberg.

Beano went anyway, returning an hour or two later looking like a drowned rat.

"I may be drenched," he declared, "But it was certainly worth it."

The only other thing of note should have been good news but was dampened by the miserable weather. After dinner, as we all sat around the table, the Major announced that we were to be re-equipped with new aeroplanes.

"We are getting the new R.E.8," he informed us.

This caused a bit of a stir. The R.E.8, like the B.E.2, is a Royal Aircraft factory design. I'd seen one once, and it was an ugly brute of a plane, but it was certainly a step up from the Quirk because it had been designed for war flying, even if the designers seemed to have produced it by committee.

"As you may know," the Major told us, "the Harry Tate has the newer R.A.F.4 engine, and it can reach up to one hundred miles per hour. It also has a higher ceiling than the Quirk, and it has two machine guns; one firing through the propeller, the other on a Scarff ring around the rear cockpit."

We all knew this, but the Major continued to expound the wonders of this new kite. Some pilots were not overly impressed because we had heard some horror stories about the "Harry Tate" as it was universally known. It was designed to be stable, like most R.A.F. designs, which allegedly made it cumbersome despite its better speed than the B.E.2. It also had a habit of bursting into flames in a crash, and we'd heard some rumours of a tendency to keep going if it ever fell into a spin.

Still, the R.E.8 was a damned sight better than the ancient B.E.2c we were flying at the moment. Best of all as far as I am concerned, it has two machine guns. With the pilot sitting in the front cockpit, all the problems of the Quirk are removed, and this would certainly give us a better chance against the Huns.

The problem, of course, is the weather, and the Met boys say the current wet front will be with us for at least another day, so we won't get our hands on the new machines for a little while. Even so, Sibbald told Beano to head down to Candas and fly back in the first R.E.8. Each of our Flights is to get one of the new machines, with the rest following as soon as they can be brought over from England and assembled.

I can hardly wait. There will be no more flying over Hunland with no way of defending ourselves. Just as I had told Richardson, the journalist, the tide was about to turn.

Wednesday 18th April, 1917

Today has been a miserable day in more ways than one.

The rain continued unabated, turning the ground to mud wherever men tried to walk. Even venturing to the Mess involved a soaking, and I could not but help feel sympathy for the men who were out in the trenches.

This time, when a few of the lads decided to take a tender into Barly, I went along with them, although I had no intentions of visiting the brothel with them. Instead, I asked to be dropped off just as we entered the town.

"Where are you going?" asked Falconer as I jumped out of the back of the tender.

"He's off to the hospital," declared Bates. "Going to see his nurse again, I'll bet."

I ignored them, pulling my cap down low to keep the rain out of my eyes and adjusting my greatcoat with what I hoped was a casual air.

"Give her a kiss from me!" called Swanningsby, one of B Flight's observers.

"And something more from me!" laughed Bates.

Then the tender splashed its way along the road, leaving me in the rain. Tugging up the collar of my greatcoat, I set off for the chateau which housed the hospital.

It was a horribly wet journey, for the road had more puddles than cobbles, and several ambulances passed me on the way to the main entrance, each of them splashing me with yet more filthy water as they raced past.

Not before time, I reached the open gates and trudged up the wide approach avenue. The chateau has extensive grounds, and the front façade looked much as it must have done in centuries past except for the prominent Red Cross flag flying from the roof, and the succession of ambulances coming and going, churning the gravel path into a series of muddy puddles which I had to avoid as I weaved my way up to the main door. My efforts were not very successful, and my boots and puttees were sodden by this time, making every step unpleasant.

The ornamental pond still formed the main feature, with a thicket of woodland off to my right. I knew from my flights over the place that there were several Nissen huts at the rear of the building. These were either extra wards or were where the medical staff were billeted. I debated heading round to discover for myself, but the rain was drumming so hard on my cap, and my boots were sloshing through so many puddles, I made for the main door instead.

Nobody paid much attention to me. An ambulance raced off after delivering a couple more stretcher cases, and other stretchers were already being carried inside. I followed, climbing the few steps and gratefully escaping from the downpour.

The entrance hall was a hive of activity, with a doctor examining each new arrival and despatching the bearers to whichever ward he thought appropriate. The wounded men had already received emergency treatment at Casualty Clearing Stations, so immediate surgery was not normally required. Instead, this hospital would assess each patient more thoroughly, then carry out any further surgery or treatment before sending the men back to England once they were well enough. The few cases I saw this morning did not look well at all. One had been gassed, his face a ghastly yellow, his eyes wrapped in a bandage, his breathing hissing and hoarse, while another had lost an arm and was stoically fighting the agonising pain. It was another reminder of the horror of this war which is consuming everyone's life in one way or another.

I didn't want to get in the way, so, still dripping rainwater, I went to the office off the main entrance hall where I knew from my previous visit that much of the administration was done.

This time, the occupant was a Private. He gave me a welcoming smile as he asked, "What can I do for you, Sir?"

"I'm trying to locate a friend of mine," I told him, using the tale I'd invented as an excuse for being here. "Second Lieutenant Morris of the King's Own Rifle Regiment."

The Private forced a smile, letting me know I was interrupting valuable work, but he condescended to check through some long lists of names typed neatly on official forms.

"Morris, you say, Sir? First name?"

I hesitated, then managed a smile of my own, using the first excuse I could come up with.

"You know, I always knew him by his nickname of Beano."

The Private shrugged, as if the relationships of officers were a mystery to him. He checked the list again.

"I'm sorry, Sir, we have a Captain Morris of the Oxford and Bucks Light Infantry, but no other officer of that name."

I frowned, "Damn! My information must have been wrong."

Rummaging inside my greatcoat, I withdrew a small package I had assembled from parcels I had received from home, along with my official rations of cigarettes. I'd also put in a little bit of chocolate and a small block of cheese my parents had sent me.

"I made this up for him," I explained. "You may as well have it. Pass it on to someone who might appreciate it, would you?"

"Of course, Sir," he said, taking the package cautiously as if it might contain a bomb.

I straightened up.

"I was in here myself recently," I told him. "Only a minor wound. I met a Nurse Routledge. I don't suppose you know where I can find her? I'd like to thank her properly for patching me up."

He gave me a sharp look, as if he'd guessed my true intentions.

"You'd need to ask the Nursing Sister, Sir," he told me. "Up on the first floor."

With a knowing smile, he added, "She's a bit of a tyrant, Sir. I'd be careful."

"Thanks for the warning," I said.

I left the office and stood to one side of the busy entrance hall, wondering what to do next. I did not fancy tangling with a Nursing Sister, for those women had formidable reputations, so I hung around for a few minutes, creating a small puddle as water continued to drip from my coat.

I had hoped to find Nurse Jennifer Routledge before lunchtime, intending to invite her to a local *estaminet* if possible. If she was busy, I had another small package of treats to give her, having exchanged some of my cigarettes for chocolate. I checked my watch and discovered it was almost mid-day.

Just as I was plucking up the courage to explore the hospital in the hope of finding her, she came down the stairs, already wearing a coat over her voluminous dress, and carrying an umbrella.

Smiling, I moved to intercept her.

"Nurse Routledge?" I said as I moved in front of her.

She stopped, frowning, and looked me in the face.

"Hello," she said. "Can I help you?"

There was no hint of recognition in her eyes at all.

Taking off my cap, I said, "We met a week or so ago. You helped treat a small wound in my back. Kerr. Arthur Kerr of the Flying Corps."

Her smile brightened as she said, "Oh, of course! You flew over the hospital the next day. I remember that. The doctors were not happy at all, so I'd better not let on it was you."

I was disappointed that she had not remembered me initially, but I supposed she must see hundreds of wounded men passing through this place, so I took a deep breath and plunged in.

"I came looking for a friend I thought was wounded, but he's not here. Still, since I'm here anyway, do you fancy going out for a spot of lunch? If your duty allows, that is."

I knew she was off duty, for she was already wearing a coat and hat, but she shook her head.

"Thank you," she said a little stiffly. "But I already have a lunch engagement. In fact, here he is now."

I turned to see the main doors swinging open to admit a tall, well-built officer entering the hallway. Even with his greatcoat on, I could see the red tabs on the collar of his uniform jacket. He had blue eyes, a small, toothbrush moustache, and short, dark hair under his military cap.

"Jennifer!" he boomed as he strode over to us. "Are you ready? The car is outside."

"Hello, Hector," she replied, stepping in to greet him with a kiss on the cheek. "I only have an hour, so we'd better be off."

And so she left, ignoring me completely and sweeping out into the rain with the tall staff officer named Hector.

Feeling a sinking sensation in my stomach, I went to the doors, watching as they climbed into the back seat of a gleaming staff car and drove off, leaving my dreams shattered.

I could not face going to the brothel to cadge a lift back in the tender, so I walked all the way back to the airfield, the rain soaking through my greatcoat and dampening my uniform. All the way, I told myself that enduring this hardship would somehow prove something to Nurse Jennifer Routledge. I knew I was being petty, for she had obviously not remembered me well enough to recognise me, but it was galling that she should instead be lunching with a red tab, a man who probably never came closer to spilling his own blood than when he was shaving.

I returned to the hut, changing out of my wet clothes and pulling on my R.F.C. Maternity Tunic as the flat-fronted jackets were known. I peeled off my boots and puttees, unwinding the long strips of linen which, when wrapped around the lower leg, preserve you from catching your trouser legs on anything. I hung them up on a peg to dry. Then I sat down to write this journal to get my feelings of frustration out. I was interrupted by Vaughn, who dashed into the hut, dripping wet but in as good a mood as I had seen since Dish's death.

"Hello, my boy!" he beamed. "I thought you were off to the knocking shop in Barly?"

"No," I said. "I changed my mind and came back."

He saw my wet uniform hanging on the pegs on the wall, but he made no comment about any conclusions he may have drawn.

"You should have come with me," he grinned.

"And where did you go?" I asked, knowing he was going to tell me anyway.

"Into Fosseux," he told me conspiratorially. "I visited Lucille's *estaminet*."

"On your own? I hope you had a good meal."

"I had a sight more than that," he grinned, giving me a suggestive wink.

"With Lucille?" I gasped. "Or her daughter?"

"Lucille, of course," he said. "She can be very choosy, but she needs any extra money she can earn."

I stared at him, unbelieving.

"I'll make an introduction for you if you like," he offered.

"No thanks," I said. I recalled Lucille's plump, matronly figure. However willing she might be in the absence of her husband, I wasn't going to get involved in that sort of relationship.

"You're mad," I told Vaughn.

"It's a mad world," he shrugged. "We are out here trying to kill men because our rulers fell out over some family squabble or other. At times like this, you need to take what you can get when it's offered."

He laughed, then clapped me on the back and said, "Come along to the Mess. Let's have a drink and make a toast to madness."

Which is what we did. I brushed off the leering questions from Bates and the others who had gone to the brothel, telling them the nurse had been on duty, so nothing salacious had happened.

"Are you going back?" Bates pressed.

"No," I eventually admitted just to shut him up. "No, I don't think I will."

Thursday 19th April, 1917

We had a binge last night because the weather boys insisted the rain was going to last at least another day. I don't remember much about it, to be perfectly honest. There was a great deal of horseplay, and some furniture was smashed up. Without Beano, the piano remained unplayed, although some of the lads poured their drinks into it just for the sake of keeping up the tradition. Even without the music, we sang a lot of songs, and we got royally drunk, so my head was thumping this morning.

It was afternoon before I could face the Mess, and I did not eat much, but I was feeling restless despite my hangover so, when Bates suggested we take the chance to go to Barly once again, I found myself accepting.

"Good man!" Bates grinned. "The rain won't last forever, and when it stops we won't have a chance to do anything much except fly."

So we went to the brothel, where a very pleasant woman in her forties took our money and allocated us to our rooms.

I won't say much about what happened. I was very nervous, and I think that was obvious to everyone, particularly the dark-haired girl who was waiting for me.

I learned quite a few things from that encounter. One was why pilots always refer to the wind sock at the airfield as an "effel". This tube of cloth, tied to the top of a tall pole, is blown by the wind to show us which way we need to take off and land. It is very similar in shape to the protective sheath the girl helped me put on. These sheaths are referred to as French Letters, the first two letters of which are F and L, so we get effel.

The other main thing I learned was what girls actually look like beneath their clothing. Most women wear long skirts or dresses, and bulky blouses which only hint at what lies beneath. Today I found out, and it was an amazing experience.

I also learned why the Army maintains these places, or at least turns a blind eye to them. Life is for living, and that requires a number of our basic needs to be satisfied. In a time when we face death on a daily basis, perhaps the act of love is more needed than ever. So, while some people may regard this as a sordid bit of my personal history, I must confess I felt good afterwards. Perhaps that is wrong, but I cannot help how I feel. The next time Beano or any of the others calls for an outing to Barly, I'll be happy to go along with them.

And that is all I am going to say about today. Tomorrow, we should be able to fly again at last. It may sound odd, but I am actually looking forward to that. Nurse Routledge may prefer staff officers who live in cosy chateaux, but some of us need to fight this war and win it. Our offensive has stalled, partly because of the rain, partly because of the difficulty of supporting the most advanced troops. The news from further south is that the French assault has had little success. There has been no word of the French troops having mutinied, so it seems Richardson's fears were unfounded, although there has been a lot of grumbling in the Mess about the attitude of our French allies, and many disparaging comments made about their lack of moral fibre.

Bernard stated, "They've lost so many of their regular troops that all they've got left are second-rate conscripts. Winning this war is going to be up to us."

Personally, I don't know enough French people to make any meaningful comment on this. The few I have met have been mostly women and old men who do seem fed up of the war. But when you consider what they have been through, perhaps that is understandable.

For our part, we will accept the challenge. We'll pick up the gauntlet and take the war to the enemy. And that begins again tomorrow.

Friday 20th April, 1917

Goldberg and I did our first mission this morning, carrying out some artillery spotting for our guns in an attempt to keep the German troops at bay while our lads completed their process of digging in. It was a relatively uneventful flight, although we twice had to scarper when I spotted groups of Albatroses high above us. Fortunately, I saw them in time, and we were able to get safely back across our Lines before they could dive down on us. We waited until their fuel ran low, then we went back and completed our mission.

Poor old C Flight was not so lucky. Desmond and Fitzgerald were attacked by some red Albatroses who dived down from behind a cloud. Desmond must have been wounded, for the plane was seen to be flying erratically, but he did manage to put it down. Our Archie reckon they ended up in a crump hole a little way behind the Hun Lines, so the two of them will be prisoners now if they survived the crash.

Goldberg and I also did two photo shoots well behind the Lines. These went off well enough, with Archie being our main problem. He bracketed us with some salvoes which rocked us around a bit and peppered our wings with small holes. Despite this, we got our photographs and returned home safely both times. I think we were helped by the fact that the sky was full of British planes today. After three days of inactivity, every pilot and observer in the R.F.C. seemed to want to be up there, so we had plenty of protection from the Hun scouts. We saw a couple of planes go down, but none of the Huns got close to us.

Goldberg seems a competent enough observer, although I somehow missed Turnbull's reassuring presence. He's been teamed up with one of the new pilots, a fellow named Branwell, but I haven't had a chance to talk to him to find out how he's doing. Branwell, though, seems a little intimidated by the stocky little Sergeant.

"He's a fierce fellow, isn't he?" he said to me when I asked how he had got on with his observer during their training flight which Sibbald, as usual, insisted they carry out before he would let Branwell near the Lines.

"He's ferocious," I agreed. "But you'll be grateful for that if the Huns get close to you."

The other main attraction today was the first of our Harry Tates. Beano flew the R.E.8 in this morning, and we all gathered round to look at this new kite.

It's a strange beast, with a huge, four-bladed propeller like the B.E.2c. To keep this clear of the ground, the front of the plane points upwards at an angle, and there's an odd bend in the rear part of the fuselage to flatten it out. The R.E.8 looks as if someone has broken its back. The gaping air intake on top of the engine, combined with the two exhausts jutting up over the top wing were normal Royal Aircraft Factory design which, as usual, gave the plane an ugly aspect.

But the big thing for us is that the pilot now sits in the front cockpit, with the observer behind him. And both of them have a machine gun. The observer has a Scarff ring, a hoop of metal around the rim of his cockpit, with a Lewis gun attached. This means the gun can be swivelled all around, giving a clear field of fire behind and above. The pilot, meanwhile, can press a trigger on his joystick which fires a Vickers gun through the propeller thanks to the miracle of interrupter gears which mean the bullets pass between the whirling blades. The interrupter gear will prevent the gun firing if a propeller blade is in the way. To me, it's like magic, and I can't wait to get my hands on one of these kites.

"You'll get yours next," Sibbald told me.

"Aren't you taking it?" I asked.

He shook his head.

"The Flight Commander should be the last person to get a better machine."

My eyebrows shot up at hearing this. Both Unswood of B flight and Bernard of C Flight had claimed the first Harry Tate for themselves, so Sibbald was almost openly criticising them.

In a low voice which only I could hear, he explained, "The Flight Commander should always have the worst machine. That way, if the whole Flight is together, everyone else can keep up with him. If he has the best machine, the rest of the Flight might struggle to keep up, and he might fly into a scrap with stragglers trailing out behind him."

That made sense to me, although I felt it was more appropriate in a scout squadron where Flights always flew together. We did a lot of our work solo, but Sibbald insisted he would be the last to get one of the new machines, and my respect for him grew immensely. He might be an old granny when it comes to taking risks, but he does take care of his men as best he can.

I'm told I should be prepared to head to Candas on Sunday to pick up the next R.E.8. I'm really looking forward to that. It may be an ugly, ungainly brute, but it's a damn sight better than the Quirk.

Saturday 21st April, 1917

Paddy Vaughn was up to his old tricks again today. His dalliance with Lucille seems to have reformed his spirits, and he's been drinking less since his close encounter with her.

Today he seemed intent on stirring things, and he used Sibbald as his first target when I told him and my other hut mates about our Flight Commander insisting he would be the last to acquire one of the new kites.

"It all sounds very noble," Vaughn drawled in his sceptical voice. "But if he really meant what he said, he'd let the newest chaps get the newest planes. Instead, he's given the first one to Beano, and you'll be next. That's not really fair when you think about it."

"It's a damn sight fairer than what the other Flights are doing," I countered, aware that Bates, who is in C Flight, was likely to be on my side because he was well down the pecking order in waiting for a new machine.

"Yes," nodded Vaughn. "But why not go the whole way? Why should you and Beano get new planes? You have the experience to have a better chance than the new boys when flying a Quirk. If one of them had a faster, better equipped aeroplane, they would have a better chance of escaping the vile Hun, don't you think?"

I frowned. As usual, he had a point, and I had no real argument against him.

Bates put in, "It's just the way the Army works. The senior men get the best stuff because they are able to make best use of it."

Vaughn nodded, cupping a hand around his chin as if deep in thought.

After a moment, he said, "There is some merit in what you say, although whether any of us is a better pilot than any of the new chaps can't really be proven."

"Of course it can!" Bates blurted. "We have the experience. All the flying skill in the world is no use unless you know how to use it in action."

"Ah, but how much experience?" Vaughn challenged, making his move like a chess Grand Master who has seen an opening in his opponent's defence. "How long have any of us been out here? I have about six weeks' time, and I've been here longer than any of you."

"It still makes a difference," Bates stated.

Vaughn smirked, "Shall I tell you the real reason Sibbald has given the first Harry Tate to Beano?"

Bates, Armstrong and I exchanged uncertain glances, but we all knew Vaughn would give us his opinion anyway.

Raising a finger, he explained, "It's because of the British class system."

"What?" exclaimed Bates. "That's nonsense!"

"No it's not," Vaughn replied calmly. "You see, the British are brought up to respect wealth, power and rank. You defer to those you are taught to believe are your betters. If Sibbald allowed the new kites to go to the newcomers, more experienced fellows like Beano and Kerr might accept it in public, but privately they'd feel slighted."

I said, "No I wouldn't."

"Are you sure about that?" Vaughn challenged.

Armstrong, who rarely says much, surprised us all by interjecting, "What you say may have an element of truth, Vaughn. However, I think you ought to recognise that saying such things could well bring about accusations of having Bolshevik sympathies."

Vaughn held up both hands in mock horror.

"Me? A Bolshevik? Not at all. I prefer to call myself a Socialist."

"In the eyes of society, the two are more or less the same," Armstrong persisted. "The big difference being that the Bolsheviks seem to espouse violence."

"They are a radical group on the fringes of political thought," Vaughn countered. "Kerensky's Government won't let them come anywhere near holding power in Russia."

Armstrong smiled as he said softly, "I wouldn't be so sure about that. And if they do seize power, you can bet Russia will be out of the war. That will mean two things."

Vaughn seemed to be enjoying this challenge to his rhetoric. He waved a hand in invitation.

"Pray explain, Professor," he grinned.

Armstrong took a moment to think before telling us, "The first and most obvious thing is that the Germans will be free to transfer hundreds of thousands of experienced troops to the Western Front. The question is whether the Americans, who will all be raw recruits, can arrive in sufficient time and sufficient numbers to counter that threat. If they cannot, we face the prospect of Germany winning the war. Ergo, Bolshevism is a very real threat to our future."

"That's all Ifs and Buts," Vaughn remarked as if dismissing Armstrong's concerns.

Armstrong ignored him.

His face grave, he went on, "The second point is more pertinent to our immediate situation. It is that Bolshevism will be viewed by our own Government as an evil thing on the basis that it has led to Russia leaving the war."

He gave Vaughn a slight smile of triumph as he added, "And that means that anyone expressing views which could be regarded as being supportive of Bolshevism, or even Socialism, will be viewed as a threat to the State."

Vaughn nodded, but his expression was still full of wicked amusement as he said, "And we all know how the British State deals with such threats. It will mean mass executions at dawn."

"Rubbish!" I blurted.

Which, I regret, made both Vaughn and Armstrong regard me with expressions of sympathy for my apparent ignorance.

The thing I dislike about these arguments is that Vaughn always puts me in a bad mood, and that can affect my flying. Goldberg and I had a narrow escape because I failed to spot a group of Halberstadts who must have been stalking us through the clouds for some time. It was only the timely arrival of half a dozen Sopwith Pups which allowed us to escape unharmed. I suppose it is churlish of me to blame Vaughn for this since it was up to me to do my job no matter what, but I cannot help feeling a bit of resentment against him.

When I returned to the airfield, I found I had received two letters. Etherington brought them to me, his expression serious.

"I'm sorry, Sir," was all he said as he handed them to me.

I sat on my bed, looking at the letters. One was from home, for I recognised my mother's neat handwriting on the envelope, but the second was one of my own letters. It was the one I had sent to Vanders a few days ago, but it had a note pinned to it.

Addressee deceased. Return to sender.

I stared at it for a long time, scarcely able to believe it. Vanders? Dead?

I know life out here is dangerous, but Vanders had been far and away the most capable pilot in our training group. In fact, I would class him as brilliant. He could do things in an aeroplane that most of us would not even contemplate.

But he is dead, and I recalled what Bates had said about talent being no substitute for experience.

But Vanders?

I wonder how it happened, but there was no explanation, simply the short note returning my letter.

I mentioned Vanders's loss after dinner, and Sibbald expressed his sympathy.

"Don't let it get to you," he warned.

"I won't. It only makes me more determined. But I can't believe any Hun could get Vanders. He was such an exceptional pilot."

"Flying skill doesn't always count for much," Sibbald told me.

"What do you mean?"

He explained, "It could have been engine failure, or perhaps a weak spar snapped, breaking his machine up in mid-air. Nobody could survive that. Or he might have been hit by Archie. That's just plain bad luck."

"I suppose so," I grunted.

Sibbald went on, "But don't equate flying skill with success in air fighting. The best scout pilots are the ones who can shoot well. Nobody ever got shot down by someone flying rings round them. It's good marksmanship that counts."

With a self-deprecating grin, he admitted, "That's why I'd never make a scout pilot. I couldn't hit a barn door at fifty paces."

I know Sibbald was doing his best to help me come to terms with the loss of my friend, but I still find it hard to believe that both Greening and Vanders, my two closest colleagues in the R.F.C. have gone west.

I wonder how their families will bear the sad news, but for my part, as I told Sibbald, it only makes me more determined to win this war to ensure their sacrifice is not in vain.

Sunday 22nd April, 1917

I had hoped to cadge a flight down to Candas, but I ended up travelling in a Crossley tender which had to negotiate the busy roads. I'd set off in the afternoon, having done two photo shoots in the morning, taking pictures of the new Front Lines to provide Corps H.Q. with the latest images of the situation. To my mind, that situation was very confusing, but the funny thing is that I couldn't help but wonder whether it would be Hector, Nurse Routledge's beau, who would be studying the pictures I had taken. Or perhaps such a task was too exalted a job for him. He was probably engaged in licking the General's boots clean, or mucking out the stables where the Staff wallahs kept their expensive horses.

I confess I brooded most of the way down to Candas. Not even the thought of obtaining a new machine could throw off my mood. Sitting there, watching the military lorries, motorcycles, horses and troops, I felt very insignificant. The war was a giant machine, forcing men and some women into situations they could never have imagined in peacetime. I had my new life in the squadron, but I suddenly felt as if nobody outside our airfield had any notion of what we were doing.

It worked both ways, of course, for I had no inkling of what actually happened inside Corps H.Q., nor of the daily trials of the artillery gunners. My brief sojourn among the infantry when I had been shot down had given me a glimpse of the horror those men endured every day, but even now I felt I was apart from them, merely a cog in a vast engine. And I realised now that, just like a faulty part in any machine, if I were broken in any way, I would quickly be replaced to allow the engine to grind on.

Of course, the war machine often misfired, as it did today.

When I reached the Air Supply Depot, I was informed that I would need to stay overnight.

Candas is normally extremely efficient for such a huge base, but my R.E.8 was not quite ready by the time I reported to the main administration office. In addition, it had begun to rain again, a heavy downpour which would prevent all flying. With only an hour or two of daylight left, I have been forced to wait until morning before I could fly back.

I telephoned the squadron and explained this to Potter.

"It can't be helped, old chap," he told me. "We'll see you tomorrow."

I was given quarters in one of the accommodation huts where a gaggle of new pilots were waiting for their assignments. They assumed I was also new, for one of them asked me where I hoped to be posted.

"I'm already on ops," I told him, my tone less friendly than it should have been. "I'm just here to collect a new kite."

"What do you fly?" he wanted to know, and the others moved closer to listen in.

"From tomorrow, it will be Harry Tates," I answered. "Up to now, I've been flying Quirks."

There were murmurs of sympathy, then another young chap asked, "What's it like at the Front?"

"It's hard work," I shrugged.

In truth, what could I tell them? That their chances depended on what sort of squadron they joined, what sort of chap their Flight Commander was, and which particular group of Huns was across the Lines from them?

Above all, much hung on what type of plane they would be flying, and on how much luck they had.

I know these fellows meant well, and I also realised that some of them are older than me, but I felt immeasurably more experienced than any of them, and I could not find the energy to talk to them about a life they could not possibly comprehend.

"Just keep dodging Archie and watch the skies for Huns," was all the advice I gave them before I headed to the bar at the Mess to get a drink.

To my astonishment, I found a familiar face sitting in the Mess at a table all on his own. Wearing a civilian suit, and much older than anyone else in the place, was the journalist, Richardson. He had been staring down at a glass of whisky, but he glanced up when I entered the room, and his face lit up with recognition.

"Mister Kerr!" he beamed. "Come and join me, will you?"

I could hardly ignore him, so I took a chair opposite him while one of the Mess waiters fetched me a drink.

"What on earth are you doing here?" I asked Richardson.

He gave a dismissive shrug. He seemed almost as weary as I was.

"I've been given permission to travel around a bit to see the logistical side of things," he informed me.

"What, like auditing the paper clips?" I asked.

"Not quite that mundane," he smiled. "No, I wanted to see how the Flying Corps keeps its squadrons equipped. It's quite an amazing set up, you know."

"I've never really thought about it," I admitted.

"That's because it generally runs so smoothly," he told me. "You'd think about it a lot more if your replacement pilots and planes were slow in coming, or if you couldn't get spare parts to keep your machines flying. And don't forget there's the question of ammunition like bullets and bombs, plus the simple matter of fuel."

"I suppose so," I nodded. "But it hasn't gone smoothly today. I was supposed to collect a new bus this afternoon, but it's not ready."

"Nothing works perfectly all the time," he pointed out. "I presume it's only a short delay?"

"Yes. They tell me I can fly it back in the morning."

"Another B.E.2?" he probed, his journalistic instincts kicking in.

I shook my head.

"No, it's one of the new Harry Tates."

I grinned as I added, "It's got two machine guns. I can't wait to get my hands on it."

Richardson treated me to an indulgent smile.

"I've heard a few reports about that aircraft," he said, his tone suggesting that the reports were less than favourable.

"So have I," I nodded. "But I don't really care. It's got guns, so we can fight back when we are attacked."

Richardson remained reserved as he said softly, "You do know that an entire Flight of them was shot down last week? They went on a long range patrol and the Red Baron's crew caught them. Having machine guns didn't do them a lot of good."

I shrugged, "That sort of thing can happen. It's not as if they would have had a better chance if they'd been flying Quirks."

"True enough," Richardson nodded. "So you will take charge of this new machine tomorrow morning?"

"That's right."

"That's good," he said, nodding in a distracted way as if this news had triggered some thought process.

Then, his smile reappearing, he returned to his exposition on the R.F.C's logistical arrangements.

"Anyway, as I said, supplying front-line squadrons is a huge operation, and it generally works very well. If it wasn't for all that hard work, you'd struggle to fight the war at all. Did you know every drum of fuel has to be filtered through a cloth when a plane is being refuelled?"

"Yes. I've seen our Ack Emmas doing it."

"It's a long, slow process," Richardson reminded me.

"I'm sure it is," I shrugged.

"I'm boring you!" he grinned. "Well, such is the lot of aged reporters. We are supposed to inform and educate, yet many young people simply aren't interested."

"It's not that I'm not interested," I told him. "I know all that stuff is relevant, but my own job isn't exactly a walk in the park."

"Of course it isn't," he agreed. Then, leaning towards me, he went on, "And that brings me to a delicate subject I hope you can help me with. I think it is Fate that has brought you here."

"No, it was a Crossley tender that brought me here," I shot back.

"Very funny. But seriously, I need your help."

"To do what?"

Richardson pursed his lips for a moment before whispering, "I need to see the Front."

"What for?"

With a sigh, he told me, "I told you once before, I'm gathering information for a book I am going to write when this is all over. A book in which I shall reveal the truth, not the propaganda pieces I am obliged to churn out at the moment."

"And to do this you need to see the Front?"

"Of course! How else can I understand what it is like?"

"I can tell you what it's like," I told him. "It's bloody awful."

"But I still need to see for myself," he persisted.

I suggested, "Then ask the General to let you go forwards to the trenches."

"I've tried that," he said. "But neither the Army nor my newspaper wants to give readers the news that one of their reporters has been killed near the Front."

"So you have been denied permission?"

"I'm afraid so."

"But you want me to help you anyway?"

"That's right."

"How?"

He gave me a soft smile as he asked, "You'll be flying back to Fosseux tomorrow, won't you?"

I nodded, "Yes."

"Well, I need to return to Corps H.Q. anyway, so why not give me a lift there?"

"I suppose I could do that," I conceded. "You have official War Office permission to be here."

"Indeed I do. All I lack is permission to go up to the front trenches."

It was then that I realised what he was asking.

"You want me to make a detour on the way home?" I guessed.

"That's right," he confirmed with an assertive nod. "Just a short detour so I can see for myself what it looks like."

"It's too dangerous," I told him.

"I'm not asking you to go across the Lines," he assured me. "I just want to see what it looks like."

"Have you ever been up in a plane before?" I asked him.

"Once. It was only a five minute joyride."

I think I had already decided to help him, but I pointed out, "You don't have flying gear."

"I have my trench coat," he replied. "And the Stores here can supply a leather helmet, goggles and gloves."

I said, "I presume you would prefer not to ask official permission for this flight?"

"You presume correctly," he grinned. "So you will do it?"

"On one condition," I replied.

"What is that?"

"I want some information."

"What sort of information?"

"There's an officer at Corps H.Q. by the name of Hector. I don't know his rank, but he's a big fellow, although he looks a bit soft despite his broad shoulders."

"That would be Hector Harkness," Richardson said instantly. "Have you met him?"

"Only very briefly."

"So what do you want to know about him? And why?"

I hesitated for a moment, then said, "There's a girl I know. A nurse. She seems very friendly with Hector."

Richardson almost laughed as he said, "Ah, a rival in love, is he? Well, I suspect you will have your work cut out to turn the girl's head. Our friend Hector comes from a wealthy family who own a large part of Sussex."

"He's rich?"

"Very. And he has connections. How do you think he managed to get a job on the Staff?"

I took a sip of my whisky while I considered this.

Richardson went on, "I must say the girl shows good sense opting for someone like the bold Hector. He may be misnamed, but his prospects are certainly a lot better than those of anyone in front line service."

That remark stung, although I could understand the cold logic of it, but one part of it caught my attention.

"Why is he misnamed?" I asked.

Richardson grinned, "If you know your Homer, you'll know Hector was the greatest Trojan warrior. His name inspired fear and respect among his enemies."

"I remember that from school," I acknowledged. "But Hector Harkness doesn't live up to the name? Is that what you mean?"

"Precisely," Richardson nodded. "As far as I can tell, he's never been closer to the Front than the rear trenches. Do you know he fell off his horse a while back when a low-flying plane came roaring across the park beside the H.Q. building?"

I could not resist smiling as I asked, "Really? I hope he wasn't hurt."

"Only his arse and his pride, I think. But he was shaking with fear after it. That's what I mean about being misnamed."

This was all music to my ears, and I began trying to work out how I could show up this red tab to Nurse Routledge. But since I had a source of information, I pressed Richardson for more.

"Do you know how old he is?" I asked.

"I'm not sure. In his twenties, that's certain."

Richardson now eyed me keenly as he asked, "I expect that makes him several years older than you."

"A few," I admitted.

"How old are you anyway?" he asked.

"I'll be nineteen at the end of this month."

This information appeared to depress Richardson.

"So young," he sighed. "Like so many out here. You aren't even old enough to vote, yet you are old enough to die in the service of your country."

"If that's what it takes to do my duty," I nodded.

"And that," Richardson said with feeling, "is the worst thing about this bloody war."

After that, we moved onto other topics. He told me the French offensive had bogged down even more quickly than ours, and that he remained very concerned about the willingness of the French to continue fighting.

He said, "Even if they do carry on, I doubt they have the spirit to succeed. Nivelle's tactics have brought some small successes, but the victory he promised has not materialised. The Germans knew they were coming, and our assault did not draw away their reserves as had been hoped."

I recalled Sibbald predicting this very outcome, and I couldn't help but wonder whether he might have done a better job of running the war than the likes of Hector Harkness.

Richardson, his tongue loosened by another whisky, told me, "I can't really blame the Generals. This trench warfare is new to everyone, and nobody knows how to overcome it. Tanks might do the trick, but too many of them break down before they get anywhere near the action."

"So what is the answer?" I asked him.

"I don't think anyone really knows. As I said, I can't blame the Generals for struggling to find a solution. What I can blame them for is the appalling loss of life."

"That's hardly their fault, is it?" I frowned.

"No?" he said, cocking his head. "I suppose it depends on your point of view. But let me put it this way. You see, everyone agrees that artillery is the key to winning."

"That's true enough," I agreed cautiously.

"Yes. The theory goes that you bombard the enemy hard enough and long enough, then all your infantry needs to do is walk over and capture the trenches which are full of dead, wounded or demoralised Germans."

He gave a regretful sigh as he continued, "What none of the High Command seemed to realise is that the same can apply to the enemy artillery. While our troops are walking over, all they need do is bombard them, then send in their own reserve troops. And so it goes on, with neither side able to take the advantage because the ground has been so churned up that troops cannot advance quickly enough to take advantage of any opening the artillery might create."

Bitterly, he added, "And I hear reports that the Germans have built their defences so strongly that even the heaviest bombardment doesn't damage them."

My brief experience of walking back through the Lines had shown me the truth of this.

"They have deep shelters and strong machine gun posts," I agreed.

"So all our Generals do is throw more and more men at the problem," he said. "Most of them are cavalry officers by experience, and they are struggling to understand how to use new technology like tanks and aeroplanes. In fact, it's up to the men at the Front to come up with ideas, but even the best of those innovations is usually ignored by the staff officers. They simply have no conception of what it is like at the Front."

I chuckled, "I've heard it said that few of the Donkey Wallopers have as many brains as their horses."

"A cruel comment with perhaps a grain of truth," the journalist smiled. "But I am in the same position until I get a look at the Front. That is what you will change."

So, aided by more whisky than I should have consumed, I have let myself be talked into taking a civilian near the Front. I'm sure it will be fine as long as nothing goes wrong.

Monday 23rd April, 1917

Candas has a pool of pilots who are stationed there to test fly new machines as well as ferry them out to airfields if a squadron cannot spare a man to collect a new kite. One of these locals, a Lieutenant named Harris, gave me a short introduction to the R.E.8.

"You've read the Pilot's Manual?" he asked.

"Yes."

In truth, I'd skimmed through this document, concentrating only on the main points I thought I needed to know.

"Well," he said, "it's a bigger bus than the B.E.2c, and it's heavier, too. That makes it hard work to fly. It also means you need to land at a higher speed. She'll stall with no warning at forty-seven miles per hour. If that happens when you're coming in to land, you'll end up being fried. The gravity tank has a tendency to crumple on impact, and the fuel will hit either the hot exhaust pipes or the engine. So make bloody sure you keep the speed up when coming in. That also means your observer must remain seated during take-off and landing. If he stands up, he'll disrupt the airflow and create extra drag which could make you stall."

I had already noticed that warnings to this effect were stencilled on the rim of the observer's cockpit; bold, white lettering making the admonition very clear indeed.

"Do you have any other good news?" I asked Harris.

I was very aware that Richardson, his face pale but determined, was standing nearby, a valise on the ground at his feet, a leather helmet and goggles held in one hand. He wore a red scarf around his neck, and his long coat was buttoned tight. He looked very nervous indeed.

Harris paid him no attention as he informed me, "The new engine gives a lot more power. You should be able to get up to around one hundred miles per hour, which is a big improvement on the Quirk, but its rate of climb isn't much better because of the extra weight. What it does mean, though, is that it can carry a bomb load as well as an observer, so it's a proper two-seater plane."

I looked the plane over, noticing that the top wing was considerably broader and longer than the bottom set.

When I mentioned this, Harris nodded, "Some pilots are a bit wary of those wings. They do look fragile, and I'll admit I wouldn't want to dive the machine too hard in case they collapse."

"You're filling me with confidence," I told him wryly.

"It's not all bad news," he went on. "For one thing, it's actually quite hard to get a Harry Tate to spin, and they come out of a spin fairly easily, but I wouldn't recommend chucking one around the sky. It's a cumbersome beast at best."

I did not care. What intrigued me were the machine guns. There was a Lewis sitting on its rail around the rear cockpit, and a Vickers attached to the left side of the engine, with the cocking handle within easy reach from the pilot's seat.

"We've fitted an Aldis sight," Harris explained, indicating the long tube which sat just in front of the front cockpit. "But the guns aren't loaded. You'll need to get your own armourers to do that for you. Also, you'll need a wireless set fitted. Other than that, though, she's ready to go."

Looking at Richardson, I saw he was nervously toying with his unfamiliar flying helmet. I could understand his anxiety. Most people are wary about getting into an aeroplane, but climbing aboard a new kite with a pilot who has never flown that type before was a daunting prospect for anyone.

I told him, "I'll take her up for a couple of circuits to get used to her. When I come back down, I'll keep the engine running. Then you can get into the rear seat and we'll head for home."

"All right," he swallowed, giving me a cautious nod.

"You can always take a tender back to Fosseux," I reminded him.

"No," he said. "We'll do what we agreed."

I explained my plan to the ground crew, a couple of oil-stained Air Mechanics. They nodded their understanding, but before I could set off, Harris insisted on running over the cockpit layout with me.

"It's fairly basic," he said, "but this wheel allows you to adjust the trim of the tail while you are in flight. That's a big help, especially if you've been carrying bombs. Once you let them go, you can alter the trim while still flying."

I nodded approvingly, encouraging him to continue.

He went on, "There's also a built-in adjustment to the rudder bar to compensate for the engine torque. Without that, you'd be constantly pushing the rudder to the left to counteract the spin of the crankshaft pushing the plane into a right-hand turn. The R.E.8 can stay aloft for over four hours, and maintaining pressure on the rudder all that time wouldn't be good for anyone."

He also told me that the rear cockpit contained rudimentary controls for the throttle, elevator and rudder.

"They fold away," he explained. "The idea is to give the observer a chance of getting the kite down if the pilot is killed or injured and unable to fly."

"Do they work?" I asked him.

He shrugged, "They move the control surfaces, but I don't know anyone who has actually tried to use them in flight. They are for emergencies only."

He smiled as he asked, "Any other questions?"

I shook my head.

"I think you've covered everything."

I had no more excuses for delay, so I signalled the Ack Emmas to start the engine. I let it settle for a while, warming her up, then waved away the chocks and set off for my maiden flight in a Harry Tate.

It was, as Harris had warned, a heavy machine to fly. Even with the rudder adjustment, I could feel the torque of the powerful R.A.F.4 engine, yet the rate of climb was still fairly sluggish. I could sense the power which gave the machine its greater speed in level flight, but I did not open the throttle to its fullest extent yet. Instead, I tried a few gentle banks and turns, getting the feel of the thing.

The Harry Tate is very possibly the ugliest aeroplane at the Front. Its gaping air intake and chimney stack exhausts, added to the broken back towards the tail mean it looks ungainly. In all honesty, it's an ungainly kite to fly as well.

But I didn't care. It has two machine guns. My finger hovered over the trigger even as I flew around Candas, watching for other machines all the time.

After three circuits, I took her in for a landing, concentrating hard. I watched the airspeed indicator closely, keeping the needle at fifty miles per hour, desperate not to let her stall. As Harris had said, crashing to the ground when fifty feet up was likely to prove fatal, especially in light of what he'd told me about the Harry Tate's inclination to catch fire.

Fortunately, I got down safely, even if I did come in a little fast and made a couple of small bounces. I guided the plane to the hangar where Richardson was waiting.

Harris was also there. I gave him a wave and a thumbs up, and he went off to his next duty while the Ack Emmas grabbed the wing struts to prevent the machine rolling away when Richardson was boarding. They could not place chocks in front of the wheels because of the huge span of the whirling propeller. Perhaps I should have cut the engine, but Richardson eventually managed to clamber aboard, another Air Mechanic helping him into place and ensuring he was strapped in. Once his valise had been passed up to him, I waved everyone away, and then we were off, the engine roaring lustily as it hauled the big two-seater into the air.

It was a better day than we had seen for weeks, with fewer clouds, and those much higher in the sky, so we had an excellent view. I was so busy tinkering with the controls, I almost forgot about my passenger, but I did twist round once I'd got the kite up to seven thousand feet. Richardson gave me a thumbs up, so I headed east, opening the throttle to push the engine a bit. I got her up to ninety miles per hour with no problem, and there was more power there if I needed it. That was wonderful. We were still slower than most Hun scouts, but at least we had a bit more speed available to help us tackle them.

Before long, the Lines came in sight. This part of the Front was unfamiliar to me, but there was no mistaking where the trenches were located. Staying well to our side of the Lines, I turned northwards, letting Richardson get a good view of the shattered earth. It was odd to have the observer in the rear seat. I had to keep twisting to see him. His face was set in a grim expression, but I could tell he was studying the ground intently.

There were lots of other planes around, all British, so I was fairly sure we were in no danger. Still, I kept a close watch on the sky, spending little time looking earthwards. When I did glance down, I could see a great many explosions as both our and the German artillery exchanged salvoes. It looked as if another major attack was being put in, for I saw a couple of tanks crawling across the muddy craters, although it was impossible to make out whether our troops were making any progress. The sight of this assault did make me realise I ought to get back to the airfield in case I was needed on a job, so I pushed the throttle fully forwards and managed to get the Harry Tate up to one hundred miles per hour. At that speed, we reached Arras in only around ten minutes. I was delighted with this, but it was time to end our little jaunt, so I eased back on the power and turned west towards Fosseux.

I circled the airfield a couple of times, noticing a group of Ack Emmas emerging from A Flight hangar at the sound of my engine. Experts all, they had clearly discerned the throatier roar of the R.A.F.4, and had come out to witness the arrival of their new charge.

I brought the Harry Tate down in a fairly good, if not perfect, landing.

Dunlop and Green ran out to meet me, as did Sergeant Stirling. They were surprised to see I had a passenger, but they turned a diplomatically blind eye, instead concentrating their attention on the new aircraft.

"She's flying not too badly," I told them. "The left wing is a little low, but that's all."

Sergeant Stirling said, "We'll get a wireless set fitted, Sir. And we'll arm the guns. She'll be ready in a few hours if you need to take her up."

"I'll need to check with the R.O.," I replied. "but at the very least I'll want to take her up for another test flight, probably with Mister Goldberg."

Leaving them to fuss over their new toy, I walked with Richardson as we crossed the field.

"I'd better head back to H.Q.," he said. "The less fuss we make over this, the better."

"Fair enough," I nodded. "Did you see what you needed?"

"I think I saw too much," he said softly. "It looks like Hell."

"It's worse when you are down there," I assured him.

He shook my hand, saying, "Thank you, Mister Kerr. I wish you good luck."

"And you."

With a grin, he added, "And if I can find a way to puncture the bold Hector, I shall do so."

"That would be nice," I laughed.

I found I was in a much better mood than I had been yesterday, but my good humour was evaporated by the news that Paddy Vaughn had been seriously wounded during my absence. I heard the details from his observer, Marston.

"We were attacked by three Albatroses," he told me. "They were the older D.II type. We never had a chance to outrun them because they came down around some low clouds and were on us straight away."

He shook his head as he continued, "I thought we were going to go west, but Vaughn turned to meet them instead of running away."

"Towards them?" I gaped.

Marston nodded, "I couldn't shoot, of course. I'd have blown off our own propeller. All I could do was hunker down behind the engine and hope they would miss us. There were bullets striking us everywhere, but I think the move surprised them. We closed too fast for them to do anything but let off some short bursts. One of them came straight for us, but he zoomed over our top wing when Vaughn refused to break away."

He moved his hands to indicate swivelling a machine gun.

"I got off a short burst at him, and he wobbled a bit, so I think I may have wounded him. Then Vaughn put us into a spin to lose height. Unfortunately, one of the other Huns stayed with us. When we pulled out, he got a straight shot at us from dead astern. Poor Paddy was hit several times. He slumped forwards, and we went into a steep dive. I must admit I thought that was the end, but he recovered consciousness enough to pull us out and head for home."

Marston again shook his head as he went on, "I don't know how he did it, but he brought us back and got us down in one piece. Then he passed out. His back was covered in blood when they lifted him out of the cockpit. Potter heard he'd been shot three times in the back, and once in one arm."

"Poor Paddy," I sighed.

"At least he's still alive," Marston said.

He was trying to give me some hope, but his tone told me he did not believe Vaughn would survive long.

This news rather depressed me. Vaughn may have been an annoying character, but he had been a more or less permanent fixture since I had arrived. For him to vanish from my life while I had been away for only a single day made it seem somehow unreal.

But what really struck me was that I am now the longest-serving officer in Hut Three. Bates and Armstrong both arrived after me, yet I've only been here three weeks. Vaughn's absence also means B Flight is very short of experienced pilots, but the entire squadron is like that. It is becoming harder to keep up with the names of the new men.

Vaughn's replacement is a chap from Cumbria called Elphinstone. He seems frightfully keen, which is just what the squadron needs.

Goldberg and I went up on a training flight this evening. Sibbald insisted on this, telling us we would need to work out how to communicate now that I had my observer behind me. Shouting to one another is not wholly reliable because of the noise of the engine, plus Archie and perhaps machine guns adding to the racket. However, we quickly realised that Goldberg could warn me of hostile aircraft by firing a short burst with his gun. I could rock the wings to alert him, and we soon had an agreed set of signals we could use if we could not hear one another.

So tomorrow we go back to war in our new machine. It may not be the most nimble of kites, but it has some genuine firepower, so I'm looking forward to taking it up. If Paddy Vaughn had had a forward-firing gun, he'd have had more of a chance against those Albatroses. This makes me determined to make use of my gun if we are ever attacked.

Tuesday 24th April, 1917

The next phase of the offensive has begun, so Goldberg and I flew a close contact patrol, using a klaxon to ask the troops on the ground to give us their positions, then heading back to Divisional H.Q. to drop our message bags.

It was the usual hellish experience, with shells whizzing past us, explosions hurling up great plumes of earth with no warning, and machine guns firing at us from all directions. This time, though, we went armed with some bombs. I dumped a few on what looked to me like a newly built machine gun nest, although I don't think I hit the target. However, our bombs must have made the Germans scuttle for cover, because when we circled back we discovered that some of our lads had got close enough to throw in a grenade or two, killing the gunners.

I was soon sweating and tired because, although the R.E.8 is faster than the B.E.2, it's a heavy machine to lug around. This only added to the nervous tension of the low flying, and I will readily admit I would not mind at all if we were told there was no need to do any more of these missions.

One thing I did enjoy was using our machine guns. If I saw any Huns at all – which isn't easy given their grey uniforms and the endless mud of the combat zone – I squirted off a burst at them. Goldberg, too, stood up to swing his Lewis gun. He emptied two of his five drums, and we returned to Fosseux well pleased with ourselves, although our new Harry Tate had collected a fair few bullet holes. It was also leaking oil from where a bullet had nicked the engine, so we were out of action for the rest of the day.

As usual, close contact work resulted in some damage. Beano limped back with a coughing engine but no injuries, and a couple of other crews returned with their Quirks full of holes. There were no fatalities, thank goodness, but poor Armstrong took a bullet in the thigh and lost a lot of blood. His pilot, Marshall, got him back safely, and he was whisked away in an ambulance.

"Poor old Professor," said Bates. "I'll miss him."

I nodded. With Vaughn and the Professor both gone, our hut has a strange feel to it. Armstrong's replacement, Gardner, arrived after dinner, which gave Bates and me time to pack up the Professor's stuff and parcel it to be sent home. Unlike some aircrew, there was nothing we felt ought to be held back to save undue embarrassment to his family, but we did find a gold pocket watch which we decided should be taken back by whoever went on Leave first.

"The base wallahs will nick it if we send it back through the normal channels," Bates declared.

He was quite correct, although goodness knows when Leave will start up again. With the offensive under way, nobody has been allowed a break for the past few weeks. Sibbald, the longest-serving pilot in the squadron, is long overdue his Leave, but there's nothing to be done about it at the moment, so the Professor's watch will need to be kept safely by Potter for the time being.

Gardner seems a decent sort, although I rather think Bates scared him with some of his tales about C Flight's exploits.

"Captain Bernard is a real go-getter," Bates announced to the slightly bewildered Gardner. "He'll have you shooting down Huns in no time at all."

This was a reference to the day's big talking point in the Mess. Bernard, who had been on a distant patrol taking photographs, was flying one of the new Harry Tates. He returned to the airfield claiming that he had spotted a scrap between some Nieuports and Albatroses. Armed with his forward-firing machine gun, he had charged into the fray. He insisted he had hit a Hun who was painted in bright yellow and blue. He said the Albatros had dived away, the pilot obviously wounded.

Bernard's observer, Sergeant Miller, confirmed they had seen some Albatroses, but said he had been too busy blazing away with his Lewis gun to see whether Bernard had actually hit the Hun.

Potter had phoned around the nearest Nieuport squadrons and found one who confirmed they had seen an R.E.8, but one of their pilots had already put in a claim for driving down a yellow and blue Albatros.

Bernard was not pleased, and spent much of the evening insisting that he had hit the Hun.

"Methinks the Captain doth protest too much," Bates had whispered to me, misquoting Shakespeare.

Sibbald was more generous.

"An aerial scrap is a confusing thing," he said in his calm, unflappable way. "Everything is moving very fast, and it's easy to focus on one thing, so you are not aware of other aircraft around you. It's perfectly possible both Bernard and the Nieuport pilot shot at the same Hun and neither of them was aware of the other."

"So what will happen?" I asked him.

He shrugged, "Potter will put in the claim and some staff wallah at Flying Corps' H.Q. will decide. It might depend on how many Huns the Nieuport chap has got already. They may think it will be a boost to morale to give the victory to the pilot of a two-seater, or they might feel a new scout pilot could do with a boost to his own morale."

"That will keep Bernard happy," Bates sighed.

I did not really care whether Bernard got the credit or not. He'd shown some guts to take a lumbering crate like the R.E.8 into a dogfight. But what Sibbald had said made me wonder about his past.

"Have you been in many scraps?" I asked him.

He gave a barely perceptible smile as he nodded, "One or two. I used to fly the old Vickers Gunbus. It was a predecessor of the F.E.2b pusher, with the engine behind me, and a gunner in front. We mixed things with some of the old Fokker monoplanes once or twice."

"Did you get any?" I pressed, eager for some information about his past.

"We got a half share in one once," he confirmed. "We had two machines escorting an observation kite, and both gunners blazed away at one of the Fokkers who tried to get to the B.E.2."

With a self-deprecating smile, he added, "To be honest, I don't know whether either of them actually hit him, but he spun away and dropped into a cloud, so we claimed the victory."

I know this may seem strange to some people, but it's not easy to confirm whether a falling aeroplane has actually crashed. Much of the action takes place thousands of feet up in the air, and since we always fly over Hunland, it's often impossible to tell whether a machine has actually been shot down. So, while the Huns only count machines they know they have destroyed, the Flying Corps credits us with various categories of victory such as, "Destroyed", or "Driven down", or "Driven down out of control". Sibbald's half share would have come under this latter category.

"How many tours have you done?" I asked.

"Technically, this is my third," he said, "although my second one was cut short when I broke my arm in a crash."

"That was at the Somme?"

Sibbald rarely spoke of his past exploits, so I wasn't going to give up the opportunity to find out more about his career while he was in a talkative mood.

He nodded, "That's right. It wasn't a bad break, but it took me out of action for a couple of months."

"I'd have thought you were due a period on Home Establishment," I said.

He nodded, "That was a possibility, but I was put back on active service just at the time this squadron was being formed. They needed some experienced men to lead the Flights, so I got my Captaincy and came back out to France."

"Can I ask one more question?" I asked when I noticed he had finished his one and only drink of the evening. Normally, after one glass, he retired to his hut.

"That depends on what it is you want to know," he replied gruffly, his former reserve reasserting itself.

"Can I call you Bertie now? It's nearly the end of the month."

"Wait until May Day," he told me, rising to his feet and heading for the door.

I wasn't at all sure whether he was being serious, but Sibbald is not a man to ignore, so I'll do as he says.

Bates remarked, "He's a strange fish."

"Yes," I agreed. "He is. But I like him."

Wednesday 25th April, 1917

Goldberg and I had a genuine scrap today. We'd been sent out on a photographic mission to check on the Hun rear areas, so we were a few miles into Hunland. It felt odd to be flying in a straight line to take the photographs but to have my observer operate the camera while I scanned the skies for any signs of Huns. Still, we completed the job and we were just heading home when a bunch of Albatroses dropped down from on high, diving onto our tail like hawks.

Goldberg's warning came just in time, a quick burst of Lewis fire to alert me to the danger, so I immediately tramped on the rudder and swung the Harry Tate into as steep a bank as I dared, turning towards the Huns to force them to steepen their dive even further. I heard Goldberg shooting away for all he was worth, then I saw tracers flashing past our port wings. I heard a brief rattle of Spandaus, then a shadow flicked over us as one of the Huns roared past. I maintained the bank, turning the R.E.8 as tightly as I could.

A second Hun twisted as he tried to get on our tail, but the speed of his dive took him past us before he could get a bead on us. A third and fourth were already pulling up, and one of them flew across in front of us, so I squeezed the trigger and heard the satisfying rattle of my Vickers gun. I doubt very much that my bullets went anywhere near him for he zoomed past in a fraction of a second, but it was nice to be able to shoot back.

Our troubles were far from over, though, for they were re-grouping. The speed of their steep dive meant they had zoomed high above us again, and this time we knew they would take more care over their attack, the first, quick pass having failed.

I could not keep turning forever, so I came out of the turn and dived for home, opening the throttle as far as it would go. The engine bellowed in protest, and the exhausts belched out clouds of dark fumes, but the Harry Tate headed west as fast as it could go, the altimeter rapidly unwinding as we plummeted down. I recalled the Candas instructor, Harris, warning me not to dive the crate too steeply in case the wings fell off, but I had no real alternative if we were to escape the Albatroses.

The wind was howling in our wires as we dropped earthwards. I heard Goldberg blazing away with the Lewis, and I saw tracers whip past us, so I applied rudder to swing the nose. This was dangerous at the speed we were going. According to our airspeed indicator, we were diving at something approaching a hundred and twenty miles per hour. I didn't think the Harry Tate was designed for such reckless speed, but we had no chance of tackling four Albatroses on our own. All I could do was try to prevent them getting on our tail. Goldberg, of course, helped immensely with this, for he was shooting at any of the Huns who tried to get close to us. With his Lewis having a wide field of fire, he was able to prevent any of them lining up an easy shot without risking being hit themselves. He must have emptied his drum, for there was a pause in the shooting, but he had four replacement drums in his cockpit, and he soon began firing again.

I was forced to keep banking in order to give Goldberg a chance to shoot at any of the Huns who tried to get under our tail. That was our blind spot, so I kept weaving and dodging as best as I could, hoping to deny them the chance of an easy shot at us. This meant, though, that I needed to ease off on the speed, for the old bus would never have taken the strain of such manoeuvres in a rapid dive.

The Lines seemed a long way off, and the ground was drawing ever closer, but then I realised the shooting had stopped again, and Archie was giving us his attention.

I brought the R.E.8 out of its dive, easing back on the throttle but making some directional changes to throw off Archie. Then I twisted round to check on Goldberg.

He had his right hand clamped to his left forearm, and blood was staining his flying jacket, but he gave me a grim smile and shouted, "Nieuports!"

He tried to jerk his head to indicate where I should look, but I could see nothing except scattered clouds and empty sky.

I headed straight home, firing off a warning flare to call for medical attention as soon as home came in sight. By the time we had reached the hangar, an ambulance was already waiting. Goldberg was still conscious, although his face was pale.

"I think a bullet broke my arm," he explained when I asked how he was.

"What about the Huns?" I asked. "What happened?"

"They scarpered when they saw three Nieuports coming to help us," he replied. "I don't think they fancied the odds."

He was whisked away to hospital, leaving me to make out the report while our photographs were developed.

"We encountered four H.A.," I told Potter and the Major.

"We are supposed to call them Enemy Aircraft now, not Hostile Aircraft," Potter reminded me.

"In that case they were bloody hostile Enemy Aircraft," I retorted. "If it wasn't for Goldberg, we'd never have got back."

"You did well," the Major assured me. "You brought the photographs back, and that's the main thing."

A Flight had another casualty when Branwell, our newest pilot, suffered engine failure shortly after taking off. Luckily, he remembered to keep flying straight ahead rather than attempting to turn back. At low height, and without full airspeed, turning back to the airfield is almost always fatal, for the plane loses lift and airspeed, then drops into a spin and hits the ground before the pilot can do anything. Branwell remembered his training, but he ended up in a ditch at the far end of the next field, and he broke both his ankles on impact. His observer, the redoubtable Sergeant Turnbull, escaped with only a couple of bruises.

Sibbald told me, "I'm going to team you up with Turnbull again. I'll take Goldberg's replacement when he gets here, and Montague is now our most experienced officer observer, so he can show the new pilot the ropes."

I was, obviously, delighted at this news, although it seemed odd that Sibbald was changing his usual tactic.

He must have seen my uncertainty, for he explained, "Sergeant Turnbull nearly always gets the job of partnering the new pilots. I reckon it's about time he had a chance to show what he can do with a Lewis gun in a Harry Tate."

I found Turnbull later, down at the hangars where he was busy loading bullets into Lewis drums, checking each cartridge carefully to ensure it was not misshapen. Faulty cartridges are the main reason for guns jamming, and a crew with a useless gun often becomes a dead crew.

"Hello, Sir," he said with a smile. "I hear we are to work together again."

"Yes," I grinned. "And this time we will both have a machine gun."

"Let the Huns beware," he laughed.

Sadly, it was not a day for laughing in the squadron. As well as A Flight losing two good men, even if they were only injured, B Flight lost Stern and his observer, Sergeant Charles, who were caught by some red Albatroses in much the same way as Goldberg and I had been. Unluckily for Stern and Charles, the Red Baron's gang are more adept at shooting than the Huns we met, and the B.E.2 was hit on the first pass. We heard from our Archie that it had dived vertically from six thousand feet and gone straight in.

C flight also lost a crew. Fitzjames and Henshaw, in their first flight in a Harry Tate, tangled with yet another group of Albatroses and were shot down. They managed to glide as far as the Lines, but there was no clear spot for a landing. They crashed into a crump hole and the petrol tank caught fire, killing them before they could get out.

Dinner this evening was a sombre affair, although the news that Appleby of C Flight has been promoted to full Lieutenant did lift the mood a little. He is one of the few pilots who is still around from when I first joined the squadron. The turnover has been quite horrible, and I began to wonder when it would be my turn.

Once again, I joined Sibbald for after-dinner drinks. This time, Beano Normansby sat with us. I was pleased that I now seem to be regarded as one of the veteran pilots even if Sibbald refuses to let me address him by his first name. Perhaps he is right, for I've not yet got through my first month out here, so the thought of being classed as a veteran is quite laughable.

As usual, Sibbald seemed able to read my mind.

He said, "I know it's been bad recently, but it's largely because of the Push. We've been going over two or three times a day for weeks now, and the Huns have had plenty of shooting practice."

"The Harry Tate at least gives us a small chance of holding them off," I put in. "Having a machine gun protecting our tail makes a huge difference."

Sibbald nodded, "Yes, it's not a great kite to fly, but it's a lot better than the Quirk for war flying."

Normansby said, "Then you should take the next one, Old Bean. You're still flying a Quirk."

"I'll get one soon enough," Sibbald shrugged. "I'd rather give the new lads a fighting chance."

Our new pilot, Fotheringham, received the usual pep talk from our Flight Commander. He's been paired with Montague who seems relieved that he will have a day or two out of the firing line while he shows the new lad the ropes.

As for me, I feel worn out. Flying the Harry Tate is gruelling work, and it feels as if I have been out here for months, not the three weeks I have been through so far. Sibbald insists things will get better, but I'm afraid I can't see further than the next day ahead. I'm aware that my entries in this journal have been growing shorter because one day now seems much like another, and the victory we all expected seems just as distant as it did before this campaign began.

There are some rumours we may move to a new airfield closer to the new Front, but the Major insisted he had heard nothing official.

"It's business as usual," he assured us.

Meanwhile, the re-equipping with Harry Tates continues. A Flight now have three of the new machines, and nearly half of all the crews now fly in a proper two-seater. What we lack is the experience to use them effectively. I know from my discussions with Vanders that our scout pilots are warned never to attack a Hun two-seater single-handed because the two guns mean it can shoot back from virtually any position, especially because the rear gunner has such a good field of fire. What Turnbull and I need to do is learn how to use our Harry Tate the way the Hun crews use their machines. I've decided to have a long chat with the Sergeant tomorrow and see if we can work out the best way to use what we have.

Thursday 26th April, 1917

Any plans I had for using our new kite more effectively against Hun scouts came to naught because Sergeant Turnbull and I managed to escape the attentions of the many Huns who were out hunting today.

We did two artillery spotting jobs, trying to track down Hun batteries and directing our own heavy guns onto them. Both patrols required us to spend over three hours over Hunland, yet not a single Hun scout came near us. I think there were too many British machines in the air today, and the presence of so many of our scout planes must have scared off the Huns.

Down on the ground, the second phase of the battle has come to a grinding halt. The Germans have dug in deeply, and they are grimly hanging onto every square yard of mud, while our infantry cannot make any further headway.

I felt worn out by the end of the day, but at least the spotting jobs were less dangerous than the close contact patrols. Flying a big crate like the R.E.8 at low level is tiring enough, but when you have every Hun shooting at you, and you are also running the constant risk of being struck by an artillery shell, either British or German, you come back drenched in sweat and with frayed nerves. Today, we were spared that, which is something to be thankful for.

The trouble is that, after these weeks of bombardment, and all the lives lost, all we have to show for the enormous effort is an advance of a few miles. Our ground troops may have thrown the Huns off the high ground, but the war is already returning to one of digging trenches. It's all a bit dispiriting, I must say.

Even so, the war goes on, and the R.F.C is taking the fight to the Germans as we always do. No matter what, our aeroplanes cross the Lines. Our two-seaters do the reconnaissance work, drop bombs and direct artillery, while our scouts hunt down the enemy whenever he puts in an appearance. I cannot deny we are suffering heavy casualties, but so are our ground forces, and we remain determined to fight on.

I must admit, though, that some of the new arrivals are finding things tough. Gardner was looking rather shocked after his first trip over. He'd been on a couple of photographic jobs and had been shocked at the ferocity of the Archie sent against him and his pilot.

"I know the feeling," I told him. "I was injured on my first trip when a shell burst right above me. But you soon get used to old Archie. As long as your pilot keeps making course adjustments, he probably won't hit you. And if he does, that's just bad luck. It's the Hun scouts you need to watch out for."

As I mentioned earlier, the Huns were not much in evidence today, so the squadron got off relatively lightly. The worst incident was when poor Elphinstone and his observer, Fitzroy, were attacked by some red Albatroses who had adopted their now familiar routine of diving from a great height to speed past our own scout patrols and so pounce on the lower-flying two-seaters before our scouts can intercept them.

Flying a B.E.2c, Elphinstone had no option but to try to dodge and weave his way home while Fitzroy did his best to blaze away at the pursuing Huns. Unfortunately, a burst of bullets struck their engine on the very first pass, and they lost all power. Elphinstone, showing remarkable presence of mind considering his inexperience, stalled the Quirk and dropped into a spin.

"I was lucky I had time to do it," he explained. "We were sitting ducks for a few seconds, but the Huns had come down so fast they were still trying to regroup for another attack."

He had spun down, apparently out of control, hoping that the Huns would believe they had killed him and would return home to drink some celebratory schnapps while he made good his escape.

"I pulled her out only a few hundred feet up," he said. "Then we glided back across the Lines and ended up in a shell crater just behind our trenches."

He shook his head in wonderment as he said, "It's bloody awful out there. I don't know how the P.B.I. cope with it."

Bates told him, "You don't need to tell Kerr about that. He spent three days in the trenches a while back."

"It was two days," I corrected. "And I spent most of it walking back home."

"In between killing dozens of Huns with a machine gun," Bates grinned.

"I didn't have much choice about that," I told him. "And I agree with Elphinstone. We may have a dangerous job to do, but at least we can come back to decent food and a reasonably comfortable bed. The Poor Bloody Infantry don't have that luxury."

"Quite right!" agreed Elphinstone.

Then, with a thoughtful expression, he added, "The odd thing is that one of the Huns must have followed us down, for he flew over us after we crashed. I distinctly saw him wave to us once he knew we'd both got out alive."

Bates said, "Huns are strange beasts."

Elphinstone frowned, "It does seem very odd. One minute they are trying to kill us; the next he's waving goodbye and letting us live."

"It's a sort of chivalry between airmen," I told him. "They share the same dangers as us, I suppose."

"Yes," said Elphinstone. "But by letting us live, it means we can go back and try to kill some of his fellow countrymen tomorrow."

I asked, "Are you suggesting he should have dived down and shot you on the ground?"

"I would have done," Elphinstone asserted.

"That would be murder!" I objected.

At which, Bates laughed and, reminiscent of Paddy Vaughn, declared, "The whole war is bloody murder!"

I suppose they are right, but the thought of shooting unarmed and defenceless men does not sit comfortably with me.

This evening, I read a piece in The Times by Richardson. He must have sent it back almost as soon as he had returned to Corps H.Q. after I'd flown him up from Candas. I must say it was quite a good piece, praising the efforts of everyone in the R.F.C., from General Trenchard down to the lowliest Ack Emma. And yet, while I was reading it, I could almost hear Richardson pouring scorn on his own words. It was a wonderful bit of propaganda without being jingoistic, for it told people about the herculean efforts being put in by everyone to ensure a steady flow of machines and equipment to the front line squadrons, while also acknowledging the dangers those squadrons faced. Unlike Richardson's earlier work, this article seemed very real. I began to wonder whether he might really be intending to produce a warts and all book once the hostilities are over. The problem with that, I reflected, is that few people would believe just how awful the truth is. Civilians can have no conception of what life in the trenches is like.

As for us, everyone in the squadron knows the risks, but we remain defiantly cheerful. As Beano has been heard to observe, "If your number is up, there's sod all you can do about it, Old Bean. Live life to the full, that's what I say. So drink up, then we'll head into Barly and visit the girls."

While reading the newspaper, I also scanned the casualty lists. The newspapers are full of them every day, and with the Push having taken place over the past weeks, the lists have grown longer and longer. This, I think, is the only indication the people at home ever see of just how bad things are out here.

Scanning the lists, I looked for Vaughn's name, but could find no mention of him. I suppose that is a good sign for it means that, despite his awful wounds, he may yet survive. I do hope so. I never thought I'd say it, but I rather miss him. I wonder how he and the Professor would have reacted to Elphinstone's bloodthirsty comments about shooting unarmed aircrew once they were on the ground. Was that any different to dropping bombs on an airfield? I say this because, tonight, some German planes flew over during darkness and dropped some bombs nearby. They may have been aiming for Corps H.Q., or they may have been aiming for us, but fortunately, none of the bombs fell anywhere close to us. But if one had, say, hit our hut and killed us while we were sleeping, would that be any different to Elphinstone's Hun having machine gunned him when he got out of his crashed kite?

I really don't know the answer to that. It's too philosophical a topic for me, so I'll just leave the question and get some sleep. The offensive may have ground to a halt, but the war goes on.

Friday 27th April, 1917

I can hardly write this for excitement! How things can change in a day. Yesterday, I was full of grim determination to continue the war, with mixed emotions over the idea of what level of brutality is acceptable, and today I am almost bouncing for joy.

The day began as normal, with hard boiled eggs before the early show which was another artillery shoot, with Turnbull tapping out his codes on the wireless set while I flew the Harry Tate in figures of eight, adjusting height from time to time to throw Archie off his aim. It was a long job, lasting nearly four hours in total, but we did manage to bring down some accurate howitzer fire on a German strongpoint which probably housed several machine guns. We also spotted what we thought might be a supply dump of some sort, and we directed several salvoes onto that as well, so it was a good morning's work.

I think the Huns must have been having a lie in again today, for we barely saw any of them all morning. Other crews reported the same. Sibbald told us it was because we outnumber the German scouts who cannot be everywhere at once, and if we had got off lightly, it meant some other poor sods had probably seen plenty of the Huns. He may be right about that, but I think the fact it was a horrible, murky sort of day could have contributed. Either the Germans had decided it was too filthy to fly, or they had been up but we hadn't noticed them because of the poor visibility.

What Sergeant Turnbull and I did see, though, was a big, fat observation balloon. I think I mentioned that our offensive had taken most of the high ground in this region from the Germans, so their artillery was blind without observation balloons.

This one was new, for I am certain it had not been flying when we began our patrol, yet it was there when we turned for home.

I don't know why I decided to have a go at it, because my last experience of attacking balloons had been a terrifying one, but we had completed our mission, I had a full belt of ammo for my gun, and it is our job to attack the enemy. General Trenchard's communications always emphasise this.

So I put the Harry Tate into a dive and went for the balloon as quickly as I dared.

Naturally, Archie tried to stop us, and a veritable barrage came our way, balls of black hate exploding all around us. There were even a couple of flaming onions which whirled past us in fiery splendour.

The ground crew manning the winch were hauling the balloon down, but we seemed to have caught them a little by surprise, for it was still a couple of thousand feet up when it came in range.

I saw the observers leap out, their parachutes blossoming like white flowers, but I ignored them. Whatever Elphinstone might think, I wasn't going to deliberately shoot at unarmed men dangling from a parachute.

Heading straight for the balloon, I pressed the trigger, grinning in delight when my Vickers gun began chattering. I had no special explosive Buckingham bullets, but even ordinary .303 ammunition gets hot when it is fired from a gun. I closed to within a hundred yards, tramping on the rudder to spray bullets at the balloon. Holes appeared in our wings as the ground machine guns let rip at us, but I felt almost invulnerable. I cannot explain why this was so different to other times I have come under fire, but I somehow felt, almost for the first time, that I could do something to harm the enemy. Up until now, my contribution had been mostly at second hand, either giving my observer a chance to shoot or by helping direct artillery fire. These are vital roles, but being able to actually shoot at an enemy in the air was a new experience for me.

At fifty yards, I saw a red glow within the balloon. Half a second later, the whole thing went up in flames as the gas exploded. The writhing fire fell as the remnants of the bag and its wicker basket tumbled earthwards, and I hauled back on the stick to leapfrog over the dying balloon. We had come so close to it that I felt the buffeting air of the explosion as we passed above our victim.

The German machine gunners pelted us as we made our escape, and Sergeant Turnbull fired off several bursts from his Lewis gun. At first, I thought he was warning me about Hun scouts, but all he was doing was shooting at the gunners on the ground. I doubt he had much hope of hitting any of them, but like me, he was taking the opportunity to hit back.

We got clean away, and I was jubilant when we landed. Even the sight of some bullet holes very close to our cockpits could not diminish my joy.

"Bloody good job, Sir!" Sergeant Turnbull told me. He was grinning from ear to ear and bouncing excitedly from foot to foot in a most uncharacteristic way.

The Major was full of praise, too, and made a point of getting Potter to seek confirmation from our own Archie who eventually agreed that they had seen an R.E.8 attack an enemy balloon and send it down in flames.

I was the toast of the Mess at lunchtime. Even Sibbald congratulated me, and Bernard gave me a grudging, "Well done."

I think he's still annoyed that his own claim of driving down an Albatros has not yet been awarded as a victory, for his face betrayed more than a hint of jealousy.

But that adventure was as nothing compared to what happened in the afternoon.

Turnbull and I were assigned another long distance photographic mission. I'm not sure why Corps H.Q. want so many pictures of the Hun rear areas. It is pretty obvious to everyone that our offensive is not going to break through the new defences the Germans have dug. I wondered whether it might be Hector Harkness behind this, perhaps seeking a way to send me into danger in order to eliminate me as a rival for the affections of Nurse Routledge, but I knew he probably didn't even know my name or that I had any interest in her. This job was probably just the result of some bored staff wallah wanting to colour in some blank area of his map.

Whatever the reason, we had to fly five miles over the Lines. Our scout patrols often go much further, but two-seaters rarely go that far unless on a bombing raid.

We did not even reach our assigned target area before we encountered the Huns. They must have woken up at last, for we saw some Albatroses dancing with a Flight of Spads several miles further south, and then we met three Halberstadts.

They were higher than us, perhaps at twelve thousand feet compared to our nine thousand, and they were coming at us from ahead and to the left. It must have been a chance encounter, for even the least experienced Huns generally try to attack from a more favourable position, but the day remained rather murky, with lots of clouds and a haze giving relatively poor visibility, so it was as if we had accidentally run into each other.

Emboldened by my victory earlier, and also recalling how Paddy Vaughn had responded when he had been attacked, I did what the Huns least expected. They probably thought I would turn to my right and put my nose down in an attempt to put some distance between us. In a Quirk, I may well have done exactly that, but this time I waggled my wings to warn Turnbull, then turned to meet them head on as I pulled our nose into a climb while opening the throttle wide.

The three Huns split apart, two of them flying wide as if to circle around us, but the third came straight on. I saw the muzzle flash of his machine gun, and his tracers arced towards us. At first, I thought they would strike us, but they fell away at the last moment, dropping beneath us. His aim was slightly off.

I squeezed the trigger, peering through the Aldis sight in an effort to get my bullets on target. I had few tracer bullets, but I did see more sparks erupt on his rounded nose, and I knew I had hit him with at least a couple of bullets.

All of this took less time than it takes to write, for we were closing at over two hundred miles per hour. Once again, I recalled the advice of my instructors.

"Never break off in a head on challenge," they told us. "If you do, you give your opponent an easy shot at you."

I hunkered down behind the engine, hoping that the Hun's bullets would not cause too much damage. But he was a rotten shot, and the closest he came was sending a stream of bullets just above our top wing.

I kept firing, and I held my course. I think I actually closed my eyes at one point, convinced we were going to collide head on, but he pulled up at the last moment, his wheels whizzing just above us. I'd kept firing, and I'm sure I could not have missed him, even though I only caught the briefest glimpse of his underside. He was so close I could see the streaks of oil staining the bodywork beneath his Mercedes engine, and his wheels must have missed us by only a few feet.

I hauled the Harry Tate into a cumbersome turn, losing height as I did so in an attempt to gain some speed when I came out of the turn. Even as I did so, I heard Turnbull's Lewis gun chattering in the familiar short bursts Turnbull preferred.

It seemed to take an age to drag the bulky R.E.8 around, but when I did, a glorious sight met my eyes.

The Hun who had dived on us was now dropping steeply earthwards, a stream of vapour trailing behind him. Then there was a glimmer of flame beneath his engine, and the next moment the entire crate was engulfed in fire as his petrol tank exploded.

Fire is the airman's worst fear, but I felt a thrill of exultation at the same time as I experienced a sense of horror at his fate.

We had another victory!

The Halberstadt was little more than a ball of tumbling flame as it fell to the earth thousands of feet below us, a long finger of black smoke marking its final descent. There could be no doubt about this victory.

The other two Huns must have stood off, watching their leader and no doubt expecting him to shoot us down. Now they circled warily as if uncertain what to do. One turned his nose towards us and let off a long burst which came nowhere near us. Turnbull squirted some bullets back at him, and then I turned to face the Halberstadt. At that, he dived away, no doubt heading for home. His companion soon followed.

I was so excited I almost forgot we had been sent to take photographs. However, as soon as I turned eastwards, another group of Huns came into sight, seven of them up high, moving to intercept us.

Discretion, I thought, was the better part of valour, so I circled round and headed for home. I heard Sergeant Turnbull operating the camera as we crossed the Lines, exposing the plates so we would have something to show for our efforts.

Once again, we pumped our fists with joy when we landed, and I clapped the stocky Sergeant on the back.

He told me, "I think you'd already damaged him, but I gave him a close range squirt as he went over us. I could hardly miss at that range."

We had, we agreed, both contributed to the kill, and that was how we reported it.

Potter was able to speak to the Spad squadron whose patrol had been tackling a bunch of Albatroses, but they had not seen our fight. However, a Nieuport squadron got in touch to say that one of their Flights had seen a Harry Tate take on three Halberstadts and shoot one down in flames.

"Two victories in one day!" the Major exclaimed. "You'll be overtaking Albert Ball if you keep this up."

Sibbald was less enthusiastic when he heard what had happened.

"That was very well done," he said. "But don't let it go to your head. The R.E.8 is no match for a scout when it comes to agility. If you meet a good pilot, he'll run circles round you."

"Not if I shoot him first," I replied, full of confidence. "Anyway, the G.O.C. is always telling us to take the fight to the enemy."

"I know," Sibbald nodded. "But don't get reckless. That's all I'm saying."

My respect for Sibbald has been growing of late, but I think he's wrong to be quite as cautious as he is. Everyone knows most Huns are not aggressive. They tend to put all their best pilots together in one unit like the Red Baron's Jagdstaffel. That means the ordinary pilots are very ordinary indeed.

I'm sensible enough to know that we had been lucky our opponent today was flying a Halberstadt. The heavier, faster Albatros with its two machine guns might have hit us before we had a chance to get him, but even so I'm not going to let Sibbald spoil my day.

Naturally, Bernard's nose was even further out of joint when he heard the news.

"I suppose this will get you a mention in Comic Cuts," he grumbled.

To which Normansby shot back, "It might even earn him a gong, Old Bean."

That's a nice thought, but I don't really expect to receive a medal for this. Still, it was nice to receive the plaudits of my fellow pilots and observers, and I didn't need to buy a drink all evening.

Saturday 28th April, 1917

Today was far less exciting than yesterday. Turnbull and I were keen to tackle more Huns if we could, but the closest we came was when a D.F.W. two-seater passed us about a mile away, diving for home with a couple of Nieuports on his tail. We turned towards them, but they were too far away and travelling too fast for us to catch them. The Nieuports didn't have much better luck, for the D.F.W. managed to evade them by diving too steeply for them to follow without risking their wings collapsing.

As for Turnbull and me, we were once again on artillery spotting duties. And again we had been tasked with seeking out German batteries as the artillery duel continued. After a while, Turnbull reached out to tap my shoulder, indicating that he had spotted something, and we flew up and down around a wooded area, but we could see no sign of any big guns. If there was a battery concealed there, they must have heard us and were staying very still.

We contented ourselves with directing fire onto a crossroads which was soon transformed into so much rubble and mud, hopefully making life difficult for the Germans to bring up supplies, but I will admit it was not a very successful mission.

Other members of the squadron had mixed luck. Cranston and Ponsonby of C Flight were shot down behind the Lines. There was a fearful scrap all around them, and we received a report from a Spad squadron that they thought Cranston had survived the crash. Even if he did, though, he's now a prisoner.

Elphinstone's luck continues its bad streak. He suffered engine failure while out on a photographic shoot. He managed to glide back across the Lines to land safely enough, but it took a while for the Salvage Team to rescue him and his kite.

Captain Unswood, B Flight's commander, did use his R.E.8 to attack a Hun plane. He stumbled across a lone Albatros, perhaps a beginner who had become lost. Unfortunately for Unswood, Archie spotted him and fired some warning shots. The Albatros woke up and dived away, apparently unwilling to tangle with a two-seater even though his plane is faster and more agile.

The weather does, at long last, seem to be relenting. The bitter cold has gone, and we can see definite signs of spring. This also seems to have heralded a pause in the fighting on the ground, for the Lines are static once again.

Our re-equipping with Harry Tates continues, with another new one arriving today. In A Flight, only Sibbald and our newest pilot, Fotheringham, are still flying Quirks. The other Flights are in much the same situation, with ferry pilots from Candas flying out their old Quirks when they deliver a new Harry Tate. We should be fully equipped within a few days, which will make a terrific difference to our ability to do our work. I can't help wondering how many of our casualties might have been avoided if we'd had them earlier. Still, there is no point in crying over spilt milk.

One bit of very good news is that Albert Ball is back at the front. He's now a Captain in 56 Squadron, and he's already shot down four Huns in the past few days.

"That'll show the bloody Red Baron who's the top man!" declared Bates.

Ball is flying the new S.E.5, another product of the Royal Aircraft Factory, although this one seems to be a decent enough machine, and we are all hoping it will prove a match for the Albatros. There are also rumours of a new Sopwith design which has two machine guns. It is as I once said to Richardson, the tide is going to turn. At long last, the R.F.C. is being equipped with new machines which will give us mastery of the air. It may take a while for the new kites to make a full impact, but I'm sure the day is coming when we will drive the Huns from the sky.

For the moment, though, our routine continues as normal. Sibbald warned us for another bombing raid tomorrow.

"We've to go back to that railway junction we hit a couple of weeks ago," he informed us. "It seems Jerry has repaired the damage, so we've to go and blow it up again."

He will be leading the raid, but decided that Fotheringham should not join us.

"He hasn't got one of the new kites yet. I don't want him struggling to keep up if he's flying an unarmed Quirk on his first mission."

Personally, I'm quite looking forward to this. It will be nice to go on a raid carrying bombs along with an observer who can guard my tail with a Lewis gun.

Sunday 29th April, 1917

Sibbald came up with a plan for a formation which would give us the best chance of protecting each other. He still has his old B.E.2c, so he'll be leading the Flight. Beano will then fly above and behind him, with Maycroft and Falconer on either side of him in a standard vee formation. My role is to fly behind and slightly below them, thus creating a diamond formation with me slightly lower than the others to prevent my kite being buffeted by Beano's slipstream.

"This gives all four observers a good field of fire," Sibbald explained as he outlined the plan. "Stick to that formation and we'll be able to hit any Huns with four Lewis guns. If they try to attack from ahead, three of you will have Vickers guns to meet that threat."

I was a bit put out by this part because I was the only pilot who would not be able to use his Vickers by virtue of Sibbald himself flying directly ahead of me.

"What if they attack from below?" Beano asked.

"Kerr and Turnbull will have a shot at them if they try to get beneath any of you. If they target Kerr, the rest of you should be able to bank your wings to give your observers a shot at them. As long as you hold position, someone will get a shot at them whichever way they come at us."

After that, he insisted on taking us up to practise this new formation. We did not have enough time to become expert, but it gave us some confidence that we could work together.

The raid was to take place in the afternoon. Sibbald wanted to use the westering sun to provide some cover for our approach.

"We'll have a Flight of Pups as escort," he told us.

That was less encouraging. The Sopwith Pup is a lovely aeroplane, but it is outclassed by the Albatros except at very high altitudes. Even so, we hoped that six of them flying a few thousand feet above us would provide sufficient discouragement to any curious Huns who might try to stop us.

Each of our planes was laden with two of the heavy 112lbs bombs. This gave us fewer eggs to lay, but Sibbald felt that our lighter bombs had not caused sufficient damage last time, and he wanted to be sure of wrecking the junction properly this time.

"Make them count," he ordered as he finished his final briefing.

We took off around three pip emma, heading eastwards and meeting up with our escort at the assigned spot just above Arras. The Pups danced around, forming themselves into two vics of three, and stayed above us, the first Flight about three thousand feet higher than us, and the second another two thousand feet higher yet.

We clawed our way up to nine thousand feet before crossing the Lines. Due to the lack of success in the recent offensive, the Lines had not moved much at all since our previous raid on this target, so it was still about ten miles into Hunland.

I checked the sky constantly, and I knew every one of us was doing the same. There were lots of other planes around, mostly British. Some were doing artillery shoots, while Flights of scout planes patrolled the sky, hunting for the enemy. I also saw half a dozen F.E.2's lumbering over on a raid of their own, and I felt sorry for the crews of those bulky pushers. They were no match for even a Halberstadt, but I'd heard they had come up with a way to fend off attacks. If Huns came near, they would form a circle, going round and round like wagons in the Wild West, thus allowing each gunner to protect the tail of the plane ahead. As long as they had sufficient fuel to outlast the Huns, they could stay relatively safe against all but the most determined attackers.

Today, though, the Huns were largely absent. The only sign of them I saw was several dots high up and way to the south. I was pretty sure they were Albatroses, but they did not come close enough for me to positively identify them.

Shortly after crossing the Lines, Sibbald put his nose down, leading us in a shallow dive towards the railway junction. Archie saw us, so we had to jink a little on our way to throw him off his aim. Fortunately, Sibbald had foreseen this, and we'd done a bit of practice in this manoeuvre as well.

I kept my eyes on Sibbald now, watching him closely. Down we went, the altimeter winding away the height.

Eight thousand. Seven thousand. Six thousand feet.

At a little over five thousand feet, Sibbald levelled off. We were flying quite fast for a Quirk because of the speed we had gained in the dive, but the four Harry Tates could have flown considerably faster. Sibbald, I reflected, should have borrowed an R.E.8 from one of the other Flights. If we'd all been in new machines, we'd have been in and out much more quickly. Sibbald being Sibbald, his pride had probably not allowed him to do that.

Archie rocked us, explosions filling the sky around us, but we had our target in sight now. The two railway lines joining together at the junction. The shattered signal box was still in ruins, but the track itself had been repaired, and the Germans had set up a couple of machine gun posts to protect it from further attack. Those guns now began firing at us, and I felt the familiar tingle of fear and excitement. I wanted to dip my nose and spray a burst back at them, but Sibbald had drummed into us the need to remain in formation in the hope that all our bombs would hit the target together.

We were relying on his experience now. He brought us in across the tracks, crossing them diagonally as he had taught us. Then he waggled his wings, the movement clumsy because of the weight of the bombs, and I readied my hand on the release switches.

Now!

Sibbald's bombs fell away, and I hit the switches, feeling the Harry Tate lift as the heavy load fell away. Bombs from the other machines were also falling, and I had a scare when Beano's two bombs almost hit me. I swerved and banked, and they tumbled down, missing us by a few yards. I told myself I would need to inform Sibbald of this flaw in his plan if he ever wanted to adopt the same formation in future.

After that fright, I dragged the R.E.8 back into formation as Sibbald began climbing away.

The junction was behind us now, and I had no time to check what damage we had done, but I saw Sergeant Foxton, Maycroft's observer, giving a big thumbs up, then clapping his gloved hands in triumph. I guessed that meant we had hit the target with at least one of the bombs.

And then it happened.

It was so unlikely, I still cannot believe it. Machine guns on the ground are extremely dangerous if you go below five thousand feet, but we were well above that now. It must have been a lucky shot, but Sibbald was hit. I saw his Quirk stagger in the air, then falter and slowly drop from its position.

I felt my heart sink like a stone as I watched in horror. Sibbald was alive, because I could see him waving one arm, ordering us to head for home without him. And I also saw the dreadful sight of a thin trail of vapour streaming out behind him.

Beano refused to abandon him, and we all circled above him as we watched him try to stretch his glide to get back across the Lines. His engine was still going, but he had obviously lost a lot of power, for the B.E.2 was wallowing like a floundering fish as it slowly inched westwards.

Then there was a glimmer of red flame. Before we knew it, those flames had spread, bursting out to engulf the front of the aircraft. Sitting in the rear cockpit, Sibbald continued to fight his fate. He dropped into a side-slip, trying to let the wind blow the flames away from him. This worked for a few seconds, but the fire was inexorable. It spread to the lower wings and began to devour the empty front cockpit, with thick, black smoke flying back into Sibbald's face and leaving a finger of writhing vapour to mark his fall.

I continued to watch, my throat constricted, my heart thumping wildly. If he had possessed a parachute, he could have saved himself, but he was condemned to falling in a burning crate. The whole of the front of the Quirk was ablaze, the dope used to varnish the canvas being highly flammable, and the wood of the airframe burning easily.

I knew he could not reach the ground before the flames engulfed him, and Sibbald must have known it too.

He had three choices left. He could stay with the kite and let the fire burn him to death; he could jump out and let gravity kill him when he struck the ground; or he could use the pilot's final, dreadful option.

I saw it distinctly, even though he was now a long way below us and smoke was billowing all around him. His right hand came up, moved close to the side of his head, and I knew he was holding his service revolver. I saw him jerk as he pulled the trigger, and then he stayed with the flaming machine as it tumbled to the ground.

Beano took charge, leading the rest of us homewards. A Flight of Albatroses came poking around, but the sight of our escort deterred them, and they contented themselves with diving on the topmost Pups, then zooming away again. It was an odd tactic, but one of the Pups fell into a spin and did not recover. Turnbull later confirmed to me that he'd watched it all the way down. It was a sad loss, but not nearly as heavy a blow as our own.

I think we were all in shock when we returned to our airfield. We had indeed blown the junction to pieces again, but losing Sibbald struck us all hard. He was a dour, pessimistic character who fussed over us like an old granny, but his solid determination had made him a rock amidst the chaos of war. For all his faults, I knew we would miss him, and would remember his death all our lives.

Casualties are part of war, and the death of close comrades is something we are accustomed to, but Sibbald's dreadful demise was so unexpected it shocked every one of us.

Even the Major could scarcely believe it. He demanded to hear the full story several times before sighing and telling us he would telephone R.F.C. Headquarters and ask for a replacement Flight Leader.

"You're in charge of A Flight until we get a new Captain," he told Beano.

Beano looked at me and said, "That makes you Number Two in the Flight."

That is quite a prospect considering I've only been out here a month, but Beano geed us all up, drinking a toast to Sibbald after dinner, then telling each of us we needed to get on with our job.

"The war still needs to be fought," he said.

He is right, of course, and the Major reiterated that sentiment. Sibbald will be a hard act for anyone to follow, but nobody is indispensable when it comes to air fighting. A new Captain will be sent here, and we shall continue to take the war to the enemy.

Now, of course, I have an added incentive to harm the Germans. I would not describe Sibbald as a friend, but he has certainly been a mentor, even though I've often disagreed with him. But, like Paddy Vaughn, Dish Tattersall and all the others, he is gone. What I need to do is make sure their sacrifice is not in vain.

I must admit it has been difficult to shake off the memory of Sibbald's fate. To distract me, I totted up my log book and found that, in the four weeks I have been at the Front, I've brought my total flying time up to one hundred and seven hours and twenty minutes. It would have been more had it not been for the days lost to bad weather, and my time spent returning home through the trenches, but it's quite a satisfying number all the same.

I shall stop writing now. It is late, and even the sound of the artillery has diminished now that the offensive has ground to a standstill.

I'm sure tomorrow will be another big day, and for me it is a little special. It will be my nineteenth birthday. I intend to make it a day to remember.

Monday 30th April, 1917

Appended Letter

Dear Mr.Richardson,

I found this journal among 2nd Lieutenant Kerr's belongings. Having read it, I thought it better not to send it to his parents. After some reflection, I thought you might be able to make use of it, even though it does mention you several times, and not always in a flattering light. However, since you claim to be seeking the truth, and want to hear the genuine voices of those involved in the war, you may find this diary of some use.

  I regret to say that Kerr was shot down and killed on the morning of 30th April. He and Sergeant Turnbull were on a long-range reconnaissance patrol when they encountered several Albatroses. There was quite a scrap, with their escorting Spads losing one of their Flight as well. Kerr and Turnbull did their best to fight the German machines, with Kerr flying to meet them, and Turnbull using his machine gun to fend off any Albatros which tried to get on their tail. Unfortunately, one of the Germans dived below them and zoomed up, shooting them at close range. I suspect both were either killed or wounded in that attack, because their aeroplane was seen to fall into a vertical dive. We do not know exactly where it crashed, but one of the Spad pilots reported seeing the wings fall apart as the plane fell, so there is no chance that either of them survived.

  I don't know what else to tell you. Kerr was a serious fellow, lacking in humour, but he was dedicated to winning the war, and he certainly was not afraid of the enemy despite what he may have confided to his diary. Sadly, he is now just another statistic in April's log of death. Perhaps if you use this journal, you may help to keep alive not only his memory but that of the others he mentions who have fallen in the service of their King and Country.

Yours sincerely,

T.R. Bates, 2nd Lieutenant
-- Squadron, Royal Flying Corps.

Epilogue
By Basil Richardson

I was too old for Army service when the war broke out. Arthur Kerr's estimate of my age was pleasantly underestimated, but the young often have trouble guessing at the age of others. I did manage to arrange to be sent to France as a war correspondent, and I soon became appalled at the loss of life, as well as with the uncaring attitude towards the casualties of those in command. In my experience, the outlook of the officers at Corps and Army Headquarters was very firmly entrenched in the Victorian era, and few of them seemed to have much understanding of the new techniques required in modern warfare. That is not to say they did not appreciate that machine guns, aeroplanes and tanks were important, but many of them seemed to believe that the trench warfare was an aberration, a phenomenon which would not recur in any future war. Those future conflicts, many appeared to believe, would see cavalry dominate once again. Most of the senior officers still rode horses regularly, and cavalry regiments were always in reserve, waiting for a breakthrough which never came.

My disillusionment with the conduct of the war persuaded me that I must record the truth. I was determined to write a book telling the public what had really happened. I never did manage to do that, but part of the reason was Arthur Kerr's diary which was sent to me by his fellow pilot after Kerr's death. It sums up most of the things I wanted to say, so I have contented myself with adding this short epilogue.

In the years after the war, I tracked down as many of the people mentioned in the diary as I could. I began with Kerr's parents, a homely and sincere couple who still grieve for him. Mister Kerr is an accountant by profession, while Mrs. Kerr teaches at a Girls' School in Edinburgh. I debated whether to give them their son's diary, for I was not convinced it would ease the pain of their loss. Eventually, though, I was forced to admit that this was the source of my information and the reason I had traced them. So, having made a diligent copy of the journal, I gave them the original. Whether it provided any comfort, I cannot say.

Regarding the pilots and observers in the squadron, many more died over the succeeding months, although some did survive. Bates himself lived to see the Armistice in 1918, having completed his tour, then spent several months as an instructor teaching new pilots how to fly, before returning to another R.E.8 squadron late in 1918.

Beano Normansby also finished his tour, but he was killed in a flying accident when flying B.E.12 aeroplanes trying to tackle the Gotha bombers which were raiding England in the latter part of the war.

Captain Bernard, the much-maligned Commander of C flight, was shot down and killed in June of 1917, while Captain Unswood of B Flight was wounded and sent back to Home Establishment. He survived the war, but was left with a permanent limp.

Major Jones has remained with the Royal Air Force, as the Flying Corps became in April, 1918. He was reluctant to speak to me about his time leading the squadron during the month that became known as Bloody April. All he would say was that it was a difficult time, but that he was proud of the squadron's accomplishments.

Captain Potter, the Recording Officer, left the R.A.F. and emigrated to Australia. I contacted him by letter, and he wrote back. Unfortunately, his memories of Arthur Kerr were fragmentary.

"There were so many of them passing through the squadron," he explained. "It is difficult to remember them all. But I do recall Kerr shooting down that balloon, and then bagging a Halberstadt the following day. That was quite an achievement."

He did say that Kerr had been a young man full of promise, and he remembered Major Jones being particularly upset at his loss.

Private Etherington, the batman, had more memories of all the men who served in the squadron. He had a particular fondness for Kerr, and was very upset at his loss, although he could add very little to Kerr's own story except that the pilot probably drank a great deal more than he confided to his journal.

"They all liked a drink," Etherington told me. "I can't say as I blame them, because they risked their lives every single day. It was awful to see them fly off and not come back."

The Air Mechanics, Green and Dunlop, also remembered Kerr as a man they thought was lucky. Both had been devastated by his death, for they thought he was destined for greater things. Green returned to civilian life as an upholsterer, while Dunlop eventually found employment in a motor garage.

As for some of the others, Paddy Vaughn spent many months in hospital. When discharged, he could still not walk, and he spends his time in a wheelchair. Despite this, he has himself become a writer, producing political pamphlets advocating a free and united Ireland. I was not able to speak to him, for to do so would have brought me to the attention of the British Police as a possible subversive. However, I did manage to exchange letters with him. He recalled Kerr very well, and confessed he was upset to learn of his death.

"He was typical of so many young men back then," he wrote. "He was sincere, determined to win the war, yet unaware of the wider issues which had resulted in the fighting in the first place. That is why I now devote my time to campaigning for Irish liberty. I see no reason why any more Irish men and women should suffer and die to satisfy the demands of a King and Parliament of another country."

Ashton, who did indeed lose the sight in his right eye, died during the Spanish influenza epidemic in 1918, as did Goldberg.

It was not difficult to trace Hector Harkness, for he survived the war having earned several medals, although I could find no record of him doing anything more valorous than using a telephone to issue the General's orders. Harkness went on to become a Conservative MP, but he did not marry Nurse Jennifer Routledge. I spoke to her at length. She recalled Arthur Kerr when I reminded her about him flying low over the hospital, but her experiences in the war had left her mentally scarred, and she admitted that she often fell victim to depression. She remained a nurse, and she remained unmarried.

"Another war will come along soon," she told me. "I don't think I could bear to lose a husband. I saw so many young men die."

When I asked her about Hector Harkness, she simply shrugged, "He was very rich, but I wanted rather more than that."

Many people wanted rather more than life gave them, and that is particularly true of the airmen who flew during Bloody April. Day after day they crossed the Lines in full knowledge that they may not survive. Every single one of them deserved a medal for that. Instead, all they got was a poppy worn once a year by a public who have little conception of what they went through. And yet, as Kerr's diary shows, they went willingly, prepared to die for King and Country, as far too many of them did. Those who survived were promised a land fit for heroes, but hard as I look, I can find little trace of that land. Unemployment, poverty and disease were the fate of far too many of them.

But that is another story, and one I shall perhaps tell in my own words one day.

Basil Richardson
30th April, 1920

Author's Note and Acknowledgements

April 1917 is known as Bloody April for a good reason. In this month, the Royal Flying Corps lost 245 aeroplanes, 211 aircrew killed or missing, and 108 taken prisoner after crashing behind German Lines. The losses were so bad that questions were raised in the House of Commons, with mentions that it was akin to murder to send inexperienced young airmen into battle in inadequate machines.

As the figures clearly reveal, a majority of the aircraft shot down must have been two-seaters, and that means they were very probably the antiquated B.E.2c, a plane which was totally unsuited to aerial warfare. One can only marvel at the courage of the men who flew these virtually defenceless aeroplanes over the Lines every day in full knowledge that the Germans were waiting for them.

The German Air Service was numerically inferior to the R.F.C. and the French Aviation Service, so it had taken a decision early in the war to fight a defensive battle in the air, mirroring the stance of their troops on the ground. They also grouped together their best pilots in several elite units, providing them with the best aircraft available. While this meant that many units within the German Air Service contained pilots of no better than average quality, the result was that the likes of Manfred von Richthofen's Jagdstafel 11 were able to shoot down British aircraft in droves. Von Richthofen himself shot down no fewer than twenty-one British planes during the month of April, 1917, propelling himself to the top of the all-time list by taking his score to fifty-two. He would go on to claim eighty victories until he, too, met the all too frequent fate of First World War pilots when he was killed a year later in April, 1918.

The Red Baron has often been criticised by British war commentators and writers for picking on the hapless two-seaters. The inference is that he was not really as great as his score suggests because he always chose easy targets. What these comments fail to appreciate is that von Richthofen, and the German Air Service in general, realised that it was the two-seaters who did the really important war work. These planes dropped bombs, took photographs and directed artillery on German ground forces. By shooting them down, the Germans were protecting their infantry and support troops. It is hardly the fault of von Richthofen that the British persisted in using antiquated aircraft. To paraphrase a current footballing comment, "You can only fight what's in front of you". It is also noticeable that those who criticise von Richthofen never apply the same criticism to the likes of British ace James McCudden who made a specialty of shooting down German two-seaters. Admittedly, the Germans were equipped with far better two-seater aircraft than the B.E.2c, but McCudden's tactic was to sneak up beneath these high-flying machines and shoot them down before they spotted him. Militarily, this makes perfect sense, and one should not criticise McCudden for this any more than one should criticise von Richthofen for adopting tactics which allowed him to attack British two-seaters with near impunity. He had, after all, served some time in the German cavalry, so he knew how important it was to destroy British two-seater planes, and he certainly did more than any other German pilot in this regard.

It is often cited that the average lifespan of a pilot on the Western Front at this time was a mere three weeks, but such statistics can hide a lot. I may have slightly exaggerated the losses in this story, but not by much. During my research, I discovered that at least four British planes were struck by their own artillery shells on the first day of the Battle of Arras.

When I first conceived the idea of writing a diary-style narrative of a pilot involved in Bloody April, I began sketching out the story from the perspective of a pilot in a single-seat fighter squadron, or scout squadron as they were known then. I quickly realised this would turn the book into a re-hash of many other books, so I soon decided to tell the tale from the point of view of a two-seater squadron since the aircrew who carried out the primary role of the Flying Corps are generally unsung heroes. As far as I know, very few books have been written by or about them, so I hope this story will go some way to redressing that imbalance.

I am very aware that the situation in which my fictional protagonist is placed allows very little scope for sub-plots and inter-weaving threads. However, all I wanted to do in this book was convey just how dangerous life was for these young men. And some were very young indeed. The book is not really about Arthur Kerr or his fellow aircrew; it is about the war in which they fought, and all the horrors it entailed.

Brigadier-General Sir Hugh Trenchard, the General Officer Commanding the Royal Flying Corps, adopted a very different approach to his German counterparts. He insisted that aeroplanes must be used aggressively, and he hammered this message home to all members of the Corps. The pilots and observers never failed to respond, and it must be said that, ultimately, Trenchard was proved correct. Aircraft are best used as an offensive weapon. The trouble was that Trenchard's men did not have the right equipment to carry out his orders without suffering huge losses, and the price was appallingly high. Like his counterparts who commanded the ground troops, Trenchard's principal tactic was to keep throwing men and machines at the enemy in the hope of wearing him down. This approach, combined with Trenchard's refusal to allow aircrew to have parachutes, cost far too many lives.

Of course, the tide did turn. As outlined in the story, new aircraft were produced which were markedly better than the Albatros with which most German units were equipped. During Bloody April, only the French-built Nieuport 17 and the rare Sopwith Triplane could hope to match the Albatros, and both of them were outgunned by the heavier German machine. In April, 1917, that situation began to change. The S.E.5a, another Royal Aircraft factory design, soon proved to be the best aircraft that odd design factory had ever produced. Most of the aces of the R.F.C. flew the S.E.5a at some point in their career. Albert Ball, who is mentioned several times in this story, was one of them, but he was shot down and killed on 7th May, 1917, only a week after this account ends. Officially, the Germans credited Lothar von Richthofen, brother of the infamous Red baron, with killing Ball, although that claim is probably incorrect. Nobody knows how Ball met his end. He is still remembered as a great hero of the Royal Flying Corps, and there is no doubt he was a hero to the men of the R.F.C. for his bravery and skill.

Another pilot mentioned in this book is Billy Bishop, a Canadian who began flying Nieuports in April, 1917 and went on to fly the S.E.5a, being officially credited with seventy-two victories. He survived the war.

Later in 1917, the two-gun Sopwith Camel arrived at the Front, and it is renowned as being responsible for shooting down more German aircraft than any other British type.

The never-ending roundabout turned again in 1918, with the Germans producing the incredible Fokker D.VII, a machine so good that it was specifically mentioned in the Treaty of Versailles as being part of the equipment the Germans must surrender. However, like the Albatros of 1917, the Fokker was always outnumbered and, ultimately, it was numbers that told.

It is, of course, easy to look back and criticise the decisions of those who were in charge during the First World War. Much of that criticism is deserved, but some is perhaps unfair given the resources available. What cannot be criticised is the sheer bravery of the men who climbed into their cockpits day after day and went out to fight an enemy who held all the advantages except that of numbers. If this story helps only one reader to appreciate the sacrifices of those men, then it has achieved its purpose.

For the benefit of any readers who have not managed to work out some of the terms used in this book, I should perhaps make some comment on the rudimentary phonetic alphabet used by the British Army during World War 1. As far as I have been able to ascertain, most letters were simply pronounced as normal, but with increasing use of telephones as a means of communication, some letters were differentiated to avoid confusion. This soon gained widespread use even during face to face discussions, and some of the more common terms have cropped up quite frequently in this story.

The most commonly used ones were: Ack for A, Emma for M, and Pip for P. So, for example, an Offensive Patrol would be referred to as an O Pip, and the afternoon (p.m.) would be Pip Emma. Rather confusingly, this meant that the morning (a.m.) would be Ack Emma, but the same abbreviation was also used for an Air Mechanic. This use of the phonetic alphabet also resulted in the airman's name for a couple of two-seat aircraft used by the R.F.C. in 1917 and 1918. The Armstrong-Whitworth company produced the F.K.3 which was then replaced by a larger version officially known as the F.K.8. As a rule, these two machines were known as the "Little Ack" and "Big Ack" respectively because of the Armstrong name.

As always, I have several people to thank. Stuart Anthony spent a lot of time looking at maps and aerial images to confirm the layout of the terrain, identifying an area around the village of Fosseux where an airfield might have been established. As far as I know, there was no airfield there.

Thanks also to historian and author Ken Wayman for letting me pick his brains on several points of detail, and to Douglas Pinkerton for allowing me access to his library of books on World War 1. These helped me a great deal in fleshing out the background to the story.

There is very little written about the detail of the work of the two-seat reconnaissance aircraft of World War 1, but I did manage to find a very helpful publication by the RAF Historical Society which gave some invaluable information on the work of these squadrons.

Away from the research, my usual team of helpers reviewed the drafts and helped locate the innumerable typos and grammatical errors. Thanks to Moira Anthony, Stuart Anthony, Ian Dron, Stewart Fenton and Liz Wright for their help. Any remaining errors are down to me.

GA
February, 2021

Other Books by Gordon Anthony

All titles are available in e-book format from the Amazon Kindle store. Titles marked with an asterisk are also available from Amazon in paperback.

In the Shadow of the Wall*
An Eye For An Eye*

Home Fires*
Hunting Icarus*

The Calgacus Series:
    World's End*
    The Centurions*
    Queen of Victory*
    Druids' Gold*
    Blood Ties*
    The High King*
    The Ghost War*
    Last Of The Free*

The Constantine Investigates Series:
    The Man in the Ironic Mask
    The Lady of Shall Not
    Gawain and the Green Nightshirt
    A Tale of One City
    49 Shades of Tartan

The Hereward Story:
    Last English Hero*
    Doomsday*

The Sempronius Scipio Series:
    Dido's Revenge*
    A Long Shadow*

    A Walk in the Dark (Charity booklet)

About The Author

Born in Watford, Hertfordshire, in 1957, Gordon's family moved to Broughty Ferry in the early 1960s. Gordon attended Grove Academy, leaving in 1974 to work for Bank of Scotland. After a long but undistinguished career, he retired on medical grounds in 2008 without having received any huge bankers' bonuses.

Registered blind, Gordon had more time on his hands after retiring so, with the aid of special computer software, he returned to his hobby of writing and had his debut novel, "In the Shadow of the Wall" published in 2010. Gordon's books are now being read by a world-wide audience. As well as his historical adventure stories, he has ventured into crime fiction with some spoof murder mysteries in the "Constantine Investigates" series. He is also kept busy with speaking engagements, visiting libraries, schools and community groups to talk about his books.

In addition to his novels, Gordon devotes some of his time to raising funds for the RNIB. As well as visiting schools and social clubs to talk about his sight loss, he has self-published a charity booklet titled, "A Walk in the Dark", a humorous account of his experiences since losing his eyesight. The booklet is available from Amazon Kindle Store. Gordon will donate all author royalties to RNIB.

Now completely blind, Gordon continues to write stories and, in his spare time, attempts to play the guitar and keyboard with varying degrees of success.

Gordon is married to Alaine. They have three children and two grandchildren. The family lives in Livingston, West Lothian.

You can contact Gordon via his website or by sending an email to ga.author@sky.com

Printed in Great Britain
by Amazon